DEPUTIZED

DEPUTIZED

T. L. DAVIS

FIVE STAR
A part of Gale, a Cengage Company

LIBRARY OF CONGRESS CATALOGING-IN-PUBLICATION DATA

Names: Davis, T. L., author.
Title: Deputized / T.L. Davis.
Description: First edition. | Waterville, Maine : Five Star, [2021]
Identifiers: LCCN 2019057094 | ISBN 9781432869724 (hardcover)
Subjects: GSAFD: Western stories.
Classification: LCC PS3554.A93776 D47 2020 | DDC 813/.54—dc23
LC record available at https://lccn.loc.gov/2019057094

First Edition. First Printing: March 2021
Find us on Facebook—https://www.facebook.com/FiveStarCengage
Visit our website—http://www.gale.cengage.com/fivestar
Contact Five Star Publishing at FiveStar@cengage.com

Printed in Mexico
Print Number: 01   Print Year: 2021

DEPUTIZED

CHAPTER ONE

It seemed as if I would spend the whole day by the public well,
drinking water, until I was bloated with it, and still my throat
ached for more as I fought the effects of a deep and serious
hangover.

The whiskey of the night before came out in torrents of sweat.
My head was pounding as I stumbled away from the well and
up to my horse for a little hair of the dog, as they say. I dug
around in the saddlebags, looking for the bottle. It was missing.
Damn thieves!

I reached into my pocket and pulled out cash from the trail
drive. Most of it was there. Ol' Skinny Jacobsen knew how to
treat a man. He bought us drinks most of the night and then
fired us. The work was done, and we knew it was coming; some
looked forward to it.

Blinking against the heat and brilliance of the summer sun, I
recognized the saloon and started toward it. I had to cross the
street in my blind, desperate desire for relief and nearly got run
down by a man with a handsome black gelding. The man jerked
back on the reins and stared down at me.

"Look where yur goin'," the dandified man hollered as I
turned away to fend off the volume of his words.

The dandy rode on and pulled his horse up at the saloon. He
tossed the reins in a quick, easy fashion and they spun around
the rail. The show-off. I could do that, too, if I wanted.

I watched him shake some of the dust from his clothes and

enter the saloon. I followed in his tracks.

Grateful for the shade, I entered the dark building. The place seemed different from the night before. Sunlight streamed through the fly-specked windows and threw itself against the dirt floor. The piano sat silent and the place was empty, but for the dandy standing at the plank bar.

There were some broken pieces of furniture in a barrel and a thought occurred to me. I felt the back of my head and ran my fingers over a soft lump of flesh. Perhaps it was less whiskey and more injury that had led to my throbbing head.

The dandy wore fancy clothes, colored red with trail dust. I figured he'd been riding awhile. He stood sharp-eyed at the bar, looking back toward me as I entered.

After letting my eyes adjust to the interior, I strolled up to the bar and laid some coins on it. The dandy kept staring at me, so I touched my hat toward him and grinned. He just looked away and waited for the bartender.

I pounded the bar with my fist.

"Service here," I hollered into the back room, where I could see the fat bartender sitting on a chair. I heard the chair release a groan as he stood.

"You, get on outta here," the bartender said, pointing toward the door.

"Heave up a bottle, first," I replied, nudging the coins closer to him.

Grudgingly, the bartender reached behind and got hold of a bottle's neck. He slammed the bottle down next to the coins; they bounced and settled with a metallic hum.

"All right, Snake, don't stand there starin' at it. Take it and git."

"Name's Frank," I said, hefting the bottle and jutting my chin in pride. I walked aimlessly toward the door and stopped to look at a picture on the wall, just to tease him.

"Git!" he screamed.

Everyone called me "Snake," but my real name was Frank Whittaker. I got the silly name from a time out on the trail, when I grabbed a snake in mid-strike. It was a trick taught to me by my uncle in Kansas. If a man had fast enough reflexes, he could bait a rattler with one hand and when it reached out to hit the one hand, a man could grab it behind the neck with the other. It took some gumption to try it, but even if a fellow missed, he could always try again. Snakes are stupid that way.

With bottle in hand, I went up to my horse and leaned against it. I stared at the brown liquid swirling around inside the glass. Would it cure me, or kill me? The back of my mouth began to water just looking at it.

I looked out over the street again and noticed the dandy walk from the saloon and take up the reins of the gelding. That was a fine horse, sure enough. It looked like it would run from hell to sundown and never let up.

"You're a good ol' hoss, yurself," I said, patting my dun-colored mare. She'd taken me all the way to Dodge City and back without a whimper. So, she didn't look as fine as the gelding, didn't cost as much either, I'd bet.

The man led the gelding down the street, but he didn't tie it to the rail. He stood there, holding the reins and looking past me, to the other end of town. I cast a glance behind, to see what had caught his attention. There wasn't a thing in the street, but a haggard dog sniffing around. I looked back at the man and he stared at me with frightening eyes. I couldn't hold his gaze and looked back down at the bottle.

Live, or die, I had to try a drink. I pulled the cork and smelled it. I could feel my face bunch up in revulsion. I swallowed the vomit that came to the back of my throat. My breath came shallow as I thought of the taste. There wasn't a good bottle of whiskey in the county, anymore.

Taking a peek at the man down the street, I noticed he continued to stare past me. I glanced back, one more time, and rubbed my face with my hand. I looked at the bottle and took a swig. I brought it down and bent over to let it back out, along with what little I had to eat the night before.

When I straightened up, I saw the man walking his horse between two buildings. I looked behind me and saw four horsemen nearing the far end of town.

I had to hold some of the whiskey down, or I knew I'd die. The sun was boring a hole into my back, my stomach rumbled and jumped inside. Lord, I didn't remember being that hungover before. None of the usual remedies were working.

I took a big drink and clamped my teeth tight against the eruption. I covered my mouth with my hand. When I was confident I wouldn't blow liquid again, I looked back toward the far end of town. The riders were gone. Glancing about, I tried to locate them. Had they slipped by, while I fought sickness? If they had, where were their horses?

Oh, I felt bad. In anticipation of emptying my stomach again, I knelt down beside my horse. I kept swallowing to keep it down. It felt better to rub my mouth, so I did.

While in that position, I heard two shots and a sudden pounding of hooves. I looked under the mare to see five riders charging down the street. Among the horses' legs, all I could see from that angle, four of them were black. I turned with the riders, as they passed. The dandy rode hard along with four other riders.

Rifle shots issued from the direction they had come. I stood up. A portly gentleman stood in the middle of the street aiming a Winchester at the fleeing riders. One more shot whizzed past.

"What happened?" I asked, calling to the man, but he just cussed and kicked at the dirt.

One more drink, then I'd be fine. I tipped the bottle up. I

swallowed and coughed. Yelling commenced up the street and I looked over my saddle at a crowd gathering about the rifleman. I stowed the bottle in my saddlebags and wandered up to have a look.

". . . Shot my clerk!" I heard the rifleman say as I came up. "Stole a bunch o' money. Where's the sheriff? Somebody has to go after 'em."

A bank robbery, now that was something. I looked down the street and followed their path, trying to see beyond the dust at the diminishing dots on the horizon. Bank robbers, I thought, shaking my head. So that's what they looked like.

Over my shoulder, the crowd grew and the rifleman loudly proclaimed the evil of the times and the laziness of the sheriff. I rubbed my jaw and glanced at my horse. I had to blink a few times to be sure, but there seemed to be a bill under his left-hind hoof. I rushed over and slipped it out of the dirt.

"Good horse," I said, patting her haunch and staring at the twenty. I stuffed the bill into my pocket and gathered the reins. I figured I ought to move on before things began to heat up.

I had just thrown a leg over the dun when I heard a shout from the crowd. I pulled my hat low and glanced in the direction. Were they yelling at me? I didn't want to know, so I wheeled the horse around and started to walk it out of town.

"Hey, you! Come back here!"

I wanted to put the spurs to the dun and get clear of Santa Fe. Someone saw me get the money and wanted it back. If I took off, they would think I was in cahoots with the robbers, but I didn't want to give up the cash. I thought over my options.

"Hey, feller. Come over here."

Feeling like a schoolkid who's just been caught putting a frog on the teacher's chair, I reined the dun around and walked it up to the crowd. The rifleman stepped out from those assembled and pointed at me when I was a few feet away.

"You saw 'em. Tell the sheriff what they looked like," he said, pointing at a scraggle-bearded man, whose revolver hung next to his thigh. It seemed a bit showy, to me. I carried my Army Colt .44 in my waistband where it had always been handy enough. I didn't see a reason to buy a holster. If I was to be generous, I suppose he had more reason to pull his than I did mine.

"You all was shootin' at 'em," I said. "You must've seen 'em better than I did."

"I saw their backs. They rode in yur direction."

"I was lookin' at the ground, then," I said.

"What can you tell me?" the sheriff asked in a kind, cajoling voice.

"One rode a black horse," I replied, trying to sound feeble. I didn't want to be put in a witness chair and I could see they were aiming to do just that.

"You musta seen more'n that," the rifleman said.

"Nope."

The sheriff lost interest in me as a witness and started asking for volunteers to form a posse. I backed the dun out of the circle of people that had formed around me and reined her around. Just then, I saw the bartender waddle up to the sheriff and point me out.

"Hold on there, fella," I heard behind me. Again, I wanted to dash off, but I knew they would group me with the robbers if I did.

"This fella here," the sheriff said, "he says you talked to the man. Says you were real friendly with him in the saloon."

I pulled the horse around to stare my accuser in the eye. The fat man blanched.

"That's a blamed lie. The only fella I saw in there was a dandy. Had a suit and all, but I didn't say a word to him." I blinked for effect and let it seem to hit me all of a sudden. "You don't mean it's the same fella? Well, what do ya know about that?" I scratched my head, to make it more believable.

"Consider yourself deputized," the sheriff said, pointing a finger at me. "You, you, you, and you," he said to four others standing about.

"How much are ya payin?" I asked but received only a stern look for my attempt. "Well, I ain't no citizen o' this here town."

"You are, now," the sheriff replied, and swung aboard a gray. The other fellas mounted and we started off.

I probably would not have gone along, but I figured we had debated over everything long enough that the robbers were long out of the county, or near to it. That and I thought I could shame the sheriff into buying a few rounds of whiskey when the deed was done.

Any fool could see we weren't going to catch anyone. The bank robbers were professionals. They knew how to go about a bank robbing and what were we? We were nothing but a bunch of temporary deputies and a no-account sheriff. Likely as not, the sheriff only set out to keep the townsfolk off his back.

Yeah, I would ride posse. We would go about twenty-five, thirty miles and throw our hands up. Might even camp out a night, just to show we had good intentions. Then, we would come back into town, haggard, dusty, and the town would be grateful enough to fill us with beans and whiskey.

That's how I had it figured from the start.

CHAPTER TWO

Our little group of amateur deputies followed the sheriff out of town. We raced through the streets and out onto the broad plain. I checked the faces of the others as I rode next to them, to see how they were taking the responsibility. Three of the quickly assembled force wore stern, grim looks of determination. The other was downright eager for the chase. The sheriff, was not.

After we'd ridden hard for a bit, and the sheriff started to slow, I rode up next to him.

"Better save a little horseflesh, huh?"

The sheriff nodded and we slowed to a walk along the rocky terrain. Of course, the most zealous fellow had to put in his two cents.

"Hadn't we to keep after them, Sheriff? They're liable to get away."

"You been a deputy long?" the sheriff asked, smirking.

"Don't need to be a deputy to know, when chasin' a feller, it's best to keep a strong pace."

"More than one way to chase a feller, or a steer, for that matter," I said, to help the sheriff out. "One way is to follow him as fast as ya can, chasing him faster and further away from ya. The other way is to figure out where he's goin' and get there first. Ain't that right, Sheriff?"

The sheriff nodded, then looked about at the ground. He stared off into the distance.

14

"What'd that feller look like?" he asked, staring at me. "Look to be local?"

"Can't say for sure, seein's how I ain't local myself," I responded. "But, he was as dusty as my throat about now."

I unscrewed the top of one canteen and took a long drink of Santa Fe well water. I dallied the strap back to the saddle horn and laid it atop the other canteen. Out in Nuevo Méjico, as the old-timers called it, a man was smart to carry plenty of water.

The sheriff nodded and studied the ground.

"Makes sense," he said. "Any local would know a southeaster route led outta the county quicker than north. I suppose these fellers saw that line of hills yonder and figured makin' there would get 'em hid, anyway. If they get there first, they could make it rough on us."

The sheriff had a pretty good plan. We could scout out the mountains, ignore the tracks leading dead north, and be back in town by the next afternoon. I nodded my approval.

One of the others, the zealous one, spoke up to contradict. "It's closer to the county line heading due west than it is to the cover of the mountains."

"It's closer to go southeast," I spoke up for the sheriff. "If these men had an idea where the county lines were, they'd have gone south. Seems to me, they don't think in county lines, but in terrain. Ain't that right, Sheriff?"

He nodded.

"There ya go," I said to the zealous one. "What's yur name anyway?"

"William Macon," he said.

"You ever been on a posse before?"

"Can't say as I have."

"Then, let the sheriff do the figurin', will ya? It ain't yur job and you ain't gettin' any reward, so rest yourself."

"I was called to serve the public and I aim to do it the best I can."

"Then, do it with your mouth shut."

Macon surveyed me a moment, taking stock of my size and manner.

"You aim to shut my mouth, mister?"

"Stop it, now!" the sheriff yelled. "Save whatever fight you all have for the bank robbers."

I put my finger up to my lips and grinned at Macon.

"They'll turn off toward the hills, soon. We need to turn now to get to cover and make our way north to flank 'em."

So, we left off their distinct trail heading north and started toward the Rio Grande del Norte. I had no reason to believe the robbers would be anywhere near the mountains, but if we followed their trail, we could wind up easy targets when we crossed the Rio Grande. As far as I was concerned it was a smart move whether the sheriff wanted to catch the robbers, or not.

When we had rested the horses long enough, we set out at a rapid pace to make the river. It was a hot, dusty day and I suffered greatly, but the few swigs of whiskey, earlier, seemed to have obliterated the hangover. But that was a temporary condition. The headache, jumpy stomach, and dry mouth would soon return.

We piled up nearly atop one another at the river. It was running about average height, but some were reluctant to go in.

"Wade in, boys," the sheriff hollered.

I pushed the hat off the back of my head and felt the temptation to test-fire my weapons, but refrained due to the serious nature of the endeavor.

A few miles distant, the line of mountains rose up from the basin.

"What say, we wind-dry these fellers?" I asked the sheriff.

He nodded and we whipped the animals into a dash across the plain. My blood ran fast and my heart beat steadily. I leaned forward into the hot wind and felt parts of my clothing break loose from my skin and begin to flap against my body as they dried.

Before I knew it, we were at the base of the hills and I pulled up there to let the others catch up. The sheriff wasn't far behind. I reached behind and pulled my soggy hat onto my head. It took another moment for the others to reach us.

As soon as we had re-formed into a posse, we started up the steep incline. We had to pick and choose our way, angling upward to keep the horses on the best footing.

We spent the best part of the day making our way up and across, down and through all the various terrain. We weaved in and out of short, gnarled trees and over rocks. We stopped several times to scout out over a rise or into a valley. The sheriff called on Mr. Macon to do the strenuous, most dangerous work. Why not? The fellow seemed well motivated.

The sun decided to relieve us from our chores, by sliding down over the horizon and calling up the darkness. I had been looking forward to the moment all afternoon. I went to my horse and untied my bedroll. I chose a quiet spot and flipped it onto the ground.

Macon was put on wood detail and we watched him gather it. Another one of the fellows put rocks in a circle to guard the perimeter of the fire. It was much too dry to be letting a fire burn as it might.

On the trail drives, we didn't have to worry so much over fire. We most often camped by a river and could extinguish an errant blaze in seconds. Up here, it was different.

We only needed the fire for coffee, anyway. As soon as everyone had their fill, we would be done with it.

I didn't think there was anything more enjoyable than sitting

17

about a campfire sipping coffee. A man could relax, knowing that the work was done for the day and sleep lay just ahead. More often than not, it lent itself to storytelling and other pastimes. I thought I would cast about for some entertainment while the coffee brewed.

"A man once told me that these here hills were haunted by the ghosts of dead Injuns," I said, searching the faces of the others for effect. "Ol' Tiny Williams once found hisself naked as an Injun buck up here. When he woke up, there was an Apache lance beside him, stuck right in the ground. They'd taken off with his horse and everything else the man possessed. Said he didn't hear a thing. Claimed it was ghosts.

"It happened," I said, looking about, pretending to recognize landmarks. "Why, hell, it happened right about here!"

I saw a grin push slowly up at the sheriff's broad mustache. He had to cover his mouth with his forearm, so as not to reveal it. Macon rolled his eyes, but the other three took the news with a glance at the surrounding rocks and trees.

" 'Course, Tiny lied a bit. Likely as not, he was drunk and just forgot where he put his clothes and let his horse run off. Mighta got drunk while takin' a bath and passed out, for all I know."

"Maybe," Macon interjected, "Tiny don't exist at all."

" 'Course he does."

"Where is he, then?"

"Well, I guess that makes you a bastard, don't it?"

Macon leaned a little closer. His eyes narrowed and glowed with reflected flames.

"You'd better do some fast figurin' to explain that, mister."

"I don't see your daddy nowheres about, must mean you ain't got one," I said, staring back at Macon. "Just 'cause a feller ain't here, don't mean he don't exist. There's a Tiny Williams, all right."

"Don't listen to this man," Macon said to the others. "I've seen his kind in every trail town in the West. He ain't nothing but a braggart and a liar."

The sheriff looked at me to see how I weathered the insults. I cast a mild glance at him to let him know I had heard worse.

"Seems to me," I said. "You just told these boys a lie. Now, who are they supposed to believe?"

"I don't lie," Macon announced.

"Just done it again."

Macon stood up, his chest heaving.

"You'd better explain yourself, mister," he said, pointing a finger at me, " 'fore I come over there and knot your head."

I sat content on my bedroll. Whatever Billy Macon could do to me, it had been done before. But, what I could do to him, hadn't. I understood Macon in ways he could never understand me.

Billy Macon was a good man. He would wind up a lawman somewhere, I imagined, if he lived that long. He was full of righteous indignation, probably went to church every Sunday. He believed in the law and making examples of bad men. Yeah, I understood him well enough. There were plenty of men like him in cemeteries scattered from San Antonio, Texas, to Helena, Montana.

There were others, too: men who had made a life out of the law, U.S. marshals and the like, who seemed to stay clean in the bloody business of dispensing justice. But, there always seemed to be something a little cockeyed about their reasoning of right and wrong. A catchall set of beliefs that justified whatever amount of brutality they employed.

"Well," Macon inquired, stalled in place by my thoughtful silence.

"Sit down, William. I didn't mean nothin' by it."

"You better not," he said, taking his seat and looking at the

19

others, as if to say: "That's how you deal with men like this."

When the coffee was done, we all thrust our cups out to be filled. The sheriff poured the cups full, then poured out the remainder over the fire. The embers hissed and smoke billowed up.

"How many Injuns you suppose are watchin' us, right now?" I asked the sheriff. He looked somewhat annoyed but glanced about.

"Not more'n ten or twelve."

I chuckled at the shocked looks on the men's faces. All but Billy Macon, who sat still and shifted his eyes quickly from side to side.

"Who's standin' first watch?"

"Macon," the sheriff said. "If there's trouble out there, I'm sure he'll find it for us."

I nodded and leaned back on one elbow.

With the fire out, darkness pushed closer in, until the moon rose up and shed some scant light onto the camp. Most of those gathered about were decent men of the town. They talked together, whispered and chuckled in the darkness.

Before going to sleep, I went and situated the dun. I took off the bridle and put on a halter. I tied it to the picket rope strung between two trees. I removed the saddle and the blanket and took them over to my bedroll. Later that night, I dug through the saddlebags and slipped some whiskey into my coffee cup. Just a drink, or two. Then, I went to sleep.

CHAPTER THREE

I slept peacefully in the knowledge that the bank robbers were far from us. Most likely in Colorado Territory, I thought. Therefore, I felt it was rude for Macon to kick my feet sometime around midnight, to stand the rest of the watch.

"I'm up," I said, trying to clear my head. I sat up and glanced at the figure walking through the darkness, as if a shadow. I picked up my saddle and carried it over to the dun. When she was saddled and ready, I started to plan my revenge.

It was a stupid thing for Billy to bother me, just before he bedded down. Doing so, he let me spend those dark hours in slow contemplation.

I grinned at the thought of it and pulled the Winchester out of my scabbard. I checked it over for cartridges and checked my revolver as well. Who knew what sort of animals dug around in the mountains at night? I wandered from the campsite to have a look around.

Walking in a slow circle, I thought of all the ways to get back at Billy. I circled the camp, drifting up high into the hills and then swinging down low until I came upon the scattered bedrolls. I stopped at the dun for a drink. The whiskey felt good going down and I had another.

Before I left to take up a position further up the hill, I stopped and stared at Billy. I could smash his skull in, if I wanted to. Then a better idea came to me. Why not show the boy a little humility?

I moved carefully away from him and went back to my saddlebags. I pulled the bottle of whiskey out and carried it over to his bedroll. I lightly sprinkled his bedroll with the liquid and what parts of him were sticking out. The next thing was the hardest. I had to dump the bottle out and lay it beside him. It sure was a waste to pour the contents into the dirt, but it was the best way to suggest he had been drinking enough to pass out.

The rest of the night, I watched the camp. Just before daylight, I snuck back in and crawled into my bedroll. I lay there, faking sleep with a smile on my face. Then, I waited for the sheriff to wake and realize no one was keeping watch. An hour passed.

"Holy Jesus Christ!" I heard him roar. Everyone stirred to the ringing voice. The sheriff rushed over to me.

"You were supposed to be keepin' watch. What're ya doin' in bed?"

I wiped my eyes for a decent amount of time and looked about, startled.

"No one woke me up."

"Like hell, I didn't," Macon snapped back.

The sheriff went over to Macon.

"You're sure you woke him up? Did you see him get up?"

"I swear it, Sheriff."

The sheriff saw the bottle and bent over to smell Macon. He backed off, quick as a cat.

"Whew! You're drunk. What the hell you think you're doin'? You can't get liquored up on watch. What sorta fool are ya? For all you know, them robbers coulda come down and cut our throats and you'd have been drunk as a dog."

"I ain't drunk!" Macon protested.

The sheriff kicked the empty whiskey bottle and sent it smashing against a rock. Then, he did something I had not considered. The sheriff pulled his revolver and cocked it. He put the muzzle up to Macon's forehead.

"I'm callin' you a liar, now. Go ahead and get tough with me, boy, and I'll put pieces of yur skull all over this mountain."

Poor Billy Macon, he went to sleep in a world he was awful sure of and woke up to a nightmare. He probably didn't even know who he was, not with that .44 poking at his brow.

Feeling a bit guilty for all the trouble, I walked over and put my hand on the sheriff's shoulder.

"We still have some robbers to catch, Sheriff. We best keep as many men as we can."

The sheriff put his thumb up to the hammer and let it back slowly. He holstered the weapon and turned on his heel. As the sheriff went over to get his horse ready, I stared down at Billy.

"Don't make the sheriff mad, Macon. He don't seem to be as easygoin' as I am."

"Goddamn you, I woke you up and you know it!"

"Did ya?" I asked, walking away.

Before we got too deep into the day, I had to let the sheriff in on the scheme. It wasn't fair to send a man out looking for outlaws, not knowing what sort of men he had with him; besides, an uneasy feeling that you could've been killed in your sleep is the sort of thing that nags on a person all day long.

"I was watchin' the camp last night," I said, moving up to the sheriff. "I just wanted to take old Billy down a peg, or two. It was my whiskey and all."

"I know it," the sheriff said. "You think I'd take a bunch of strangers out into the desert, on posse detail, without keepin' a close eye on 'em?" He shook his head. "No, sir. That wouldn't be smart, would it?"

"I reckon not."

"I'm grateful to ya . . . what's yur name?"

"Frank Whittaker."

"Folks call ya 'Snake,' do they?"

"Some do."

"I'd like to see that trick, sometime."

I grinned.

"Well, Frank, we both know Mr. Macon needed to fit his place out here and I suppose you put him in it. I'm grateful for that. Now, maybe, he'll take orders like everyone else."

Wouldn't bet on it, I thought. The sheriff put the spurs to his mount and disappeared through the foliage. His statement caused me some concern, however. How long did he expect us to be out here? By my figuring, we should be on the way back to Santa Fe. What more could we do? Ride the length and breadth of the county?

Billy Macon rode up beside me.

"You did it to me. I won't forget this," he warned.

"Yur still drunk," I replied and watched his eyes glow red with hate.

The sudden crack and echo of a rifle spun both of our heads to the north. We kicked our horses into a run and charged along, weaving through trees and over rocks. A bullet whipped through the branches above our heads, sending debris filtering down.

We came upon the sheriff crouched behind a rock firing down the hill. I swung off the dun and tied her to some high bushes. I pulled the Winchester out of the scabbard and crawled up to the sheriff's position. Peeking over the smooth crown of a rock, I saw down the hill to where a group of men were gathered. A white puff of smoke issued from one of their rifles. A bullet landed with a thud into the dirt just below us. Then the delayed report issued from below.

"Hittin' anything?" I asked.

The sheriff didn't answer but rose up on his knees and let go a shot.

"Just keepin' their noses in the dirt, for now. The other three are off gettin' in position . . . I hope."

"That, or hightailing it for Santa Fe."

I looked over my shoulder to locate Billy. He was snugged up against a tree, using it to steady his aim. He sent a piece of lead down the hill. I peered over, looking at their horses.

"Seen the black, yet?"

"He ain't with this bunch."

"Good Lord, Sheriff, how many are there?"

"Don't know," he replied, letting off another round. "You gonna talk, or shoot?"

"I'll shoot if ya tell me to, but I don't think we're shootin' the right fellers, Sheriff."

"Shoot 'em, anyway. They're shootin' at us."

I raised the Winchester and popped a shot at one of the men. From the tree, Billy took a shot. We kept them busy from the front, while the others made their way to the sides. Just as lead got to flyin' pretty thick, a white flag of truce was raised up on a stick.

We stopped firing and stared down at the handkerchief.

"Aw hell!" the sheriff said, knowing that no outlaw would raise a truce, not without being shot a few times, and we hadn't hit anyone.

One of the men stood to full height, though still mostly hidden by a large boulder. There was a white flash. It looked like he had fired at us from his chest, but there was no whizzing of a bullet, no dull report.

"We've been shootin' at the law!" Billy said, in disgust. He stared at the sheriff, showing a curled lip of indignation. "I mighta known you'd do me this way."

From down below: "Come on out, Leonard. Ain't no way out."

"Do you what way?" the sheriff asked, standing to face Billy.

The voice from below droned on as background noise to the

action on the hillside, the way a piano plays in a saloon after a fistfight breaks out.

"Makin' me look like a fool."

"You don't need any help," I added.

"And, you. I know you put that whiskey on me and went back to sleep. You're all a bunch o' slobs."

The sheriff busted him upside the head with the butt of the rifle. Billy's knees buckled and he slumped to the ground. Blood issued from a gash in Billy's cheek and dribbled into the dry, sandy earth as he lay crumpled on the ground.

I shook my head.

The sheriff looked at me.

"Damn, that boy's got a mouth to him, don't he?"

I nodded.

By then, the voice down below was growing hoarse from screaming up into the air at Leonard, whoever that was. The sheriff walked up close to the rock and looked out over the top.

"There ain't no Leonard up here. This here's Sheriff Ben Fowler, of Santa Fe County. We've got a posse up here, so you'd better have a damn good explanation for shootin' at us."

"Sheriff?" the man below asked and let out a string of profanity. The tiny figure threw his hat on the ground and kicked dirt into the air.

Behind me, Billy moaned and tried to pull himself up to his knees but fell back again.

"The hell you shootin' at me for?" the distant man asked. "I'm a U.S. marshal. Come down here and explain this, Sheriff."

"I ain't explainin' a damn thing," the sheriff muttered to himself, then walked to his horse. "Get that man atop a horse and bring him down with ya."

I got my hands under Billy's arms and raised him up, but he could not stand. I let him back down and brought his horse over. It was a job, but I got Billy thrown over my back and laid him over his saddle. He looked up with a swollen face and babbled something. Then, we started down the hill. I rode beside Billy and occasionally had to adjust him to keep him from tumbling out of the saddle.

When we rode up to the scene, Billy came to and pulled himself upright. He straddled the mount, but his head hung low, as if the swelling were heavy and drawing his face downward.

"You fired the first shot," the marshal said, pointing a stiff finger at Sheriff Fowler.

"I'm lookin' for five men that robbed the bank in Santa Fe. You all seem to be about five, don't ya?"

"Don't mean we're outlaws."

"Don't mean ya ain't, neither."

The two went around and around until they were satisfied that no blame could be attached to one party, over the other. Then, they settled down to do some dickering.

"This here's my jurisdiction," Sheriff Fowler said.

"The whole goddamned U. S. of A. is my jurisdiction, Sheriff." The marshal looked the horizon over. "We've done alerted every outlaw in the world with all this firin'. Hell, don't you even know who you're lookin' for?"

"Bank robbers, is all I know," Fowler replied.

"At least, we know who they are. The leader rides a fancy, black stud."

I grinned and caught his eye.

"What're you grinnin' at?" he snapped.

"Not a thing, Marshal," I replied, knowing the horse was a gelding, not a stud. I wondered how much he really knew about the man he sought. "Who is this feller, anyway?" I asked.

"Leonard Braswell, but he goes by any number of names. Leonard's his real one. He's a gambler, mostly. He wears fancy clothes and rides a fancy horse. When the money runs out and

27

his luck's been bad, he robs a stage, or a bank. Held up a riverboat awhile back and jumped right off into the Mississippi River. The money liked to have sunk him, but he had a boat waiting and got away."

"Ever seen him up close?"

"Son, if I'd gotten that close to him, I'd have shot him."

I nodded.

"You're welcome to tag along, Sheriff, but we're keepin' after this dog until we put a leash around his neck and hang him from the nearest tree."

"Or cliff," I said, looking around at the short trees.

The marshal shot me a keen stare.

"You're welcome to tag along, Marshal," Fowler returned, "until we get to the county line."

"Look here, Sheriff, I'm a U.S. marshal. I'm in charge of this expedition. You can ride under my badge, but I'm runnin' things."

"Not in Santa Fe County, you're not."

The various deputies stood about uneasily while the two leaders hashed out the pecking order. Billy looked up with a lopsided, swollen head and one bloodshot eye. He stared at the raging debate.

"What on earth happened to him?"

Fowler looked over his shoulder at Billy's pathetic face.

"Challenged my jurisdiction, you might say."

CHAPTER FOUR

Our little posse had grown to a formidable force, with the addition of U.S. Marshal Dayton Howard and his deputies. The marshal wasn't pleased to be under the direction of Sheriff Fowler, but the sheriff put the situation into proper terms.

"Any time you think I'm goin' the wrong way, Marshal, you just take yourn and go another way. But, don't start shootin' at us no more."

By noon, I was thirsting for the long-departed whiskey. I looked up at the sun. The brilliance of it was like a slap in the face, and I ducked my head in repentance.

We rode out the ridge of mountains and wound up near the town of San Miguel without finding any sign of Leonard.

"Looks as if I've come too far," Fowler said, peering at the town from under the shade of his hat brim. "C'mon boys," he said, waving a hand for us to follow.

"Hold on there, Sheriff," the marshal called. "Now that we've been trackin' together for a spell, I'd be obliged if you'd stick it out a bit longer. Leonard may be holed up in that town."

"That town ain't in Santa Fe County. I've done gone outside my jurisdiction as it is."

"How about leaving me some of your men?"

"That ain't up to me."

The marshal looked about at the three others, ignoring Billy. All of them shook their heads. When he came to me, I stared at him.

"How much you payin'?"

"Fifteen dollars a month."

I spit into the dust and thought it over. Riding wages for a top hand was twenty.

"Twenty," I said.

"I'm not authorized to bargain. Those are set wages by Washington."

I could do worse than riding around looking for Leonard. Without cattle to tend, it might be enjoyable. Not as enjoyable as lying around a saloon with money in my pocket, but a sight more profitable. Anyway, the marshal didn't seem any more able to find Leonard than Fowler was.

"Seems to me you don't need another deputy. What you need is a guide. I charge twenty dollars a month."

"A guide?"

"Yes, sir. If you didn't know San Miguel's outside Santa Fe County, you could use a guide."

I didn't know enough about the country to be a guide, but I had been up and down the Santa Fe Trail enough to know my way around. Besides, it didn't seem like the marshal knew as much as I did. If he let me ride with him long enough, I would know how far I could push it.

"What if I'd only pay fifteen dollars for a guide?"

"Then, I'll take a badge and keep my mouth shut, like these other deputies. If you want my opinion on things, it'll cost twenty."

"What do you know about this man, Sheriff?"

Fowler looked me over. I suppose he was trying to figure out which one of us he felt a greater loyalty to, the marshal, or myself.

"He's a good man. I can't vouch for his abilities as a guide, but he knows his way around."

We split company there, Fowler going back to the comforts

of Santa Fe, and me, off with a U.S. marshal and I wasn't even under arrest. Imagine that. That was a hoot, and I started my new career off on the right foot and led us to the general store in San Miguel, to replenish my stock of whiskey.

"What the hell're we doing at a store?"

"I suppose you're right," I said, dismounting. "That Leonard feller's too much of a bible-totin' critter to buy himself a drink after robbin' a bank and losin' the law."

I came out moments later with a bottle in my hand.

"No, sir. They ain't seen him."

"What's that bottle for?"

"Drinkin'," I replied. "Desert nights get awful cold."

I saw one deputy shake his head, lean over on his saddle horn, and stare at the ground.

"Maybe you best see if you can catch the sheriff," the marshal said, stony-eyed and staring straight ahead. It didn't seem he was so much against whiskey, but he didn't want to be led around by a drunk.

"Fine with me," I replied. "Where's my twenty dollars?"

Another one of the deputies blew air through his teeth and looked at me in exasperation.

"You ain't earned it. All you've done is shown us to a town we already knew was there," the marshal said, this time staring right at me.

"Well, now," I said, taking a step back to survey the situation. "I've contracted to work for a month, but if you only want me for the day, I'll give you the day rate."

"How much is that?"

"Twenty dollars."

"I won't pay it," he said.

"A dollar a day, then."

"That's thirty dollars a month."

"Or, two dollars. Depends on when we catch him, don't it?" I said, thinking I'd make it a month if I had to circle all of New Mexico to stretch it out.

"I could decide not to have a guide at all."

"That's the best idea I've heard yet," the third deputy said.

Marshal Howard glanced at him for reassurance.

"We've come this far without one and New Mexico ain't that much different from Texas."

"Damn right," the third deputy nodded his agreement.

"You're right about that," I agreed. "Except for the mountains. Knew an old boy set out to Colorado once. Found him froze to a tree up yonder. 'Course, not 'til spring. Got off the trail, ya see," I said, winking.

That gave the bunch of them some pause, but I could tell he would get shut of me as soon as he could find a replacement.

"I ain't all that bad," I offered. "Once we get the price set."

"I'm offering twenty a month. Take it or leave it."

"Hell, that's all I ever asked for, Marshal."

"Mount up," he said.

When I'd gotten into the saddle, they all stared at me.

"Well, which way?" the marshal asked, exasperated.

I looked about at the terrain and thought about it a bit. I rubbed my jaw and looked in all directions.

"Seems to me, if I was Leonard, mind you, I'd head out of New Mexico. That bank he robbed held the governor's money. Not only that, he's a travelin' man and most likely headed for Colorado Territory," I said, mostly, because I wanted to go to Colorado. "Gambler, you said?"

The marshal nodded.

"There's a fair amount of gamblin' in Trinidad." I had spent a few days there and had a hankering to see it again. I knew some places there that would justify the trip.

"You'd better be right about this."

"Can't say if I'm right, or not. You ain't hirin' a gypsy. I can only say what's likely. You get a better idea, I'll follow you."

After riding for several miles one of the deputies, a man named Pete McAllister, pulled up alongside.

"Best not be foolin' with the marshal. He's a mean feller, when he wants to be. Shot three men in Texas and stabbed two others with that big knife of his. All they done was curse in front of a woman. At least, that's what I heard," he said. "No, sir. There ain't no tellin' what goes on in his mind."

"Appreciate the warning," I said, extending my hand. "Name's Frank Whittaker."

He told me his name and pointed out the others.

"That fella with the black Stetson, that's Will Dobson. Next to him, with the droopin' mustache and side whiskers, that's George Brimson. He's pretty fast with that Whitney revolver. The other one off to the right there, sniffing around for sign, is Little Jimmy Carroll."

"What brings you fellers up from Texas? Seems there's enough trouble down that way to keep the law busy."

He shook his head and let out a little laugh.

"You ain't heard of Marshal Howard?"

"Not 'til this mornin'."

"They know him right well in Texas. Fought in the war with Mexico and the Civil War. Only reason he ain't a general is he fought for the Confederates. When they needed a good man to take up chasin' outlaws, the Yankees forgot about his Southern loyalties and give him a badge."

"You still ain't said what brings you to New Mexico."

"Now, who else would they send after Dandy Jim Beudreaux?"

"I thought we was lookin' for Leonard somebody."

Pete winked and nodded his head.

My stomach went sour. The name Beudreaux had been with me since childhood. When I was sixteen, I fancied following in his footsteps. It sounded like an interesting life to ride the riverboats, gambling. I envisioned dance hall gals sitting on my knee, while I played a hand of stud for thousands of dollars.

When I left home, I set out to do just that. I had played with friends until I could win at will. Then I went into larger towns to try my luck. The fact that I had fallen back on cowboying to keep myself alive attested to my inability to pursue the dream. Every now and then I would sit in on a hand, but any thought of making it a career was forfeited in interest of a full stomach.

Since those days, I had learned more about the man. At first, I rejected the reports of his crooked games and the men he killed when he lost. But later, in Abilene and Kansas City, I had come to know gamblers of his kind and could see how my vision had been clouded by childish idolatry.

Still, I followed Beudreaux's career with interest. He was a grand character in my eyes and I felt sad to be chasing him down. But then, I had faith in my hero. He wouldn't let the likes of me catch him. Hell, no one could catch the famous Dandy Jim! Not even Marshal Dayton, by god, Howard.

I thought back to the day in the saloon. He didn't look a thing like his picture on the cover of the book. He was, by then, old, but keen-eyed and serious. I shook my head at the thought that he might be living by the skin of his teeth, dodging the law and robbing banks. It did not seem right that a man I had grown up thinking of as an honorable man would turn to such extremes to keep up his high-living ways.

But then, other men I had looked up to as a child had proven themselves to be unworthy of my quick worship. When the veil of childish ignorance was lifted, I could see that the funny, kind men I met on the street were just drunks. That the rough, surly men I disliked were actually good fellows to work for. So it was for Dandy Jim. Instead of a larger-than-life Robin Hood, he was a gambler, thief, and murderer. I couldn't quite hate him for it, though.

I thought about turning back, right then. I wanted no part of stringing up the man I had admired. If others had to do it, I would square myself to the outcome, but I did not want to be a part of it. Then, it occurred to me that it might be the only time I would have a chance to see him up close. Different from the time in the saloon, this time I would know who I was looking at and I would take advantage of it. I might even ask him what caused him to change, if indeed, he had.

I looked over at Pete.

"You think you'll ever catch Dandy Jim?"

"Marshal Dayton Howard doesn't fail, because he doesn't give up. We got involved in this when Leonard shot one of our party. We had Leonard near cornered in San Antonio, shortly after the episode on the river. Poor Douglas Smythe was sent in to get the lay of the place before we burst in to capture the gambler. Unfortunately, Leonard saw what Douglas was up to and he shot him. He escaped in the turmoil.

"We've been on his tail ever since. He surprised us with the robbery, because he knew we were only hours behind. We thought he'd make straight for Arizona, but he turned north and robbed the bank in Santa Fe. But then, if he was predictable, he'd have been caught long before now."

Pete was silent for a moment, then he looked on up ahead.

"His time's running out and he knows it. Dayton says he'll get desperate and sloppy now. Says he'll try to kill us all maybe. Sneak up in the night if we let him. But the marshal will stay on him, even if he has to go all the way to California. That's just the sort of man the marshal is."

"That right?"

Pete solemnly nodded, as if knowing his fate lay with the desires of the marshal and the cunning of the gambler.

I felt it, too. We were pawns in the overall game being controlled by the white king and the black king. They would use us to get closer to, or further from, the other. They kept our lives in limbo, while they maneuvered about the chessboard of the West pursuing the crucial advantage that would present them with victory, or death.

Well, I would play along for a while. Soon, they would move off, out of my little square, and I would go back to punching cows. But I would always be able to tell of the time I helped Marshal Dayton Howard chase down Dandy Jim Beudreaux.

CHAPTER FIVE

That night, we camped several miles outside of Raton along the eastern edge of the Rocky Mountains. I had been quiet most of the day thinking about Dandy Jim and his exploits. I thought about my place in the posse and found that I had been lacking in my duty. I had never been one to take the lazy way, so I figured I ought to pitch in and give it some effort.

Sure, I had taken the job as a guide to get back at the sheriff for dragging me away from the saloon. I felt cheated somehow and wanted someone to pay for my inconvenience. But the marshal agreed to pay my wage and I owed him some effort for it.

Where would Dandy Jim be? What sort of place would attract his need for high living and still provide an atmosphere of drunkards and gamblers? I stared at the fire, as if the answer lay within the flames.

"So, what's your story, Frank?" Pete asked. I noticed that the others, even the marshal, were anxious to hear what gave me the credentials to be a guide in this rugged country.

"I've punched some cows throughout this area and down south for John Chisum. I've taken several trips up north to the mining camps in Colorado and to forts along the way. Chisum has several government contracts around here. I just got back from drivin' steers to Kansas City for Skinny Jacobsen, though.

"I know most of the places a man can go for shelter and diversion. There's bordellos and saloons from Mexico to

Montana and I've seen most of 'em at one time, or another."

"If you ain't a regular lawman, what were you doing with the sheriff?"

"Well, that was unfortunate," I said, thinking back on it. "I'd just gotten into Santa Fe from takin' a herd to Kay Cee. Next thing I know, I'm part of a posse heading out looking for bank robbers."

"Why'd they choose you?" the marshal asked.

"Handy, I guess."

The marshal seemed a bit disappointed in my answer. He pushed at the fire with a stick and let himself become entranced by the sight of the glowing coals of fractured firewood. He tossed another few sticks on the fire and it flared up.

"I'm waiting," the marshal said over the sound of sizzling sap.

"For what?"

"The rest of it." He pointed a flaming stick in my direction. "Don't play me for a fool, cowboy. I could tell you how I know there's more to it, but that's none of your business. Get on with the rest of it."

I felt guilty, I imagine. The marshal seemed to know things about men, the way I knew cattle and horses. He had a knack for it and summed men up by looking them over, taking note of every aspect of their dress and manner. Then, he would cull out the bad ones and leave the good ones be.

"Well," I began, a bit hoarse. I cleared my throat and swallowed pent-up saliva. "I saw him, Leonard, at the saloon that day. I was the only one to get a look at him."

"There ya go," he said, his eyes softened. I felt he was pleased with me, as if I had done something special. I was happy to oblige.

"So, you say your name's Frank Whittaker?"

I nodded.

"There's more to that, too. Ain't there?"

What did he mean by that?

"Hell," he continued. "I've never met a cowboy yet that didn't have a nickname of some sort. You mentioned Skinny Jacobsen. Surely, his parents didn't give him that name. So, what's yours?"

"Aw, hell," I said, feeling myself blush. "Some folks call me 'Snake,' I reckon."

"Snake, huh?"

"That's right."

"And, why's that?"

"On account of a little trick I showed this feller, once."

"You mind if we see it?"

"No, sir, but you need to have a rattlesnake for it to work."

"Maybe, you could just tell us about it."

"I could, but I usually make money with the trick and it don't seem right getting these men curious without being able to satisfy their curiosity. Hell, they might start callin' me a liar if I couldn't prove what I said."

"I'm sure they'd believe you," the marshal said, looking around at his men. I watched as they nodded.

"Tell ya what. If we run into a rattlesnake, I'll show it to ya. But I'll have to charge something for it. Otherwise, folks'll be wanting me to show it free all the time and it's dangerous."

"Fair enough," the marshal said, filling his cup with coffee and easing back into the shadows.

I looked over at Pete. He and the others fell back away from the fire and melted into the surrounding darkness. I reached out and poured myself a cup of coffee. Feeling alone and making quite a target for a sharpshooter in the darkness, I picked up my bedroll and moved into the night.

I lay on my bedroll thinking things over. The marshal was a clever man. He knew just how hard to push, just what to do, to get a man to tell him what he wanted to know. I felt a bit used afterward, as if I'd been tricked into revealing more than I should have. I couldn't help feeling like he'd picked my pocket or burst into my room unannounced. I knew one thing by then, I was glad I wasn't the man he was after.

"Marshal," I said, into the night, knowing he lurked there waiting for me to confess everything.

"Yeah, Frank?"

"I know a place about thirty miles west of here, a town called Cimarron. There's a real fancy hotel there. Being on a spur of the Santa Fe Trail, it attracts a lot of wild characters, outlaws and such. I think Leonard might be there."

"Why's that?"

"Well, sir, if Leonard's also Dandy Jim Beudreaux, he'll be attracted by the gambling and the fancy livin' quarters. They say ol' Lambert was a chef for Abraham Lincoln and he makes some mighty fine dishes."

"I hope you're right. Good night, then."

" 'Night, Marshal."

I had some personal reservations about going to the St. James Hotel. It was famous for housing some of the toughest hombres in New Mexico, and those were the townsfolk. The drifters were worse. Even so, it was smart to cover all angles before heading across Raton Pass to Trinidad. If I was going to take pay for being a guide, I figured I ought to put some effort into it.

I woke early, while still dark, and lay staring up at the wild outreaches of heaven. Tiny stars winked down upon the broad plain and I watched as they faded with the growing dawn, the way life fades with the slow progression of days.

The little fire lay cold and I looked around for twigs to bring it to life. I leaned up on one elbow to have a better look and realized that all the other bedrolls were empty. Jumping to my feet, I drew my Colt and scanned the area beyond the camp. Off to the right, the group of them were gathered, talking. I let out a sigh of relief and replaced my weapon.

I suppose they had to have their private conversations. They were a gang themselves, in a way. A law gang and they were protective of their own. So, I stoked the fire to life and called over to find out who had coffee and who had extra water for the pot.

"Don't you have coffee and water?" Will Dobson asked, his black Stetson moving about in the gray of early dawn.

"I ain't carryin' no store for this bunch," I hollered back.

"Look in my saddlebags," Little Jimmy Carroll said.

I went over to his paint and found a bag of coffee. I unwrapped the strap of his canteen from the saddle horn. After making coffee and setting it on the fire, I put the articles back. His paint was a fine horse and I noticed that it had an Indian mark on the haunch.

Shaking my head, I wondered what sort of man steals horses from Indians? The marshal had himself a passel of rugged men in his posse. I was tough enough, I suppose, but I wasn't the grizzled brawlers these men were. There was a cold emptiness about them, like some of the Civil War amputees I had met. A man's never the same after some part of him is removed. There's always a longing for it, even if it isn't an arm, or a leg. Sometimes, a person can't see what's missing about a man, but he knows it's gone.

When I had gotten my horse saddled, I sat near the fire on my heels, waiting for the coffee to boil. With my empty cup in hand, I stared at the pot.

"A watched pot never boils," Pete said, walking over.

"It'll boil all right and I'm gonna be here when it does."

Pete chuckled and sat beside me. The others came by in time and took up seats. Little Jimmy Carroll sat for a moment and then gathered his horse and started back the way we had come.

"Where's he goin'?"

"Trail work," Pete replied.

I nodded, as if I knew what trail work was. These lawmen did things different, that's for sure.

George Brimson stared at me with narrow eyes. It was the boldest, most naked stare I had ever endured and it unnerved me. His bushy side-whiskers and drooping mustache seemed like a disguise of sorts. Buried in deep sockets were the blue eyes that peered out like the jab of a pin. I looked at the fire to avoid his gaze.

"You think it's likely that Leonard's at this hotel?" the marshal asked.

"Likely," I replied, keeping my eyes on the pot.

"Ever put lead outten that thar hogleg? I mean at somethin' other'n a sick cow, or a chicken?" Brimson asked, straight-faced and serious.

"You forgot snakes. I've shot them, too," I answered with injured pride. It wasn't like I hired on to the law as a career. I just wanted to make a little profit.

George Brimson leapt to his feet and took great strides to reach me. I jumped to my feet and met him next to the fire. He pulled his revolver and stuck it to my chest. He cocked it back.

"Now, George," the marshal said, mildly, as if George were an errant child.

"I mean, you ever done it like this here? To a man, huh? You ain't never kilt no one, have ya?"

"No," I said, but thinking that killing a man was nothing to be proud of.

"See there, Marshal. What you wantin' this here cowboy along with us for anyways? He'll just git hisself kilt." Then to me: "Law work ain't nothin' for a tinhorn cowboy. So, when it gits thick, you just back outten the way, boy." He held the hammer back and pulled the trigger, then let the hammer ease back in place. George whipped the gun in circles, the way I had seen trick shooters do, and landed it in his holster.

"George is right, Frank. Don't feel like you have to take part in any of the shootin'. You're hired as a guide and that's all we expect of ya. But, don't get in our way, either. The last thing we need is to be worried about you when the time comes."

"Hell," George said, turning his back on me and walking to the far side of the fire. He threw up an arm. "He cain't even tell when a man's about to walk up an' stick a revolver in his chest. How the hell's he gonna know when the shootin's about to start?"

Good question, I thought.

"Don't mind George," Pete said, leaning close and whispering. "He's pretty gruff, but he tells it straight. Ain't no backup in that one, none at all."

I poured coffee for the men and filled my cup. I set the pot back on the fire thinking Jimmy would want some when he came back. Pete sipped at his cup and looked off the way Jimmy went.

The marshal got up from his seat and went over to his horse. In a moment, he came back with a badge. He buffed it on his shirt and handed it to me.

"Better wear this," he said.

"What for?"

"It may keep someone from shootin' at ya. You can give it back after we leave Cimarron, if ya want. Sometimes, a badge'll hold a trigger finger back, that's all."

"That thar badge ain't gonna give him enough time to skin that iron, I'll tell ya that, right now," George said to the world.

The only thing I didn't like about George Brimson was he was right. It probably wouldn't give me time to draw the Colt. I wasn't a pistoleer and never claimed to be. I had no cause to shoot another man before, and the idea of it wasn't very appealing.

"Pin it on, just in case," the marshal said, giving me a nod and a wink.

CHAPTER SIX

Little Jimmy Carroll met us on the trail west of Cimarron. It surprised me to find him there, relaxed and sitting with his feet up on the withers of the horse, like some cowboy staring out over a herd. When we came up to him, he nodded quickly to the marshal and fell in with the group.

We continued on in silence. It seemed as if the mountains, standing solid in the distance, drew us in as a whirlpool draws twigs toward itself. I could see myself as a twig, being sucked into the turmoil of the area.

The sun rose behind us, spreading heat across our shoulders and casting our shadows ahead, as if warning the path of our approach. The deputies seemed lost in their own thoughts. Perhaps, they were going over the way they would handle themselves, or thinking of the technical aspects of their jobs.

I approached the valley with a conflicted heart. What would I do if I met up with Dandy Jim? What would he do if he recognized me from Santa Fe? I looked down at the badge on my shirt. I wanted to give it back. Would it save my life, or help to forfeit it? From everything I had seen, of the short time I'd spent in Cimarron a few years back, the citizens didn't give the law much thought.

About halfway to Cimarron, Will Dobson decided that he had to stop for a nature call. We all pulled up while he found a somewhat secluded place to drop his drawers.

"Don't be all day about it," the marshal said, watching him

scamper off.

Pete McAllister chuckled to himself and leaned toward me.

"Ol' Will, he must havta shit three, four times a day. If he wasn't such a steady man with a rifle, I bet the marshal'd leave him hunkered beneath a tree, one o' these times," he whispered.

I nodded.

Will had been gone for some time when we heard him cussing softly.

"Marshal?" he said, the voice coming through his teeth.

"What is it?" the marshal demanded.

"Git over here, there's . . . a snake. Hurry."

"Shoot the sonofabitch!"

"I . . . I can't. Lord, please don't let me die like this!"

"Here's your chance, Frank. Go get that snake away from Will's ass."

I hopped down from my horse, thinking I would make amends for whatever weakness I presented earlier. I came upon Will, his britches around his ankles and his white buttocks shinning in the morning sun. Tall grass surrounded his feet. I heard the rattle liven as I neared, but I still couldn't see it.

"Where is it?"

"Right there, by my six-shooter," he said, whispering and sitting in a crouch as still as could be. "Just shoot the damned thing."

"Don't you want to see how I got my name?"

"I don't give a good goddamn how ya got it, just kill the snake."

The rattler, sensing the anxiety, coiled back and searched for blood with his nose. The rattle sped up precipitously.

Now, I know when I have an old boy in a position to extract some money from him and I didn't miss the opportunity often.

"I'll take care o' this snake, but it'll cost ya one dollar. Call it a fee for seein' the trick."

"If you don't hurry, it'll cost me more than that."

"Well?"

"Deal, deal," he said, squirming to get another inch away from the diamondback.

"Gather 'round," I called back to the others. "Two bits a piece to see the trick."

"Two bits? How come I have to pay a dollar?"

"It's yur ass," I replied.

I heard the others approach and glanced behind. The other four stepped cautiously over. I had already started to attract the snake's attention to my left hand. I waved it in front of his head and heard the others whisper to themselves. I didn't listen to what they said, I was focused on the snake to judge when he would strike.

As soon as the snake took to watching my hand, Will walked away like a crab and hastily wiped himself. I could see him hiking up his britches from the corner of my eye.

When he was safely away and not likely to attract the strike in a different direction, I brought my right hand up as far away from my left as I could. I moved sideways, keeping my left hand in front of the snake's nose.

The important part of the trick was to correctly judge the length of the snake. A rattler can strike a little more than half its length. By judging its length and keeping one hand right about its striking distance, a person could force it to strike by making a sudden move.

I slowly moved my hand in a circle to entrance the rattler and to keep it from striking. When I was ready, I darted my left hand in and back out as I came around behind it with my right. As soon as the rattler was extended in midair, I caught him about four inches from the head.

The worst part was the sudden revulsion of grabbing the scaly surface of the snake. It took some resolve to keep from dropping it, but it would have been considerably worse if I had.

I held on and brought my left hand around its tail to keep it straightened out. I inched my right hand closer to the back of its jaws. The others were whooping and hollering up a storm.

"Now pay up, boys, or I'll heave him at ya."

I carried the snake around to each man and waited for them to put money into my shirt pocket. Will complained the most about forking over the cash and I had to shove the snake at him before he counted out his change.

"Now, what are ya goin' to do with it?" Pete asked.

"I've heard tell," I said, suppressing a grin. "A man can snap the head off if he takes it by the tail and cracks it like a bullwhip."

"Point it the other way," Will said, still eyeing the snake with dread.

"Cost ten dollars to see me try," I said, not wanting to try it. To my relief, none would pay and they mounted up for the ride into Cimarron.

I bent over and put the rattler's tail under my boot and reached to my belt for the Bowie knife I kept on a loop. I unsheathed the shining metal and slipped it just under my right hand. Quick as you please, I cut the head off. The jaws opened and the body dropped and coiled about my leg.

Nothing gave a man the spooks like having a headless snake coiling around a part of him. Even though I held the head in one hand, I had to look down to make sure it hadn't grown a new one. It was a queer precaution, but it eased my mind.

I tossed the head as far as I could and watched it cartwheel through the morning air. The experience was worth the two dollars I earned, but I wouldn't do it again for a hundred, not for a while, anyway.

When I approached the group, they held bemused smiles and shook their heads at my audacity, or stupidity. I couldn't help but believe they were impressed, though. I must have been grinning like an idiot, but I couldn't stop.

"Nuevo Méjico is full o' crazy sonsabitches, they say," George Brimson hollered to the sky. "And, I'll be goddamned if I ain't ridin' with one!"

Old George had changed his tune about me, for the moment, but he hadn't seen a thing, yet. We were still a good fifteen miles from Cimarron, where "crazy sonsabitches" stood plentiful. We didn't have long to wait to be introduced to the town, however. Our first meeting came in the form of a man riding hell-bent for Kansas, as far as we could tell.

The rider noticed us and directed his horse toward our group. I heard Little Jimmy Carroll cock his double-barreled shotgun. As the rider drew closer, we could see he wore neither shirt nor hat. He charged his mount right up to us and jerked back on the reins, bringing the horse down on its haunches.

"I'm beggin' ya, by Christ, don't tell him ya seen me. Ya didn't see nothin', now," he said, wild hair poking out in all directions. When he spoke, saliva dripped down his chin. His head vibrated with excess energy and he kept looking over both shoulders. Even his horse seemed scared senseless.

"Who?"

"Who? By Christ, that devil. That drunken, crazy sonofabitch, Clay Allison. Threatened to put my head on a pole! A pole! What sort of man could do such a thing? Hell, anybody asks ya, tell 'em you ain't seen nobody, understand? It'd mean my life."

Without another word, he gigged his horse and charged east, toward no town that I knew of. All of us looked about at one another, as if to see how the experience had affected the other.

"He'll be dead before sundown headin' that way," I said.

We continued on toward Cimarron, watching anxiously for whoever chased the bedraggled, harrowed man. I had heard of Clay Allison; he was given to drunken rages and was not above committing horrendous crimes. Word had it that when he was sober, he was a polite and decent man. Drunk, he was different.

A few miles further on we heard the sound of horse's hooves and looked behind us. The bare-chested man rode hard upon us. We reined our horses around toward his approach. He pulled the horse to a stop. Again, the stud slid on its haunches.

"By Christ, you didn't see me! I ain't here. I'm a spirit. You don't even see me now. Remember that," he said and charged off toward Cimarron.

All of us wore confused and concerned faces as we glanced about at each other. What was going on? Was Allison really after the man, or was he a lunatic, or both? George Brimson let out a great laugh.

"Now, that's a crazy sonofabitch," he declared, pointing at the cloud of dust slowly rising toward the blue, cloud-pocked sky.

An hour later, we saw a line of dust coming at us from the south. A lone rider came out of the dust spire, bare chested and glowing red. The sun had baked his skin while he charged about on a lunatic's journey.

"Well, now I've just had enough o' this character," Will Dobson said, raising his rifle. He sighted down the length of the barrel. I looked at the marshal. Was he going to let Dobson shoot the man, in cold blood?

The sound of the rifle echoed in my ears as I watched the bare-chested man tumble backwards off the horse. Will Dobson spit into the dust and thrust the rifle into his scabbard.

"You just gonna let him do that, Marshal?"

"Seems to me, he put the man out of his misery and spared the horse. That's all he's done."

"You got somethin' against what I done?" Will asked.

I shrugged my shoulders. If the marshal didn't care, who was I to complain? I did feel a bit disappointed to find the marshal wouldn't even scold the man.

I had always known the line between outlaw and law wasn't very wide, but this incident narrowed the line even further. From a U.S. marshal, no less! I would expect such behavior from some county posse made up of men as likely to be murderers and bank robbers themselves, but I had given Marshal Howard credit for being a more solid lawman.

"If the marshal don't care, I don't," I said to Will.

He nodded his head, as if that were the proper response.

"Shouldn't we go bury him, at least?" I asked, as we had already started toward Cimarron.

"Coyotes and wolves have to eat, same as us," George replied.

"We're in pursuit of a criminal, Mr. Whittaker," the marshal said. "I'll let neither crazy men nor their bodies deter me from that pursuit. Deputy Will Dobson shot the man out of sympathy for his crazed condition and the health of his horse. Now, shape up and keep up."

With that, the marshal made everything plain enough. I knew it was wrong, he could not change that, but I saw it from his point of view and let the matter drop.

CHAPTER SEVEN

Cimarron was as unimpressive as I remembered it. A few adobe buildings and a few businesses gathered at the base of wooded hills. There didn't seem to be enough activity to warrant a newspaper, but its office sat just off to the side of the road.

The most impressive structure was the St. James Hotel, a creation of Henri Lambert's optimism. The St. James was a two-story adobe building with a lavish interior. Lambert's idea was to build a swank hotel in the middle of nowhere that would attract the upper crust of Western society. No one knew if he planned it as a retreat, or as an attraction in itself, but planned it was.

Lambert's hotel offered some of the best meals to be had in the territory. Too often, however, the bar at the rear of the dining room was the main attraction.

I led the group of men into town, crossing a bridge over the Cimarron River and up to the hotel. After passing the newspaper office, I reined the dun around a corner and my jaw fell open. Atop one of the corral poles was someone's head.

"Good God," I said to myself, stopping the horse and gaping at it. The marshal and his deputies reined up. The sight explained a lot about the wild man out on the prairie. Apparently, the threat was more real than any of us imagined.

A Mexican stable-boy stood at the gate to the corral, grinning.

"*Es muy barbarico, no?*"

"*Muy*," I replied, riding into the corral, keeping far from any part of the head that might dislodge itself from rot and tumble down.

When we had all dismounted and left instructions with the boy, I looked at the marshal.

"I got you here, now it's yur play."

"Stay to the back and duck out when the shootin' starts. If it does."

I nodded. The others seemed edgy and stiff. I let them pass in front of me and I fell in at the rear. Whatever they had in mind was none of my concern. I was just a hired hand. I had no reputation to protect, nor law to uphold.

We had just come around the corner of the hotel, beneath the overhang supported by poles, when a lawman stopped us.

"Hold on there," he said, throwing up a hand. "What's your business in town?"

"Who the hell're you?" the marshal asked.

"Mace Bowman. I'm the law in Cimarron," he said, jutting his chin and jerking a thumb at his badge.

The marshal pulled his lapel back and showed Bowman the encircled star.

"Glad to meet you, Sheriff. I'm U.S. Marshal Dayton Howard. We're in town looking for a fugitive, Leonard Braswell. We'd appreciate any cooperation you're inclined to give us."

Bowman struck a pose, with his right leg thrust forward and a hand pushing on the butt of his revolver. "Braswell," he said, getting the feel of it on his tongue. "Don't know the name."

"He goes by several," the marshal offered. "You might know him better as Dandy Jim Beudreaux."

"Aw, hell, why didn't ya say so? I got him locked up right now."

We all looked stunned, as if kicked by the same mule.

"Where's he at?"

"Over to the jail. Come along, I'll show ya to him."

Bowman led the way across the dusty street toward the sheriff's small adobe office. He was sauntering, dawdling, as he walked, and the rest of us were stumbling over ourselves to stay behind. He stopped once to trim his fingernail and the delay liked to have driven the rest of us into hysterics.

Then, Bowman threw his head up toward the south end of town. We heard the thunder of hooves and gunshots. From around a bend, eight riders rode hard upon us. By then, all of us had our weapons drawn and sighted. Bowman threw his arms out to keep us from advancing.

"Hold your fire, boys," he said, drawing his revolver. He fired at the horsemen. One of them fell from his horse. The others slid to a stop and wheeled their mounts around to charge back the other way.

"Nice shot," Pete said.

"Hell, I didn't shoot that sonofabitch. I wasn't aimin' at none of 'em. They's just a bunch o' drunk bastards. Been tryin' to rob the hotel for a week now." Bowman holstered his revolver and waved us on. "I ain't got all day."

As we neared the jail, I saw the fallen man get up, stagger sideways, and fall again as he tried to run the other way.

"There he sits," Bowman said and flipped a hand at a short man in a bowler hat.

"That's Dandy Jim?" the marshal asked. "Frank, get up here." He reached back into the crowd of us, grabbed me by the shoulder, and pulled me up front. "Is that the man you saw?"

"That ain't him."

"Well, by God, that's Jim Beudreaux!" Bowman insisted. "I got him in here for drunk and disorderly. Tried to have a conversation with Mr. Pole. When Mr. Pole wouldn't oblige, Jim here took to shootin' at him. I can't have that, boys."

Yeah, Bowman could allow someone to sever a human head

and place it on a pole above the corral, but he couldn't allow someone to take a shot at it. That sounded like Cimarron.

"This ain't the man we're after, Sheriff."

"Well," Bowman replied, lighting a cigar. "That's all the Jim Beudreauxs I've got. Take him or leave him. Makes no never mind to me." Bowman looked over at the prisoner. "You stupid sonofabitch, you ain't even got enough smarts to be a big outlaw."

The man shrugged pathetically.

"Let me buy you a drink, Marshal," Bowman said, showing him to the door.

The group of men shuffled slowly forward, waiting patiently for a chance to exit. That left me alone with the prisoner. I glanced at him self-consciously and then felt that I ought to give him a piece of advice.

"You should use an alias, Mr. Beudreaux."

"My name ain't Beudreaux an' Bowman knows it," he said.

I studied the fellow for a moment. What did he mean? Why would Bowman lie? Then again, why would this guy lie? Lies for the sake of it, it seemed.

The doorway cleared and I followed the others over to the hotel. We got rooms and brought our things up. The stable boy promised to look after our horses. When we had a chance to get things squared away, we met Bowman and the marshal at the bar. They had the jump on us by a few drinks.

When the whiskey was poured, I listened to the conversation between the marshal and Bowman. For the most part, it was shoptalk about outlaws apprehended and sought. They compared notes on what they had heard about certain notorious men.

Then, George Brimson walked up to Bowman, his rough manner evident in his gait.

"Sheriff, if those men've been hankerin' to rob the hotel, why ain't you just put 'em in jail?"

Bowman bristled at the suggestion that he might not be doing his duty.

"For one thing," he said, pulling back to get a better look at Brimson. "One of 'em's my deputy. For another thing, they ain't done nothin', yet. Is that a good enough explanation, Deputy?"

"Not hardly," Brimson snarled. "Seems to me, any deputy plannin' to rob a hotel ought to be shot, then fired."

"Is that right?"

Brimson nodded.

"Excuse me, Marshal, but it seems you ain't got this deputy trained to mind his own business."

"Now, George," the marshal said, turning toward the two arguing across his back. "Let the sheriff do as he sees fit. It's his town."

"Damn right," Bowman said, aiming a stream of spit into a brass cuspidor. He kept his eyes on Brimson.

"Next time I see them damn fools shootin' their pistols, I'm liable to make it my business," George said.

The marshal abruptly spun around and grabbed George by the shoulder. He turned him toward a table and gave him a shove. "Have a drink."

In time, we moved away from the bar and over to the table where George sat, sullen. Sheriff Bowman excused himself after a while and went about his duties in town. As soon as he was gone, George started in.

"Damn poor excuse for a lawman," he said.

"Now, George, some things ain't what they seem. I can't say anything, right now, but there's reasons for why the sheriff doesn't arrest them fellas."

"Yeah, he's a damned chickenshit," George replied.

"I don't believe that's true, George."

56

George flipped his hand to dismiss the conversation, but George knew he was out of line.

"So, Frank, it don't seem much like Leonard's anywhere about," the marshal said.

"No, it don't," I agreed.

"You have any plans on where to check, next?"

"I imagine I ought to go upstairs and sit in on a hand, or two. Sorta see if anyone's heard tell of him up there."

"Fine piece of thinkin'," the marshal beamed, leaving me to wonder whether it was sincere, or not.

I excused myself from the group and went to the bar. As I bought a bottle of whiskey to take up with me, a thought nagged at the back of my mind. I went back to the marshal.

"Marshal, I'd like to have a few dollars to play with," I said, thinking the government should stake my hand, since I would be there on official business.

The others didn't see it that way. Will Dobson pushed his Stetson hat back on his head and stared up at me with a gaping jaw. Pete snickered.

"Well, if that ain't the goddamnedest thing!" George Brimson boomed.

Little Jimmy Carroll slumped in his chair and grinned silently to himself.

"You want me to pay you to gamble?" the marshal asked, to clarify the point.

"No, sir. I want the government to stake my hand. I ain't there to gamble, I'm there to get information."

"Git on outta here, you little scamp!" Brimson hollered, amused at my attempt.

"Now, now, George, the man has a point."

All heads turned toward the marshal, as if he were more insane than I. I stood before them determined to stick my play out.

"You just keep record of what you lose, and I'll present it with your claim for wages," the marshal said. I knew it was a graceful way out for him. If I ever saw a cent, it would amaze me, but I couldn't argue with the reasoning of it.

"If that's how ya want it," I said, pulling my hat down in frustration. "But, I ain't gonna lose if that's how it is and I don't know that anyone'll talk to a man takin' their money."

With that, I pulled the cork from the bottle and took a draw. I proceeded through the lobby, down the hall and to the staircase. Behind me, I heard the shouts of laughter from the marshal's table. I cussed under my breath and started up the steps.

At the top, I turned to my right, walked down a short hall and turned left at the next. Halfway down and on the left side of the hall was a closed door. I knocked lightly.

"This is a private game," a muffled voice called out from within.

"Private game, hell," I replied. "I've never seen a private game that money didn't make public."

"Just have," another voice replied.

I kicked the door in frustration and walked away. I stopped after only a few steps and had a pull of the bottle. As I drank, I heard the door open. I turned around to watch it slam shut. A din of squeaking chairs and hushed voices rose from the room.

"The hell's goin' on in there?" I called, I put the stopper in the bottle and let it dangle from my hand as I took cautious, curious steps toward the door.

The door opened a crack and I saw the flash of a muzzle. The bullet shattered the bottle and I dove for the wall. On hands and knees, I scampered along the floor. Behind me, I heard shots ring out. Pieces of wood splintered at the end of the hall. I got around the corner and was halfway down the steps when I met the marshal's bunch on the way up.

Pete McAllister grabbed me by the shoulders and looked me over.

"They hit ya?"

"Shot the piss out of my bottle," I said, puffing. I put my mind to searching the different parts of my body for pain. None.

"C'mon," Pete said, pulling on my sleeve, dragging me up the steps. When he said "C'mon," I'd started the other way. Then, I realized the law went to the trouble, not away from it.

A number of shots were traded in the hallway before Pete and I could get to the corner. About the time we came to it, we were met by the others coming back around, heading for the steps. They brushed us out of the way. They passed us like a train and we followed in the excited air of their departure.

The group of us met Bowman in the lobby. He tried to stop us and ask the particulars of the shooting, but he was brushed aside. I grabbed him by the sleeve and told him to come along. I wanted all the real lawmen I could find.

The marshal was the first one out the door and I saw him pull up and take aim in the sunbathed street. He let off two shots. About that time, horses' hooves could be heard coming from the south.

I made it out the door in time to see the would-be hotel robbers ride into the marshal's party. A horse reared and dumped its rider on the ground. George reached up to another rider and jerked him out of the saddle. One of the riderless horses charged up onto the boardwalk of the St. James and cleared it of spectators.

The street was awash in men and horses and dust. There was general cussing and some shots were fired. I ran into the middle of it and stared at the fleeing party. There were five horses, one as black as midnight.

"I'll be damned," I whispered to myself.

A fistfight broke out between Will Dobson, George Brimson,

and a few of the drunken hotel robbers. Will Dobson hit one of the men so hard, he did a back flip and landed on his face. The marshal was backing a man away from the center at the point of a revolver. Sheriff Bowman walked beside the marshal pleading the man's case.

Pete McAllister came around with the horses. The sight of the horses brought everyone to their senses and they got busy disentangling themselves from their adversaries. We mounted up and charged out of town hot on the trail of Dandy Jim Beudreaux.

CHAPTER EIGHT

Riding out of town, we crossed the bridge and followed the dust to the left. The wind beat against my chest and I felt a bobbing at my shirt. I glanced down to see the badge bouncing up and down in the wind. I had forgotten to take it off when I went up to the gambling room. That must've been what caused the shooting.

We were not far from town, before the marshal threw his hand up.

"Whoa!" he yelled, pulling back on the reins.

The rest of us gathered around, the horses stomping and blowing.

"Let's head on back to town, fellas," he said, reining his mount around.

"The hell for?" Brimson asked, disgusted.

"Damnit, George. You see that canyon, there?" The marshal pointed at the path leading through high walls covered with foliage.

George looked at the cover with renewed interest and we all came to realize what the marshal meant. The canyon gave but one route in and plenty of cover for an ambush. All Dandy Jim had to do was pull up and pick us off as we rode through.

"Now," the marshal began, seeing that we all understood. "You want to follow? Go on ahead, but I'm tellin' ya, there's a better time and place."

With that, we rode casually back toward Cimarron. I pushed

my mount up next to the marshal. I pulled the badge from my shirt and held it out.

"I reckon this started it all," I said, sheepishly.

"You might want to take that off when you're playin' cards with wanted men, Frank."

I looked downward to keep from meeting his gaze.

"Stupid sonofabitch," I heard Brimson mutter.

"You best keep this badge, Marshal. I don't seem to think like a lawman."

"Just put it in your pocket for now. It may come in handy."

I snorted my disbelief but stood in the stirrups and put the badge in the hip pocket of my britches.

Back in Cimarron, the street outside the hotel was cleared, but for a few men lying unconscious in the dust. Brimson reached out and slapped Will Dobson on the shoulder.

"That's the feller you knocked hell outta, he still ain't got up, Will," he said, delighted.

Will Dobson spit and said: "Better not."

Little Jimmy Carroll swung up close to the marshal when I had drifted back to ride with Pete. He whispered a few things to Marshal Howard and peeled off from the group.

"Trail work?" I asked Pete.

He nodded and we rode to the corral. The Mexican boy held the gate open with a grin.

"The hell you grinnin' at Mex'n?" Brimson asked, but the boy pretended not to hear.

"*Bienvenido*," was all he said, and closed the gate.

Pete told us to go on while he spoke with the boy about matters concerning a black horse and where it had been kept. None of us had seen it when we rode in and the others must have been kept close by, saddled. Part of our delay in chasing the outlaws was due to time spent saddling the horses.

We had just rounded the corner of the hotel, when Bowman

stepped out.

"That was a quick foray," he said.

The marshal cornered him over the remark.

"The hell's the idea of harboring a fugitive?" the marshal snapped.

"I ain't harboring a damned thing. If that man was wanted, it's news to me. Hell, there's been a party holed up in the gamblin' room for two days, now. Ain't none o' my business, lest it's on the street causin' trouble."

"And, what's the idea of lettin' criminals run loose? Those idiots nearly killed us all!"

Bowman surveyed the streets and the few men lying about.

"Seems like you held your own, Marshal."

"That ain't the damned point! We might've picked off a few, if we hadn't been run down from behind." The marshal was breathing hard and staring at Bowman. "I hope to God, you arrested some of 'em."

"Now looka here, Marshal. You bring your business into my town, you get my town. You don't like it, take your business outta my town. Understand? Your problems ain't my problems."

Bowman spun on his heel as if to go to the jail. When he did, George slapped leather as a show of loyalty to Dayton Howard and contempt for Mace Bowman. In a flash, Bowman spun back around with his revolver drawn and cocked. The speed of his draw startled us all, especially George, who hadn't intended to do anything more than show off. George hadn't even jerked his own weapon but stood like a fool aiming his finger at the sheriff.

"Next time you draw that hand, it had better damn well be loaded," Bowman said, retiring his six-shooter to the holster. He gave George a smirk and continued toward the jail.

"Damn, George," Will said, slapping him on the arm. "That fella's purt near fast as you."

"Purt near," he said, hawking up some bile and spitting into the dust. "Let's get a drink."

The two of them walked off. I stood in the street with the marshal. Pete called and came up to us.

"The boy says he had to keep the horses saddled and stashed at his house during their stay."

"Didn't he think it peculiar enough to mention it to Bowman?"

"Yes, sir, but he was afraid. Says he didn't know whether to tell or not to tell."

The sun edged closer to the tall mountains and stained the blue sky with a furious orange glow.

"Old Leonard had it figured about right, this time," the marshal said, starting for the hotel.

Pete and I stood in the street. One of the unconscious men stirred and sat up. He blinked a few times and searched the ground for something.

"Wild town," Pete said.

"Yes, sir," I replied and tugged at his sleeve to follow me into the bar.

By the time we entered, several groups were seated for their meals. The marshal was at the bar buying himself a bottle of whiskey. I was glad to see it. It always seemed easier for me to communicate with a drinking man. The others, the bible-toters and the like, I couldn't hardly speak to at all.

Will and George were seated at a table near the bar. Just behind them at the bar, a dealer leaned his head on his palm and threw back shots as fast as the bartender could pour.

"Over here, boys," Will called, waving a hand to us.

We made our way over and took up chairs.

"Looks like a lively crowd," Pete said, glancing around.

"Aw, to hell with all of 'em," George said. "Git some glasses."

I went to the bar and got a couple of glasses. When I set

them down, George poured. I could see a gleam in his eye and knew he was contemplating mischief. If I had seen it before I sat down, I wouldn't have. A lot of men dawdling around Kansas City had that look and it always led to trouble.

The marshal stopped by the table on the way to his room.

"We're leavin' early, boys. Keep that in mind."

When he disappeared around the doorway to the lobby, Will leaned close to the three of us.

"Dayton don't like gettin' beat this way. Lord knows what sort of hell them boys'll go through when he catches 'em."

"Ta givin' outlaws hell," George said, raising his glass and slamming the contents down his throat. He belched and filled the glass.

As time drifted onward, those having dinner rose and turned the dining room over to the scalawags on the fringes of decent society. No doubt, they had spent a restless night worrying over the brawls and shootings below.

Those of us left got increasingly drunk and loud. Prostitutes filtered in wearing shiny, revealing costumes of debauchery. I stared at one of them: a dark-haired girl with greenish eyes. She was plump and sweet looking.

"Ain't you never seen no damned sportin' girl?" Brimson asked, trying to get my goat.

"Hell, yeah. I've seen the likes from here to hell and back, but she's a sweet-lookin' one, ain't she?"

"Whore's a whore, I say," Brimson thundered.

Cigars and cigarettes from several sources began to fill the interior with smoke.

"Don't mind him, being married makes him irritable," Will offered.

"Makes everyone irritable," George agreed.

A few men started a game of cards in the corner and I thought I might be able to win a few hands from them. I forgot about the girl and studied the game.

"Now, that's a goddamn shame if I ever saw one," George said.

I looked at him and followed his eyes to where two negro soldiers stood at the door.

"Imagine putting a uniform on a couple o' niggers. What's the world comin' to?"

I took some exception to his opinion, having known a number of negro cowboys in my day, but arguing the point would have gotten me on the wrong side of George. That was the last place I wanted to be, knowing his mood.

Instead, I turned my attention back to the game and watched with interest. The fellow in the brown farmer's hat was losing and from what I could see of the other's hand, it must've been a tough chore.

"Excuse me, fellers," I said, standing. "I bet I could win some money over there."

George grumbled something about drinking his whiskey, but I ignored it and walked toward the table. I figured the men for a couple of yokels and I was anxious to get into the game. As I started across the aisle between tables, the negro soldiers passed in front of me.

"Mind if I sit in on a hand or two?" I asked, politely. "I've been out trackin' outlaws and such for a while. Ain't picked up a deck in ages. If you fellas don't mind, I'd just like to see if I still know how to play."

They studied me for a moment, then motioned me to a chair. They offered up their names and we shook hands. One's name was Fred and the other Florencio. Florencio was a Mexican businessman, I guessed. He wore nice enough clothes and had some manners. Fred, the man in the brown hat, he seemed to be a hired hand of some kind. Perhaps he worked for Florencio. They seemed an odd pair.

"What's the game?" I asked.

"Is Monte," Florencio said, dealing.

I nodded my head and gathered my cards.

Then, from the far corner, over the din of conversation and through the cloudy atmosphere of smoke, I heard George's voice.

"I don't give a damn what you say, Will. Nigger soldiers is a flat disgrace to the uniform, I say."

I watched the soldiers glance quickly over their shoulders.

"Ain't nothin', but Abraham Lincoln's pets, them niggers. Who the hell let 'em in here, anyway? They all ought to be strung up together, far as I know."

"What's yur bid?" Fred asked.

"Boys, I'm gonna have to let this hand go. My apologies," I said, watching George.

"Now, that's awful rude. We've already dealt," Fred remarked, then looked at George. He summed up the situation, then looked back at me. "Don't let that bother ya none. Just hit the floor when the shootin' starts. That's the way we do it here."

I glanced at him, then back to the action. One of the soldiers pushed away from the bar and turned to George.

"Mister, we's only in fur drinks. We's soldjers rights enough an' they's plenty more, too."

"Bring on all o' you woolly-haired bastards, I'll take every one!" George fired back.

Will put his hand on George's shoulder. I didn't know if it was to calm George down, or to show his sentiments. I looked at Pete. He didn't seem much like a fighter to me. In fact, I wondered what had caused Pete to become a deputy in the first place. Pete was staring at the door. I glanced at the door, then back to George.

"Naw, naw, mister, we wants no troubles here."

"Then, get the hell out!" George boomed, silencing a number

of discussions.

To each side of me, the game resumed. I looked at the door again. Who was Pete watching for?

The negro still facing the bar reached a hand back to pull his friend around. Perhaps he knew the kind of man George Brimson was. I figured he had seen plenty like him.

The first soldier pulled free of his friend's grasp and declared: "This'n be a free country!"

That brought George out of his chair and the other negro around from the bar. I didn't see George jerk his revolver, but it was in his hand. The negro came around with a belly pistol drawn. Will came out of his chair, reaching for his. Pete bailed out of his chair and started for the door. I thought he was trying to get away.

I stood out of instinct, an involuntary attraction to the impending carnage. George shot the quiet negro with the revolver. Fred and Florencio ducked under the table.

The soldier that had been doing all the talking flipped the flap on his holster and dug around for the army Colt. It was much too cumbersome a move for a saloon. George shot him in the head, taking him back and over against the bar. The other soldier got off a round from the floor, but it went harmlessly into the ceiling among a vast number of others. George shot him in the head, too.

George flipped his weapon around on his finger and holstered it. Will had barely gotten his revolver out before he put it placidly back into the holster and punched George on the shoulder.

"Coulda give me one."

"Hell, I waited fur ya on that last'n," George replied.

When it was over, I glanced at Pete. He had his weapon drawn, ready to face off any reinforcements. I sat back down and watched as the arguments started between the hotel staff.

68

They argued about whose turn it was to clean up.

"Deal," I said, directing my voice under the table.

the mattress above where he lay. It was a cheap of straw beneath. I said, throwing off a smile as the other

CHAPTER NINE

It was still dark when the knock came to my door. I pulled myself into my rumpled, smelly clothes. Reaching under the pillow, I found the heavy Colt and thrust it into my waistband. I looked the room over with a bit of regret. It was likely to be awhile before I slept on another bed.

I opened the door and passed through with my rifle resting on one shoulder and my saddlebags draped over the other. Adjusting my hat, I looked both ways down the hall. No one else seemed to be about, which meant I was probably late.

The sound of my footsteps echoed off the silent walls. I tried to quiet them as I eased down toward the lobby. I had every intention of walking right out of the place, but a man was waiting for my arrival.

"Dollar twenty-five for the room," he said, his shotgun cradled in the crook of his arm.

"The marshal's payin'," I replied.

"Not what he says."

"I don't give a damn what he says. I'm with the posse and I ain't payin' for no room."

The man raised the twin muzzles of the shotgun in protest.

"Ask him for yurself," I said, waving him toward the door.

We stepped out into the street amid the chirping of crickets. As we started around the corner, a figure in the darkness whipped his horse and yelled. He was near the newspaper office. I stopped to see the cause of the commotion.

"I won't have it, by God! Damn lies, that's all this rag's good fur!" the man screamed through the whiskey in his voice. The horse stomped and snorted in front of the building. Finally, the man got down with his rope and kicked the door open.

In a moment he backed out of the building, letting out slack. He climbed aboard the fuming, sweaty mare and threw a few wraps of rope around the saddle horn.

"Hawwww," he yelled, kicking the horse's flanks. The rope drew tight and vibrated. The horse strained against the weight, then a scraping was heard from within the building. Whatever the man had on the other end of the rope came loose with a snap and the horse bolted forward. The object, squarish, flopped and broke a piece of the door as it came out into the open.

Without bothering to look back the man rode right into the river, dragging the object bouncing and cartwheeling behind.

"There, goddamnit! Print that you sonsabitches!" he hollered, kicking his rope free and coiling it up.

"Who's that?" I asked.

"Aw, that's just Allison gettin' rowdy again," the man said, eyeing me with casual contempt.

"The feller that put that head on the pole?"

The man nodded and stared at me, as if I was trying to make conversation to delay paying for the room.

"Come on," I said, leading him out to the corral. My horse was ready and waiting along with the others.

"Damn near noon," Brimson roared, when he saw me.

"Marshal," I began, irritated. "This man says my room ain't paid for. Must be an oversight."

"Ain't no oversight. I don't pay board for guides," he replied.

I heaved my saddlebags up and thrust the rifle into the scabbard. The shotgun no longer served as a nudge, but a shove, when the man cocked the hammers back.

I put my hands out so he could see, even in the dim light,

that I wouldn't resist.

"I've got the money," I said. "Damn dirty trick," I snarled at the marshal.

I moved off to a dark corner of the corral, so as not to let on I had plenty of money. If the marshal knew that, he would make me pay for everything. I dug out a wad. When the man saw it, he released the hammers and swung the shotgun over his shoulder.

In a moment, we were mounted and heading out of the corral. As soon as Pete closed the gate behind us, we were met by Bowman. He stood in the street with several men, some of whom had been trying to rob the hotel the day before.

"Hold on there, Marshal," he said, putting up a hand. The other hand hovered around the butt of his six-shooter. I glanced at George. He puffed up a little and readied himself.

"What, now?" the marshal snapped.

"The feller that shot the soldiers is gonna have to stay put for trial."

There was an immediate eruption of voices from our group.

"Self-defense," George said.

"They drew first," Will added.

"That's just damned nonsense!" the marshal shouted.

"Saw it all," Pete declared.

"Looked fair enough, to me," I said, my voice softer than the rest.

"I'm sure all o' that's true," Bowman replied. "Don't change much, anyway. Still need a judge to say so."

The marshal swung down to plead his case. His voice dropped to a reasonable level.

"We're in pursuit of a desperate outlaw, Mace." The marshal used Bowman's first name, a dead sign that the marshal was in a bad position for bargaining. "I need this man. All of my men are experts at one thing or another and I need 'em all. We'll come back this way. You can have your trial, then."

Bowman thought it over. The marshal, thinking he had made some sense to him, pushed the argument.

"Hell, I know how it looks, but we're not like the other vermin that pass through here. We're the law, damnit. We'll abide by the ruling of a judge, but not now, Mace. Those men are gonna get away if I have to hold up here as long as a day."

"I sympathize, Marshal, but I have my problems. Those weren't just a couple of drifters. They were soldiers."

"They were niggers!" George screamed, as if Bowman didn't understand the obvious.

The marshal flushed red, knowing George had lessened his hand.

"Shut up, George. For God's sake!" Then, he turned to Bowman. "Listen, we won't be more'n a month. You can wait that long for justice, can't ya?"

"Well, I could," Bowman said, rubbing his jaw. "But I can't say the Army won't come lookin' for ya. I'd have to cooperate, say you left too soon for me to catch ya in my jurisdiction. I could say I was off huntin' Allison. That usually works."

"I'd be much obliged," the marshal said.

"I'm gonna turn my back," Bowman said. I thought he meant figuratively, but he turned his back on us. "Best not be there, when I turn around, or I'll have to hold him over for trial."

We wasted no time putting Cimarron behind us, but instead of turning toward the canyon, we turned east. Safely out of town, we pulled up.

"George, we ever get into a scrape like that again, you keep your blamed mouth shut! We have important duties to tend to, understand? This ain't no time to settle personal business."

"I coulda took him," George muttered, but in a voice that sounded small and uncharacteristic of George.

"What about the rest of 'em? And, what about the law? We

ain't outlaws. We don't shoot fellow lawmen unless they're corrupt and Bowman ain't corrupt."

"How do ya know that?" Will asked, coming to the defense of his friend.

"I do, that's all," the marshal said.

It was only then, that I noticed Little Jimmy Carroll. He'd been there the entire time, but he had a way of melting into the scenery. I was pleased to see him.

"Where to?" the marshal asked Jimmy.

"Wandered about the hills for a bit, then lit out east o' town," he replied, rolling a cigarette. " 'Bout midnight," he added.

"Ya got us this close," the marshal said, turning his gaze to me. "Where next?"

"Up over the hill, I imagine. To Colorado."

The marshal nodded and kicked his horse into a trot.

It was difficult to see how his mind could allow the shooting of a crazy man on the prairie, without remorse and even less conversation, while maintaining that he was the law. I suppose it all made sense to him, but I could not fathom it.

Yet, to demand consistency from the marshal would've been asking too much. I knew a lot of folks with strange objections to normal things, who also found outlandish acts completely reasonable. The wild and dangerous nature of the West, combined with the sheer isolation of it, lent itself to speculative notions of right and wrong.

So, we headed toward Raton and I don't think I was the only one worried about being chased by the Army. We rode hard for several miles, then slowed and pampered the horses. Then, off again.

We made Raton in early afternoon, stopping only long enough to fill our saddlebags with supplies. Then, we started up the wooded slope west of town. The hot sun was favorably hidden by thick aspen and pine. We made good time, though we had to walk the horses a spell.

It was rugged going. None of our boots were fitted for walking as much as for riding, and they certainly were not fit for walking on an upslope. Yet, we all knew the importance of pushing onward.

If we could capture Dandy Jim, we could rectify the situation in Cimarron before the Army caught us and hung us all for murderers. I would like to say I saw the worry on the others' faces, but I did not. Only in their urgent mood could I tell they were worried about the Army as much as I. Or, was it a sense that we were close to Dandy Jim?

Either way, I was grateful for the rapid pace. This game they played—upholding the law and yet, above it—left me disillusioned and hoping to part company before I started to endorse it.

We made camp high in the hills having covered some forty miles, some of which were as straight up as a man could stand. My legs ached from the walking and climbing and pulling on the reins to coax my equine partner into the endeavor. Jimmy Carroll had the best trained horse of all of us and made good use of it. He grabbed hold of the horse's tail and sent the horse up first, pulling him behind.

Our campsite was set in a small clearing. Rocks were gathered to form a firebreak from the dead pine needles that covered the ground. We used some of the dry needles to get the fire going. As soon as we could, we rolled out our bedrolls and stretched out on them with groans.

The dark of night descended upon us like the dropping of a curtain. It seemed as if we were cut off from the rest of the world. It was spooky and I got my share of uneasy feelings as I stared out at the walls of trees.

I figured I better have a look around and got up from the bedroll. If I could satisfy myself that there was not a bear, or cougar, or Indian pacing the fringes of our camp waiting to pounce, I could get some sleep. Not before.

Once on my feet, I felt of the Colt and checked it for a full load of cartridges. After only a few yards, the campfire seemed distant and eerie. My shoulders hunched as a sensation ran up my back. I drifted further away, looking down into a valley. Then, I went above our camp and tried to get a glimpse of it, to see how visible it was.

As satisfied as I could be, I started back to camp. Still, there seemed to be something just behind me, tracking me. I turned around several times to see if I could catch sight of something, but always I stared off into the dense trees and shaded sky. I wanted to run back to camp but knew how silly I would look stumbling into the firelight, alarming everyone with news of a strange feeling.

When Little Jimmy Carroll stepped out from behind a tree, I nearly lost my mind. My whole body vibrated, trying to jerk my revolver and get a run going, then realizing that if I ran, I would run right into him.

"Little jumpy, ain't ya?"

"I'm spooked," I said. "I can't even deny it. And, you don't make matters any better, follerin' me around givin' me the gooseflesh."

"T'weren't me. I just came out to see if you'd gotten lost."

"Well, there's somethin' strange happenin' in these hills."

Jimmy laughed and clapped me on the back.

"It's just the dark."

"I've seen dark, before," I replied in self-defense. "This place is just spooky, that's all. I guess I like the flat land, where a man can see a few miles. This place has me all crowded in."

"I get the same feelin' in a house," Jimmy smiled, emulating a shiver.

CHAPTER TEN

I woke stiff and sore the next day. I could barely raise my leg high enough to kick myself upright on the bedroll. Glancing around at the others, I could see I had company in discomfort.

The little fire had been stoked to a flame and a pot of coffee brewed. I pulled my hat onto my head and got my things together. I noticed that Jimmy Carroll was absent, as always.

Soon, we were on our way across the summit of Raton Pass. I led the way, but Jimmy drifted further ahead trying to cut sign. When we started downhill, we dismounted and led the horses over the roughest parts. I could hear George Brimson cuss every time I called the men to halt and dismount. It wasn't my fault.

Then, after drifting into and out of valleys, there at the top of the world, we came out high above Trinidad in Colorado Territory. The roots of the town went back nearly as far as Santa Fe, but it was blocked in by mountains.

The massive church sat center, with Spanish architectural lines. It was something to behold from that elevation. Looking out over the vast emptiness of space, I figured I was as near to flying as a man was liable to get.

The town rose higher into the sky as we descended. Nearing level ground, we again mounted up for the last several miles. There was a large meadow to cross and then a hill rose up and obliterated the town for a time. When we topped the rise, Trinidad lay before us.

That last bit reminded me of spying the railhead after a long trail drive. It made me lonesome for the long, tedious days of driving cattle across the West. Time passed slow and easy, then. It wasn't like the hectic pace I had kept up since being deputized.

In my mind, I could see the long, fat herd of cattle moving slowly along, their tails swishing at flies gathered around their backsides. I could see the dust with golden rays of sunset filtering through. I shook my head. Those were the days.

"They came through here," Jimmy said, calling from up ahead. The marshal and I kicked our horses ahead to inspect the trail.

When we got there, Jimmy was almost breathless with excitement as he knelt beside the one clear print he could find. There were others, but that one was in a bit of soft dirt, not quite mud.

"See here, this is the black. See, how his shoe isn't quite straight. And, that mark ain't very old. See, how there's no dust on it, no twigs. And see here, this droppin's pretty fresh. They spent the night up on that mountain with us. Quite aways ahead, I imagine."

"Where ya suppose they're headed?" the marshal asked, looking at me.

"Don't know," I replied, looking in the direction of the print. "Don't matter how they came into town, it's how they go out."

"Well, no shit," the marshal snapped.

"Hell, don't ask me, we're gettin' out of my area. I've been to this town and I know some places to check, but that's about it."

"Can you follow that trail?" he asked of Jimmy.

"Hell, yes."

"Let's get to it, then."

Jimmy swung aboard his stud. The others caught up to us and we moved on, following Jimmy. We hadn't gone far when their group split up, each of the five horses entering town from a different direction.

"Well," Jimmy said, getting down to figure out which trail would lead us to Dandy Jim. "They know we're trackin' 'em."

"Or, just being careful," the marshal said.

Jimmy nodded.

"I can tell ya which of these marks were left by the black, but that ain't gonna tell us who's ridin' it."

The marshal shook his head and looked toward the town.

"Aw, hell. It's an ambush either way. If we follow the black, they'll be there. If we split up, they'll be waitin'. This Leonard, he's somethin'."

Up to that point, I had just been trying to stay out of the way. I wanted to help out a bit and collect my wages. I saw no reason for me to get in the middle of it. But I had the answer to the dilemma. Dandy Jim assumed that no one in the marshal's party knew what he looked like. But I knew. Splitting up was sharp business, but only if they planned to watch us without us knowing about it. The only way they could do that is if we didn't know what they looked like.

"Marshal," I said, not wanting to go through with my offer, but knowing I had to.

"Yeah?" he asked, irritated at the interruption.

"We need to send a man in who knows what they look like." I swallowed hard. "To spoil the ambush."

He was skeptical and listened with an expression prepared to scoff.

"Well, sir. The fact is, I could go into town and look around. Even if I don't find 'em, they'll know I'm lookin'."

The marshal's expression grew thoughtful and clouded over with doubt.

"But you've only seen Leonard. What about the others?"

"I seen them, too. Well enough."

"First I've heard of it," he replied, accusing me of withholding information.

I shrugged. Did he expect me to shoot off my mouth about everything I knew? I knew a lot about horses and cattle. Did he want to know that, as well?

"I could ride in followin' the black and see if any of 'em's around and what they're doin'. I'll catch up with ya at the hotel."

The marshal nodded and I started off.

"Hold on," George called to me.

I pulled back on the reins and turned in my saddle.

"Any man can grab a snake outten the damned air, oughta be able to do a decent pull. I'll give ya a hint."

We dismounted and met at the ground. George went through some basic principles of the fast pull, like cocking the revolver on the way out of the holster and aiming from the hip. Since I didn't have a holster, he showed me how to cock the Colt before drawing and how to pull it out keeping my hand next to my body. Cocking it while still in my pants was a worrisome proposal, but I gave it a go.

"That way, thar, you can aim as ya pull, see?"

I tried it a couple of times and got fast enough to suit him. Of course, I had to endure his show of flipping and spinning the revolver on his finger. He said I could learn all of that on my own, though.

"I'm just showin' ya enough ta keep ya alive, right now."

I had the feeling George Brimson would never show me much more than I had to know to suit his purpose.

I started off trailing the black. It wasn't hard to do. Dandy Jim had obviously made his important move by splitting up and wasn't paying much attention to what kind of trail he left. I began to wonder if all the trails were that easy to follow, or if I was following the one they wanted me to follow.

I never felt more like a marked man than I did traipsing across that final meadow on the way into Trinidad. I kept an eye close on the rooftops of the buildings looking for the glint of a rifle barrel. Fortunately, I was coming in from the south. With the sun at my back, I'd be able to see such a thing as a rifle barrel catching a ray of sunlight.

I followed the trail of the black, until it melted into thousands of other hoofprints along the main street. Then, I pulled up and tied the dun off at a hitching rail. Taking my saddlebags and my rifle, I walked along the streets looking into alleys and behind buildings for the black. I stared at every man I met to see if he could be one of them.

Unable to find the black and giving up on that idea, I went into an alley and stacked some boxes and righted a barrel until I could reach the roof of a small building. I climbed up and walked gently to the front. From there, I kept an eye on the other rooftops and the streets.

Looking toward the south, I watched the marshal's group near. On the streets, several men stood at different corners. A cowboy-looking fellow leaned heavily against a post outside a saloon, staring toward the south. He seemed to be some sort of lookout.

I kept my eye on him. He stood there for a long time, then slowly pitched over and fell to the ground. He pulled himself to a sitting position and put his back to the post. He was just a damn drunk and I had been wasting my time.

The longer I watched the inhabitants of the streets, the more I became convinced there was nothing out of the ordinary. The thought occurred to me, then, that Dandy Jim might have rode straight through Trinidad and up to the town of Pueblo hoping we would spend days searching Trinidad.

If Dandy Jim knew all that I did, he would head for Fort Garland. I doubt even the marshal had enough grit to ride into an Army post with a deputy wanted for the murder of soldiers, black or otherwise. To our advantage, Dandy Jim did not know that much.

The more I thought about it, the more I was sure Dandy Jim had gone right through town. It made considerable sense, unless he thought he had given us the slip in Cimarron. I was just getting comfortable with the thought that he had come through Trinidad as a ruse, when I looked down to find a familiar horse tied to a hitching post. It wasn't Dandy Jim's, but it looked like it belonged to one of his men.

That day, on the streets of Santa Fe, I noticed one of the men riding a gray. It was covered with red dust, then. I kept an eye on the animal below, as I sifted through recollections. The four that entered from the opposite end of town were riding two chestnuts, a gray and a palomino.

My brain worked at a furious pace, trying to build memories and figure angles at the same time as I kept track of all the men who seemed to be loafing about that end of town. It did not help that Trinidad was full of loafers.

Then, a man came out of a store. He looked tall and wore a high-domed John B. Stetson on his head. A feather hung from it, signaling that he was either an Indian, or someone who did business with Indians. The saddle suggested that he wasn't an Indian, but he was dark-skinned; Mexican, maybe. He walked up to the gray and swung aboard.

When he pulled the gray around, I could see a black star on the forehead and knew it wasn't the animal I thought it was. So, what did that mean? Maybe, Dandy Jim lit out after all.

The marshal's posse was nearing, so I kept my Winchester ready. I shifted my position a number of times, keeping track of those shiftless wanderers of Trinidad. None of them paid any attention to the posse as it rode brashly down the center of the street. Their horses stepped proudly and the men stared straight ahead, except for the moment they passed by. Jimmy looked right up at me, bold as day. I covered them as they ventured further into town. Then, they pulled up at the livery and walked to the hotel.

I got down from my perch and walked up the boardwalk. I felt a thousand eyes on me but couldn't catch a single stare. It was a strange sensation, like riding into a trail town with a couple thousand head of cattle knowing the children were hidden, watching every movement from knotholes and half-curtained windows.

"Didn't see a damned thing," I said, coming up to the others, who watched the door from their comfortable positions along the bar. "I bet they went clear through to Pueblo or Fort Garland."

They all nodded and looked past me toward the doorway. The hotel wasn't bad, but nothing as grand as the St. James. Instead, it provided the necessities and catered to the common man.

A couple of Mexicans sat at one table. The bartender was also a Mexican. Except for the odd dog wandering around inside, the place was kept clean and respectable. Two card tables were set up against the back wall and a billiard table stood in front of those.

"Good thinkin', taking up position like that," the marshal said, guiding me off to a corner of the saloon. We sat at a table several feet from the others. "I'm thinkin' we'll stay here the night and get a start in the morning. You know where this fort is?"

I nodded.

"We can't go there, but you can. You're gonna have to be our guide in more ways than one now. What with George's problem, and all," he said, smirking. "You can go places we can't and ask questions of people we'd just as soon stay clear of. It's dangerous and we won't be close enough to lend a hand, so be careful.

Now, I'm gettin' rooms for all of us, except you. If you're smart, you'll take a room and get some rest.

"By the way, you'll do some scouting this evening. Just stop by some of the places you know of and see if you recognize anyone. I don't think Leonard will be about, but we need to check."

To all of it, I nodded sincerely. I was not about to take a room, though. I had spent enough money as it was and I wasn't getting paid any more than the initial twenty dollars. He had made that clear enough in Cimarron.

Then, we had some whiskey and they went to look over their rooms. I stayed in the saloon and had another drink. Dayton Howard was a stingy cuss, that's for sure. To hell with him, I had slept out most of my life. It would neither be the first, nor the last of it. I threw back a shot of awful whiskey and pushed away from the bar. I figured I'd better get my horse settled and stop in at some of the gambling halls and cockfight arenas.

CHAPTER ELEVEN

I stepped out of the saloon and looked up and down the street. I'd taken no more than three steps, before Pete caught up to me.

"Hey," he said, almost breathless. "I better come along and keep you out of trouble, eh?"

"You'd better take that badge off, 'fore ya get both of us killed."

Pete glanced down at his chest and pulled the worn, frayed lapel over the badge and buttoned the coat.

We walked along the dusty boards and crossed a side street at the end of the block. We turned deeper into the shadowed lanes and back alleys. We came upon an old barn, where cockfights were held. The wavering flicker of a coal oil lamp sent yellow beams of light through every crack and knothole of the barn, as if escaping from the blood and gore within.

Pete and I stepped up to a door that stood ajar.

"I'll go just inside. If I need help, I'll kick the door," I said. To which, Pete nodded and put his back against the outside wall.

The leather hinges groaned when I pulled on the door. I stepped in and was met immediately by a big man, clearly over six feet tall and at least four wide.

"*Que pasa?*" the man asked.

I shrugged but responded: "*Lucha de gallo.*" I wasn't fluent in Mexican by any means, but I had heard enough to get me around the worst forms of entertainment.

The man, knowing I didn't know any more Mexican than he knew English, pointed a fat finger at the center of the barn, then gave me a shove. I shuffled for balance and looked back at him in irritation.

Men were gathered about the center of the barn, bent over to get a better look at the deadly combat. They screamed to urge on their favorite. Scuffles among the onlookers were frequent, but short-lived. I circled the group, staring across the pit at the faces of those opposite.

For the most part they were Mexicans, which could as easily be said for the town. Noticeable among them were the few whites, who numbered three, or four, and were gathered together. I was shocked to find a priest sitting with them. At first, I thought it was strange that a man of the cloth would allow himself to be drawn into such a disreputable group. Then, I realized who he was and it no longer surprised me. I smirked to myself.

"Figures," I whispered.

In Santa Fe, they called the man Reverend Munnecom. There had been a scandal concerning his poisoning of another priest to get even for being passed over for a promotion. In the end, there was no conclusive proof, but the Church sent him to Trinidad. Since then, there had been more talk of his gambling and drinking and philandering.

There was something particularly repugnant about a man wearing his robes and skulking around with the lowest class of citizens, then appearing bright and cheery to preach to his righteous congregation moments removed from the local cockfight arena. I found him particularly distasteful, but I knew there were few others I could question. I made my way around to his group and swallowed my disgust.

"Pardon me, Father."

He looked up with a glassy-eyed tolerant look for a second, then turned back to the fight. When there was a lull in the action, he swiveled his head toward me.

"I've been looking for this feller that might've stopped by. I wouldn't bother ya if I knew better Mexican," I explained, while he craned his neck to look over his shoulder. He glanced behind me to see if I was alone.

"What would this gentleman look like? Does he have a name?"

"Yes, Father. His name's Dandy Jim Beudreaux, a gambler."

"Is that the sort of man you think I'd have knowledge of?"

I had been leaning over to take some of the pressure off his neck, but straightened at the comment. I looked about the barn, the dust, the Mexicans, the roosters bloodying each other in the little wooden arena, and back at him. Couldn't he see where he was? Did he not know that he was, even then, associating himself with "that sort" of crowd? Had I called on him in the presbytery?

"Oh, I realize where I am," Father Munnecom said, obviously recognizing my confusion. "Do you think I conduct Mass from here? No." He shifted his weight in the chair. "I'm visiting friends and that's the sum of it. As for the others here, I'm not aware of any of their names, aside from these men," he said, pointing to his companions.

"Of course not, Father," I replied, pretending to be shocked. "I just thought you might've heard of his passing through."

"Sorry," he said, returning his gaze to the arena. As he did, and noticing that one rooster lay dead, he passed a few bills to his neighbor and cursed into his whiskey.

Pete and I made our way about the rest of the town, with no luck. No one had seen the famous gambler, or they refused to admit it. We went back to the hotel feeling a little better. Nothing is better for lifting the spirits of a man than to know he isn't being hunted in the darkness of night by an unseen enemy.

As we entered the hotel, we stopped at the saloon for a drink.

Inside, at a table near the bar, the marshal sat with the town marshal. A few of the others were there. George wasn't. They were keeping him out of sight in case the Army came through asking questions.

Pete and I stopped at the bar for a drink.

"Bet ol' George is fit to be tied," Pete chuckled.

"Why's that?"

"Missin' the fun, this way. George loves a saloon."

I nodded and drank. Then, we lifted our newly filled glasses and pulled some chairs up to the table to join the conversation. They were discussing the goings on in Cimarron. News traveled quickly along the Santa Fe Trail that connected the towns.

The town marshal, as I was introduced to him, was Jose Juan Agrellepo de la Garza, or J.J., as he was familiarly called. J.J. Garza was a thin, light-skinned Spaniard of an old Trinidadian family. He spoke easily of the many outlaws he had sent packing for Nuevo Méjico and of the troubles he had when they returned.

Garza spoke tolerable English and seemed cut of the same cloth as Dayton Howard, except that he had an air of nobility that the marshal lacked.

"Jes, I know heem," Garza was saying about Clay Allison, when we came up. "Hees muy loco," he said, putting his thumb to his mouth and tipping his closed fist up to resemble a bottle. "But, jou know, iss muy inteligente. Hees ganado," he shook his hand, searching for the English word, then seized it. "Cattle. De hombres, no molestar."

The men gathered about the table were from either Texas or New Mexico Territory, and understood Mexican as well as the next. But I imagined a poor Northerner running afoul of Garza. I smiled at the fellow's consternation at being thusly charged and imprisoned, in what he thought was the United States, by a Mexican sheriff and tried by a Mexican jury and all of it taking place in the Spanish language.

More reason for the Northerners to stay put, I thought.

It was learned, through a conversation in Mexican, that a man of Dandy Jim's description rode through town early that morning. He stopped to take on some supplies and headed out for the Sangre de Cristo Pass. Or, so it was assumed by his general direction.

"*Muy bueno caballo. Muy negro.*"

Our heads nodded in affirmation that it was our man he spoke of. That black gelding of his would hang him one day. No man, who valued horseflesh, could forget a horse like that. I silently wondered what a man might be thinking when he clipped the berries from such an animal.

"Well, Marshal," I said, nodding at each man. "I'd best be off. I've got to figure a bed for the night."

"Iss hotel," Garza said, throwing his arms wide to encompass the building, trying to do his part for local commerce.

"Iss no gratis," I explained and poured myself another drink from the bottle on the table. I threw it back and walked to the door.

On my way back to the livery, where I planned to sleep, I thought about Dandy Jim. Most likely, he was simply too vain to be without a showy horse. Too addicted to the excitement of gambling to save himself. Perhaps, his life wasn't worth much unless he embraced such things.

At the end of the street I had to turn to the left and walk down the block. From years of working ranches and trying to keep track of rattlesnakes, I had a bad habit of looking at the ground when I walked. I paid for it when I bumped into a man on the street and looked up to say my apologies.

"I'm . . ." I began, but the words were choked off by startled recognition. There he stood, Dandy Jim Beudreaux. I made to shout and jerk my Colt, but another grabbed me from behind.

They pulled me into a dark alley. I was stripped of my revolver and knocked upside the head with it. They threw me against the wall. Fists smashed against my face and ribs. I watched their boots walk across the ground, then stop. I fought to stay conscious but couldn't.

I woke to the feel of water on my face. I shook my head to get my eyes to straighten. Another rush of water splashed over my head.

"You awake?"

"Yeah," I said.

"Snake, isn't it?"

"Frank," I said.

"Yes, Frank. That's really such a bland name," Dandy Jim said. "Snake from Santa Fe. Has a ring to it, no?"

I looked up at him and blinked against the water dangling on my lashes. They had beaten me unconscious and propped me against a building. Their faces were indistinguishable in the darkness, but there was no mistaking the piercing eyes of the gambler.

"What brings you to Trinidad?"

"It's a good town," I said, shrugging.

"That it is," he said, then grew thoughtful. "We seem to be traveling in the same social circles of late."

"Who the hell're you?" I asked, hoping he didn't know any more than I thought he did.

His grin edged at his lips, his eyes narrowing.

"I think you know."

"Look, I ain't got any money," I said.

A spark of doubt flashed in his expression.

"Hell of a coincidence," he said. "I was in Santa Fe a few days ago. I saw you there. I've since come to Trinidad and who do I find? Snake! If I didn't know better, I'd think you were following me."

"I ain't follerin' no one."

"So, I have to ask myself why you'd do that," he went on, as if he hadn't heard me.

"I ain't."

"A marshal came into town today, too. The marshal's looking for me, Snake. But he's too stupid to find me without help. You wouldn't be helping him, would you?"

"I don't know what the hell yur talkin' about."

"We'll see. Tell Buster to come over here," he said. Behind him there was some movement and low discussion. Then another man walked up.

"Is this one of them?" he asked, lifting my chin with the barrel of my own Colt. The man studied my clothes and face.

"Naw."

"You're sure?"

"He wasn't with 'em."

"Well, well," Dandy Jim said, looking me over. "A rare coincidence. You're a fortunate man, Snake." Just to be safe, he brought the barrel of the revolver down on my head again.

Hours later, I woke up with a start. It was nearly morning and my head hurt like God was tossing thunderbolts against my skull. My revolver lay in my lap, minus ammunition. I staggered to my feet and continued toward the livery supporting myself with a hand out to the nearest wall.

When I got there, I pulled the bottle of whiskey out of the saddlebags and sat down in a pile of straw. I pushed back against the wall and kicked a knee up to support my forearm. I took a drink of the whiskey. If I had ridden in with the others, I would be dead. My life hung by a sliver of doubt in Dandy Jim's mind.

It shook me. There was no reason to deny it. I knew the work was dangerous, but I felt that any confrontation would be between Dandy Jim and the marshal. I thought of myself as a bit more important than one of the horses and foresaw no reason for me to face Dandy Jim alone.

I had never felt much like a member of the marshal's posse. The whipping I took only confirmed that I would have to look out for myself. None of them would look out for me. Well, maybe Pete.

What I should do, I thought, was pull out. Who cared if I left? I didn't have any special knowledge of Colorado beyond what I knew about Trinidad. All right, more than that, but not much.

I lifted a hand to my head to feel of the soft, swollen parts. My tongue searched the inside of my mouth and found two chipped teeth and a sore on the inside of one cheek.

Less than four dollars, that's all I had earned for the beating I had taken. It did not seem worth all of the ups and downs of traipsing over Raton Pass, the sore legs, the stay at the hotel; all of it for a few lousy dollars. It didn't seem right.

Well, I knew how to make more money. All I had to do is keep my mouth shut about Dandy Jim. Let them wander about the territory blind, searching for a man they were leaving behind.

I didn't owe them a thing. Were they there to keep me from getting my head kicked in? Did they let me sleep in their hotel? No, I was sent out to sleep in the stable, like some dog. That was fine. I didn't need their companionship. I could make out on my own, but they were going to pay more than four dollars for what I had endured so far.

CHAPTER TWELVE

I dozed in the stall next to my horse and woke to the sounds of the others getting ready for the day's ride. I pulled myself to a stand. I had to put my hands out to steady myself. My vision was blurry. Rubbing my eyes to clear them, I looked over at the marshal. He was intent on saddling his mount with the utmost care. Everything was so precise, so carefully done, it was annoying. He looked up while I sneered at his actions.

"What'd you do? Get into a fight?"

"Got robbed," I said. The others moved slowly toward me. "Some fellas jumped me on the way back here."

"That's a damn disgrace, and you with a badge in your pocket. Wouldn't have happened if you'd been wearing it," the marshal scolded.

No, I would have been killed if I had been wearing it.

"Anything broke?" Pete asked, looking me over carefully. "Who did it?"

"Gamblers, thieves, somebody like that."

They shook their heads and went back to work. George stuck around a bit longer.

"If you'd gotten that pull down like I told ya to, ya coulda killed 'em. 'Stead, yur all beat up." He spit into the straw and turned away.

A lot of damn help you are now, I thought.

"If the marshal stood my board, I'd have been asleep," I said, just loud enough for myself to hear.

"What?" asked the marshal.

I waved him off and shoved cartridges into the Colt.

We set out before light. Our direction was given by the testimony of J.J. Garza. As we started off, I had some pangs of guilt for letting them ride off in the wrong direction. I felt sure Dandy Jim was holed up somewhere in Trinidad, watching us leave. "Us," I thought. If he were watching, he would know I had lied the night before. But, why would he care? He would know where the marshal was and that's about all he could ask for.

"You know where this Sangre de Cristo Pass is?" Marshal Howard asked.

"Yep, but you'll want to be careful coming out the back side of it."

"Why's that?"

"Fort Garland's at the other end."

The marshal rubbed his jaw. It was something to consider.

"Hell, we'll just have to take our chances."

The marshal kicked his horse ahead to talk to Little Jimmy. Pete brought his horse up next to mine.

"Sure missed a fine night's sleep," he said, grinning.

"I always sleep better when I ain't payin' for it," I agreed. "Trouble is, no one's payin' my board, but me."

My words had an edge to them. I wasn't sure if it was due to the animosity I felt at being left out of the benefits of riding with the marshal, or because I knew the journey was a waste of time. Pete caught the ill winds that were blowing and drifted back to his normal position.

I had gotten myself into a real jam. I didn't know any more about the country we were being led into than I knew about Tasmania. I was no good as a guide, nor as a deputy. But I couldn't go back, either. Dandy Jim was back in Trinidad and after watching me ride out of town with the marshal, he would be anxious to get his hands on me.

The man-hunting business was losing a bit of its luster. I was beginning to feel homesick for the wide prairies. About then, I even felt cheated of chuck-wagon grub, which was a sad statement in itself.

I had never experienced moral dilemmas trailing cattle like I had as a guide. There seemed to be something inherently sneaky and crooked about law enforcement. The marshal kept trying to get something for nothing and I had to work my tail off to keep from getting cheated or shot. I had no misgivings about hanging Dandy Jim. I had seen enough of what he had done and was willing to do, by then. His willingness to kill me in the alley sickened me and I knew he had to pay for such deeds. Not for that one in particular, but such things were common to him and his bunch.

I spit into the dust and looked out over the long miles ahead. It seemed difficult, then, to take the job as casually as I had before. I had something invested in it; time, if nothing else. The burden of knowing we were getting further away from the quarry, too.

"Que pasa?" Pete said, having snuck up on me while I was deep in contemplation. I suppose he used the Mexican to break the tension. Mexican was a friendlier language than English.

Breathing out some of my frustration, I looked at him. He was the best friend I had in the group. He was a nice fellow with an amiable personality. I doubt anyone could resist him for an entire day if he wanted to talk.

"Aw, I've just had some things on my mind. I'm a cowpuncher by trade and I suppose I'm gettin' antsy to get back to it."

Pete nodded solemnly, as if he were able to understand the problem.

"Well," he said. "That's natural. It surely is. It's different for me. I love this sort of occupation. Someday, I aim to get offered

a marshalin' job myself." He smiled. "But you've got to stay
with us until we get that damned gambler."

"What do ya suppose the marshal will do to him?"

Pete shrugged and said: "Hang 'em."

"Right then?"

He shrugged again. "Hell, might have to shoot him for resist-
in'."

"I don't think so," I said, looking toward the line of
mountains ahead.

"Why's that?"

"The man's a gambler. Likely, as not, he'll take his chances
in jail. Who knows, might get broke out, or the jury might not
convict him. He might claim not to be Dandy Jim at all, nor
Leonard Braswell."

"There's other ways of knowin' who he is."

"I suppose there is, but every day he spends in jail, it's that
much more likely he'll talk someone into breakin' him out."

Pete gave me a strange glance, as if he had to consider me
from a new perspective. I had tipped my hand and he caught it
immediately. That was his job, I guess, to talk folks into a circle
and find out what they really had to say. But he didn't push it.
He grew distant and prodded silently with his eyeballs. Every
time he glanced at me, he seemed to think the sight over a
minute and look again. Then, he drifted back.

The sun rose in the east, chasing a wave of heat ahead of it.
In an hour, sweat streaked our dusty faces, giving us a wild,
savage appearance.

We entered a valley of wide meadows. The low hills in the
distance were marked by vertical tables of rock running in a line
up the sides, like huge fences constructed by giant hands. The
others did not seem to notice the remarkable landscaping of the
place, but I was transfixed by it.

Pete pulled up next to me. I figured he wanted to do some

more questioning. I beat him to the punch.

"You ever seen anything like that?" I asked, pointing to the rock formations.

"Can't say as I have."

"Damned remarkable, if you ask me."

He shrugged and seemed to have lost the point of his visit.

As we moved deeper into the valley, a wind picked up and we pulled our hats low. I noticed that the conditions had silenced Pete's desire for conversation. I guess he liked to work from a comfortable, nonchalant manner that would not be possible if he had to shout questions into the wind.

Up ahead, Jimmy Carroll wheeled his mount around and kicked his horse into a run toward the rest of us. He pulled his revolver out of the holster and shot into the air. We all looked at each other a second before sensing danger. Before we could react, a bullet tore through the chest of Pete McAllister. A split second later the dull report of a rifle was carried to us on the wind. We dove from our saddles and for cover. Those unable to reach a rock, or a tree, drew their horses down to the ground and hunkered behind them.

I pulled Pete behind a rock. He was bleeding from a hole the size of a nickel. I stuffed his handkerchief into the hole, but it was soon soaked through. His chest was gurgling.

"Goddamnit, Will, unsheathe that thing and get to pluckin'," the marshal demanded.

"Can't pluck what I can't see."

"Frank," George called to me, a giggle in his voice. "Stand up, so's we could see where they's firin' from."

I ignored the comment and looked into the dull, roving eyes of Pete. My friend, Pete. I felt guilty for the morning silence. What might we have said to one another under other conditions? What clever thing had taken place after I left for the livery?

His tongue lolled out of his mouth and he seemed to die, then was revived for a moment, more eye roving and tongue lolling. Then, he slipped away. As I held him, he seemed to crumple from within. The wind tossed a wisp of hair, landing it sharply onto his eyeball. He did not blink, would never blink. I slid him off my thighs and closed his lids.

As Pete slipped out of his body, I slipped out of mine, in a different sense. I no longer felt the cohesion of a whole person. Some part of me detached itself from the rest. I watched myself as if from a distance and saw my actions from an impossible angle.

"All right," I heard myself whisper. The words sounded hollow and alone.

"All right," I said again, and stood up, reaching for the heavy Colt in my waistband.

"What the hell're you doin'?" I heard the marshal ask, but the words got no further than my ears.

"Holy Jesus Christ," Will said.

George snickered. "Goddamned Nuevo Méjico and all the crazy sonsabitches livin' there," he said, and stood up, too.

"George, get down!" the marshal screamed.

I looked the horizon over from end to end. Fifty yards away, Jimmy Carroll had his horse pulled down. He was wadded up into a ball behind it.

"They'll shoot the both of ya," the marshal said. "They shot Pete."

"Aw hell," George replied. "In this wind? It had to be luck. Me an' Snake here's gonna coax 'em. Get ready with that rifle, Will."

"I'm ready," Will said.

I heard the marshal cuss.

I walked over to the dun and pulled the rifle from the scabbard. Pushing the Colt back into my waistband, I checked the rifle over for cartridges. It was full. George and I started out across a meadow in front of the others.

Why weren't they firing? They could see we were trying to bait them, but they had already shot one of our men and we offered two more. How could they resist? We kept walking further from cover.

Then, two bullets whizzed past. One on each side of us, followed by two cracks, almost simultaneous. We saw the general direction of the fire and knelt to take a shot apiece.

"Gettin' 'em, Will?"

"One more time," he replied, his voice level, calculating.

Again, we walked toward the source of fire.

"Cross to the right," Will said, knowing the mind of a rifleman, knowing that the two shots were to disguise location and to get the wind. By crossing to the right, we added a lead to the equation.

"Start and stop a few times," he added. "Don't stop to fire."

"Cain't aim, if'n I don't stop," George replied.

Will laughed from behind us. "You ain't gonna hit nothin' anyway, George."

Two more shots ripped through the wind, tearing a hole in the air; two more distant cracks, then one boom from behind us.

"Get one?" George asked.

"Yep."

Four horses sprang from their scattered positions and made a run across the meadow. The lead horse was black. I stood blinking in disbelief. I thought Dandy Jim was still in Trinidad. What the hell was he doing out here?

"Mount up!" George said, tugging at me, spinning me around toward the horses. We ran back and mounted as the others gathered their mounts along with Pete's and put spurs to horseflesh. Jimmy Carroll went racing ahead of us.

We chased them up the meadow and through a long bend to the right. They had gotten the jump and were five to six hundred yards ahead. Then, we saw Jimmy turn his horse and race back, waving us off. We pulled up.

"Army!" he said, as soon as he knew his voice would carry.

"Head for the hills," the marshal demanded.

We rode hard to our right, toward a wooded hill and cover. I couldn't help feeling a bit chagrined. It didn't seem right that I had hooked up with the law; I felt that I was justified in my actions and because of George, we had to hide from the Army.

Meanwhile, the outlaw, the gambler and murderer, rode to them, got comfort from them. No, sir, justice was not being done.

Chapter Thirteen

To avoid the Army, we had to circle way up and around a hill, running our horses hell-bent through the dense trees, down into valleys and up hills. Jimmy led us along the best paths he could find, but nothing could keep the branches from slapping our faces and cutting our cheeks. By the time we came to a cluster of rocks and stopped to look over the meadow below, we looked like Indian warriors smeared with red paint.

To give the horses some rest, we dismounted and stood about by a rock formation. Our chests were heaving with fatigue and excitement. As we watched the meadow below, we saw the Army ride slowly out of the valley away from the pass and Fort Garland on the other side.

"Now we got 'em," the marshal said. Dandy Jim and his bunch were stranded in the meadow. The Army column moved off slowly, leaving them to their own devices. We held the high ground and could watch their every move.

Presently, they rode to the opposite side of the meadow and started up the hillside. It caused some difficulty in keeping track of them, but unless they wanted to turn around and go back to Trinidad, we were ahead of them.

"Let's push on, men. We need to keep this lead," the marshal said, swinging a leg over his mount.

From then on, we kept a steady pace. For two days, we rode up and down, over and through. We ate cold meat from our saddlebags and fed the horses on short, dry grass.

Through it all, the marshal pressed on. He knew we would come out of the hills before Dandy Jim. With his object so close, the marshal became single-minded. He thought of nothing but keeping Dandy Jim close. Jimmy Carroll was keeping an eye on him so he could not slip around behind us.

On the third day, we came out of the mountains some fifteen miles past Fort Garland. It had taken us nearly a hundred miles of hilly riding to go fifty miles as the crow flew. Down below, a tempting river splashed over rounded boulders. The marshal made his decision to make a fight of it at the river. It was a much better plan than continually riding into ambush after ambush.

The horses could smell the river below and stomped impatiently. We had canteens of water and found a brook now and again, but the horses hadn't had a decent gulp of water since the start. We made camp right there behind thick vegetation. The marshal thought Dandy Jim would come along the river soon.

So, we waited. The marshal went uphill a ways to set a signal that Jimmy would know. The rest of us sat about on the rocks, or leaned against trees. All of us were silent for a number of different reasons.

My silence was a product of watching Pete die. I could not get his face out of my mind, and when I stood up and started walking across the meadow, I wanted to kill all of them. Part of it was repayment for the beating, but most of it was vengeance for Pete. He was a young man with promise as a decent lawman. From what I could see, the country needed a few more like Pete.

George, he probably felt a bit guilty for being the cause of the long ride across the hilltops. We had been cussing him and his quick pull as we left pieces of our skin on sharp branches. If he just had not shot the damn soldiers, we could have settled it all in the meadow.

Will, I'd like to think he kept quiet because he'd had to kill a man. Wishful thinking, that was. He was probably upset about how long it took him to make that first shot.

While I waited, I built a little corral out of pine needles and twigs. I carefully tied long blades of grass around the small corral rails to hold them in place. I was busy at it, when George walked up.

"The hell ya doin'? Figurin' to rustle some beetles is ya?"

I kicked the little corral into pieces and stared up at him. I waited for him to say something else, but he shook his head and walked off.

The marshal came back from making his sign. He looked over the brooding men and sat down on a rock. I glanced up at him, from time to time, to see if I could make out what he was thinking. A few minutes later, he walked to his horse and pulled the rifle from the scabbard. When he started to clean it and check the firing mechanism, we all got ours and did the same.

Darkness was preceded by a bright orange glow spreading like a disease through the valley and climbing the mountain slopes, until it engulfed everything. A welcome, cool breeze kicked up around us, sending whispers of air through the trees.

A horse's neigh came loud on the wind from across the valley. We scrambled to our feet and stood with weapons clutched in our hands, breathing slowly and staring blind into the distance.

"The wind," the marshal concluded aloud, meaning that the wind carried the sound to us as loud as if we stood next to the source. In fact, it might be miles distant. We relaxed, acknowledging the phenomenon.

Then, a horse's hoof struck a stone behind us and we all whipped around. George had his revolver cocked. Jimmy Carroll appeared out of the shadows, with his hands held out to his sides.

"Hell, Jim, don't you know no better'n that?" George scolded, his thumb pressing against the hammer, letting it ease forward.

"Wouldn't a been met with no different, if I'd sang Dixie," he replied, dismounting. "They're ahind us, some," he said to no one in particular. "I figure they'll be coming along before daybreak."

Jimmy and the marshal wandered off together to make plans. I went back to my bedroll and laid down. Staring up at the star-filled sky, I thought of Pete. He was as close a friend as I'd ever had. Every time I closed my eyes, I saw his dying face: his tongue lolling out, his eyes wandering.

I didn't get to sleep for a long time. My thoughts dwelt on Dandy Jim's sudden presence in the meadow; the ambush and the sounds of that morning. Visions of death played against the curtains of my lids. Fitfully, I tossed back and forth on the ground searching for a position that would let me doze. In the end, I caught an hour's sleep. It wasn't enough, but it would have to do.

Jimmy brought me around with a nudge of his boot.

"We're movin' closer to the river," he whispered.

I gathered my things as quietly and quickly as I could. I passed Will as each of us moved about in the darkness. His face was drawn and tense.

When my horse was packed and ready, I looked around. Every other horse was ready, but tied to a bush, or tree. I tied mine and pulled the Winchester from the scabbard. I followed Will down the hill to the rest. They were spread out, keeping their heads low. I went to the furthest left flank of the group and took up a position.

The cool air of morning sent a shiver up my back. It was a clear night, but there was no sign of the moon, only the purple canopy above. What had they planned up there on the mountain? What did they expect? Would Dandy Jim just step out of cover for a drink of water? I shook my head. I didn't take Dandy Jim for a fool. I wanted to ask someone a few questions, but they were all too far away.

It felt awkward, sitting there, ready, with no instructions. If I saw someone, was I supposed to take a shot, or wait for a signal, or let Will have his shot first? Then what? I thought it awfully negligent of the marshal to leave a man in such a situation.

We waited for two leg-cramping hours behind the foliage. Mosquitos buzzed, looking for skin to attack. Gnats circled, tickled, and made a nuisance of themselves. The eastern sky began to lighten. Dandy Jim would not have waited so long. He must have found another way around. I relaxed, waiting for the others to come to the same conclusion.

Then voices, hooves, and rippling water came across the distance. I strained to see, waving at the gnats, slapping mosquitos. I shook my head to ward off the insects. The voices, hushed and secretive, drifted up the canyon wall to us. Sound was a strange thing in the hills. Shadows in the valley, barely visible, moved along the bank. Would they water their horses? Had they done so, already? When would we take them? How? I looked at the others, hoping to find a clue, but they hunkered as before. The shadows couldn't get much closer. They were right below us.

The marshal made some hand signs that I didn't understand. Fortunately, the others seemed to. They nodded, or made gestures of their own. I shrugged in case one of them expected some acknowledgment from me.

I couldn't see Will. He was too far down and hidden. Next time, I would stick close to him. He would be called on to do the shooting and I could get an idea of what was coming by watching him.

I brought my rifle to my shoulder, just in case. Below, they were starting to pass our position. It seemed a good time to open fire if we were going to, and if not, what the hell were we doing? I wiped the sweat from my forehead and repositioned the butt of the rifle. I took aim on the dim figures. Hell, I could hit a horse if nothing else.

What the hell were they doing? I could barely see the dark figures of the men below. They were getting out of range for me and none of us were very far apart. I took the rifle from my shoulder and scratched my head. Whatever they had in mind, I'd lost my effectiveness.

"Boom!" went Will's Schuetzen rifle. It was a German marksman's rifle, with a stock curved to fit the shoulder. I had never had the gall to ask to see it, up close. I heard it well enough, though.

A man screamed like his shirt was on fire and hooves beat over rocks and out of the river. Several shots rang out, but it was harassing fire. Promptly, George and I were sent down to capture the wounded man. The marshal, Jimmy Carroll, and Will sent lead to chase the others away. We slid, grabbed for bushes, and tumbled down the side of the steep hill.

When we got to the bottom, the man was flopping around on the opposite bank like a stranded trout. We came out from the vegetation and moved cautiously toward the river. The man was crying, screaming, and cursing. He kicked and rocked as we waded into the water, holding our weapons high above our heads to keep the cartridges dry.

There was more firing from the hill. I looked downriver to see if Dandy Jim was trying to rescue the downed man, but saw nothing. It was still too dark. I didn't like coming up on a wounded man, not that way.

The river reached to our waists at the deepest and the footing was slick with moss and a swift current.

"Don't let him die," we heard the marshal call from up above, like a command from God.

"The hell have we got to do with it?" I asked, whispering to George. He did not seem to hear me.

As soon as we began to rise out of the river, water poured out of small cavities in our clothing. It sounded like the draining of a washtub and caught the attention of the wounded man. He looked up at us, startled. We froze in our tracks and swayed back and forth with the current still at our knees. He winced in pain, blinked his eyes, and started looking around for something.

George drew down on the man.

"Don't kill him!" the marshal yelled.

"Don't pay no mind to that," George said. "I'll kill ya, all right."

I rushed out of the river, knowing our only chance was to get hold of the man before he found what he was looking for. The man, unable to locate a weapon, stared helplessly into the sky. Then, he rolled to one side and felt of the ground beneath him. I was nearing fast. George took measured steps out of the river. More shots were fired from the hillside.

The man's hand was clumsily moving his revolver along the ground, trying to get the butt in his hand. He picked it up by the barrel and dropped it onto his chest. He reached for the butt. I was ten feet from him.

"I'll kill ya, goddamnit!" George said.

"Don't!" came the word from above.

The man cocked the weapon, grimacing along with the movement. I could tell George was just waiting for the muzzle to turn his way before he let go a shot. But the man shoved the barrel under his own chin. I was close enough to dive for him. I hoped to knock his aim off. I saw his finger fumble to find the trigger guard. I hit him just as it went off. The bullet careened along the ground and ricocheted off a boulder. He still held the revolver in his hand, and he was trying to cock it when I pulled it from his hand. He gave out a groan and let his head fall back heavily onto the sandy riverbank.

I looked over my shoulder to see the marshal wading through the water. George eased the hammer back, whipped the Whitney around on his finger, and dropped it into the holster. The man gave out a scream of pain and clenched his teeth. His horse stood a few feet away and I went to gather him. I put my revolver into my waistband and walked slowly toward the chestnut horse. I stuffed the man's revolver into the saddlebag.

The sky grew rapidly lighter, revealing the damage done to the man on the ground and the blood on my shirt from struggling with him. The man held his hands to his stomach, trying to keep his innards from spilling into his lap.

The marshal splashed up out of the stream and came toward the prisoner. I held the chestnut's reins in my hand and walked up to George. The marshal dug inside his vest. He removed a few wanted posters and flipped through them.

"You must be this sonofabitch," the marshal said, throwing the poster at the wounded man.

The man couldn't care less. Death awaited him and he would be grateful for it when it came. He shoved the poster off his chest and stared up vindictively at the marshal, then spit. The stringy globule shot up, tethered, and swung back onto his cheek. The marshal kicked him in the head. The man's head whipped back and his hands came momentarily away from his stomach, giving George and myself a look at bluish-red guts. I grimaced and looked away. "Smart-ass sonofabitch," the marshal said. "You think ya can break the law? You can kill, steal, accost folks and no one's gonna catch ya? Huh? Smart-ass sonofabitch." The marshal kicked him again. "Where's that bastard goin'?"

The man shook his head, moaned, and lost consciousness.

The sun rose a few minutes after the man passed out, not in the deep valley, but everywhere else. The sky was bright blue with thin clouds hanging lazily overhead. We were submerged in shadows, but on the opposite bank where Jimmy and Will continued to cover us from the bushes, the sun crept slowly to them.

Every few minutes, the marshal would walk over to the wounded man and give him a kick, just to see if he were awake.

"Hey, Frank, you still got that whiskey in your saddlebags?"

I nodded.

"Take George and go get it. Hell, just bring the horses down while you're at it."

I started off back across the river with George close behind. We had left our rifles on the bank. We each kept a revolver just in case. We scrambled up the side of the hill and to the horses. Leading them back down was a chore. It was steep and slick and bushy.

To be honest, I didn't want to get back. Whatever the marshal had in mind, it was going to be brutal. How long would he keep the man alive? What would he do to him in the meantime? I didn't want to know.

Yet, I would have to watch, help, and do whatever I could. Dandy Jim had become my responsibility, in one way or the other. Maybe, I felt guilty about not telling the marshal when Dandy Jim caught me on the street. Maybe, I owed something to Pete. I wasn't sure of why, but I did as I was asked and knew I would, until Dandy Jim was dead.

Chapter Fourteen

George and I brought the horses and whiskey down. We mounted up and rode across the river. The marshal was bent close to the wounded man. He appeared to be comforting him, but I knew better. He was probably whispering threats into his ear, telling him of the pain that lay ahead unless he talked.

We splashed up onto the bank. The marshal looked over his shoulder and extended a hand toward the bottle. I dug it out of my saddlebag and tossed it to him. He pulled the cork out of the neck and took a swig.

"Warms a man's belly," he declared, pouring a good measure of the whiskey onto the man's wound.

The man jerked and jumped. His screams filled the canyon and overwhelmed the sound of the rushing river.

"Where's he goin'?" the marshal demanded of him.

He shook his head.

"Plenty of whiskey."

The man refused to talk.

"String him up," the marshal told us.

"C'mon," George said, waving me on.

We dismounted and got a rope around the man's hands. George sought out a tree and threw the remainder of the rope over a sturdy limb. He walked back and swung aboard the horse. He kicked it forward, dallied the rope, and began to pull the man along the ground.

The man screamed and moaned and gritted his teeth. I could

110

feel the back of my neck beginning to heat up, ashamed of our torture, wishing the man would simply confess. What did he have to gain by remaining faithful to Dandy Jim? He was going to die anyway. Maybe, that was the point.

"Christ, just tell 'em what they want!" I yelled at the man, hoping he would comply and get it over with. It was better than the alternative. I found myself growing angry with his stubbornness. I blamed him for making me watch, even participate, in such goings on.

Slowly, limply, the man was being raised. Then came the disgraceful moment when gravity had its way and his innards fell from the hole in his stomach. The hole wasn't large enough to let them all flop out, but some bluish tubes poked out of the hole and started a precarious journey down, between his flailing legs.

"Want a drink?" the marshal asked.

The man shook his head and rolled his eyes, fighting off the pain.

"I think ya do."

The marshal walked over to him, took another drink and stopped. He looked back at me.

"If you want any of this, I suggest ya have some before I let him have a drink. Ain't gonna be fit for the devil when he's done with it."

I shook my head.

"Suit yourself."

The marshal took a drink, then pulled a long Bowie knife out of a sheath hanging at his belt.

"Got your choice. I can pour it down your mouth, or give ya a new one."

The man thought it over and opened his mouth.

"Good, I like cooperation."

The marshal poured the whiskey into the man, who promptly

spit it back up at the marshal. He was trying anything to get himself killed. The marshal was prepared for that and stepped out of the way. He shook his head, as if truly sorry it had to be handled the other way.

"Well, hell," he said, then grabbed a piece of dangling intestine. He pulled it out of the man and held it up so he could see it. The marshal looped the intestine around the shiny blade of the Bowie. "God, this is gonna stink, ya know?"

"Nevada Territory," the man blurted, breathless and scared.

"Hell, I know that. Where at? What for?" He shouted, squeezing the knife in his hand. "I'll cut it and leave ya to die," he warned.

"Carson. He's goin' ta Carson City."

"What for?"

"The mint."

The marshal let go of the man's intestine and sheathed the knife.

"Let him down, George."

By then, the man was wasted. He seemed near death. His eyes were sunken deep into his face and blood covered his britches. I saw him shiver.

"Water," he said, his voice creaking.

George flipped the rope from around the saddle horn and the man dropped to the ground. He kicked and flinched and cried. I felt sorry for him and rushed to get my canteen.

George retrieved his rope and led his horse away from the dying man.

"Drink from hell's own river," the marshal said. Before I could get back, he raised the revolver and sent a piece of lead through the man's forehead.

I let go a breath. At least it was over. I looked around at the others. George fiddled with his rope, getting it coiled neatly and tied to his saddle. The marshal broke the revolver open and replaced the spent cartridge with a new one. Will and Jimmy started down the slope, leading their horses. Was I the only one who saw something strange about all of it? Did none of the others feel ashamed at what had taken place? I understood it was necessary, but didn't they also have that emptiness of soul? Or, were they just covering for it by tending to their ordinary routines? I knew better than to ask if we should bury him.

"There ya go," the marshal said, to me.

"What?" I asked.

"That man's worth seventy-five dollars. You want him? You can load him up on his horse and take him to the fort. They're obligated to pay. If you can find the first one we killed, he's bound to be worth somethin', too."

Finished with reloading, the marshal snapped the revolver together and worked the action a few times, then shoved it into his holster. Was he telling me to leave?

"What're you gettin' at, Marshal?" I asked.

"Nothing. You want to make some money? Take the body to the fort. If you don't, leave him here."

"Well, I'm coming with you," I said, wanting least of all to be left wandering alone after what we had done to the man.

"Come or stay. That man's your pay. It's none of my business. If you take him to the fort you could probably catch up to us later. We know where we're goin' now."

I thought it over. There was something that made me want to come along on that journey. Was it that interesting? Or, was it just an instinct for survival that warned me against turning my back on any of them?

"I've got unfinished business, Marshal," I said, hoping that would suffice.

"We'll keep an eye out for ya."

I threw the man on the back of his horse and tied his hands and feet together under the horse's belly. I had just gotten ready to move out, when a thought occurred to me.

"Marshal, why don't we carry this man with us 'til we get to a federal post?"

"What the hell ya 'fraid of, the murderer's that way," George said, pointing west.

I glanced downstream, but waited for the marshal to answer.

"There ain't no fort further on, far as I know. That man's liable to rot before we get any other place. You take him on back, if you want the bounty. Here, take this poster." The marshal bent down to pick up the bloody poster.

I took the poster and the man and headed back along the river toward Fort Garland.

We split up then, me riding east and they, west. I felt abandoned and exposed. To everything they did, there seemed to be an ulterior motive at work. I kept looking over my shoulder to see if someone was tracking me.

It was becoming apparent that I was incapable of thinking like the others. I didn't know why Dandy Jim continued west, instead of sticking to town and going the opposite way of the marshal. I didn't know why the marshal wanted to know where Dandy Jim was going. It seemed to me they had his tracks to go on and didn't need to torture a man for useless information.

Glancing back, I saw the grotesque, seventy-five-dollar load. I aimed to get the money and rejoin the marshal as soon as I could. I thought about heading south to Santa Fe, or east to Trinidad and leaving the marshal and Dandy Jim to figure things out for themselves.

At first, I thought I stayed with the marshal because of the money, or the beating I took, or to get vengeance for Pete's death. But, none of that was the reason. With more money tied to the trailing horse than I ever expected to get out of the marshal, I was forced to acknowledge that the money had nothing to do with it. If it did, I would just turn the horse to the south, or east, and be rid of the whole band.

No, whatever reasons I had, they went deeper than that. Was it morbid curiosity to see how much carnage the marshal's men could produce? Was it for the chance to witness the death of a famous man? Or, was it that as much as I denied it, I liked the danger and excitement of law work?

I had to admit it could get the blood pumping at certain times; the sound of the revolvers blazing away and the gut-wrenching feeling when a bullet whizzes through the air. It was like an intoxicant. I felt disappointed in myself. What sort of man was I, if I could relish such moments?

I kicked the horse into a trot, trying to make the best time I could. It was only twelve or thirteen miles from where we parted company, but I didn't want their trail to get cold.

The sun grew hot and the dead man was starting to attract scavengers. An eagle circled above. I saw a coyote loping along the horizon, sniffing the air. You would have thought I was trying to carry gold through a street full of thieves. I reached over and pulled the Winchester from its scabbard in case more ferocious predators were drawn to the corpse.

An hour later, I glanced back at the dead man. A magpie sat calmly on his back pecking at the open wound.

"Get off o' him!" I screamed, but the magpie only blinked its insolent eyes and pecked. I pulled the Colt out and took a shot, but the magpie flew a fraction of a second before the bullet arrived. Then I cursed myself. I jerked angrily at the reins, trying to mitigate the mistake of calling attention to myself by letting off a shot.

Looking back to check on the dead man, there sat the magpie, pecking. I shook my head and wiped sweat from my forehead. I threw my hands up in despair and disgust. As a grown man, I don't know that I had ever come so close to crying. I was frustrated, angry, and disgusted with the magpie and the sudden turn of events. I pushed on.

I caught sight of the adobe fort by late morning. It was nothing more than a few low, rectangular buildings of uncreative architecture. I neared the place with a bit of apprehension. Since riding with the marshal, I had come to think of everyone as an enemy first and a friend only after they had survived the first round of gunfire.

The wandering soldiers shot strange looks as I passed, trailing the horse, the corpse, and the magpie. What would they suggest I do? I'd tried to make the bird leave. Every time I shooed it, it circled and landed again. I couldn't shoot up the rest of my ammunition chasing a bird.

Eventually, one man turned a naked look of revulsion toward me that I thought deserved a direct answer. I stared down from my perch atop the horse with as much dignity as I could manage.

"Even magpies got to eat."

I presented the poster and the body to Captain Gerard. He looked me over with suspicion and little tolerance.

"Don't like bounty men," he said.

I shrugged. Neither did I, but a dollar was a dollar.

"Ain't lookin' for friends," I replied, adopting a bounty man's attitude. "Is this the feller in the poster, or not?"

"It's him."

"Then pay up."

"The major has to approve it," the captain replied with some satisfaction.

"Well," I said, hoping to prompt him.

"He's on patrol. There's been some activity to the east."

I brought my hands to my hips and stomped my foot impatiently. There had been a damn sight more activity to the west. What was I supposed to do? Sit around for days until the major came back?

116

"Christ almighty, you mean you can't just give me the damn money and let him approve it later? I got the man. I got the poster. I ain't exactly askin' ya to take my word for it."

"I'm sorry," he said.

"Well, if this ain't a typical mess. When you expectin' the major?"

"Tomorrow."

I slapped my hat against my leg. Tomorrow? The marshal would be long gone by then.

"Look here," I said, trying to keep from grabbing the man up by his blue lapels and shaking some sense into him. "Me and a couple of fellas are trackin' a bank robber, stole the governor's money. This fella's one of 'em and he has a poster, now we're runnin' low on supplies and ammunition. All I'm askin' is you pay me what this man is worth and help resupply me so's we can keep huntin' the rest. Don't make me report the fact that we couldn't get the governor's money, because you wouldn't just put your hand in the till and bring out seventy-five dollars." I looked his uniform over. "Huh, Captain? What's yur name anyway? Gerard? I'll recall that easy enough when I make my report."

"I've got orders . . ."

"Bad enough you makin' a lousy decision for yourself, now you're makin' one for your boss, too. I hope the both of ya got asses made of steel. Yur gonna need it when the governor talks to the general, hell, maybe the president."

I don't suppose I had ever run roughshod over anyone, except a couple of lazy cowboys. It felt kind of good, respectable.

"You'd best get to doin' somethin'," I added, causing him to rise from his desk and search madly through papers and the like. He dug out a locked box and opened it. He drew seventy-five dollars from it and held it in reserve while he scratched out a receipt on a piece of paper.

"Thank ya," I said, signing my name and pocketing the money.

CHAPTER FIFTEEN

I left the captain's small office with money in my pocket. I went outside to the corpse and cut the rawhide strips to dump the man off. He landed heavily, dried blood from head to foot. He lay there with his eyes open, staring blindly. I sighed at the thought that death was becoming routine.

I gathered the reins to both horses and started toward the west.

"Hey!" someone called from behind.

I turned around to face the captain.

"Where ya going with that horse?"

"To get some more," I said, then I spit and went on about my business. If he wanted to take the horse from me, he could, but I figured it was part of the pay for hauling the body back to the fort. Secretly, I hoped there would be some whiskey in the saddlebags. He owed me some of that, too.

As the sun set behind the mountains, I noticed the beauty of the landscape. The mountains had become nothing but a hindrance to our objective, or as cover from bullets, or cover from which to fire. Only in the silence and solitude of that day, did I appreciate the distant peak and lower hills covered with several different kinds of trees. The shading of the leaves varied from dark green to medium to light.

My mind went back to the trail drives and how, at the end of each day, the sunset brought forth breathtaking scenery. It would catch me by surprise to look up and find myself surrounded by beauty, filled with wonder at God's great work, and I would feel guilty for the cussing I had done over the course of the drive.

I rode on to the small river. I wanted to make it that far so I would have a clear idea of where I wanted to go. Also, I wanted to give the horses a good drink before setting out the next day.

Upon arrival at the river, I picketed the horses and dug through the saddlebags. There were a number of personal articles, none of which were of any use to me. Under a shirt, I felt the hard, smooth, circular feel of a bottle. Next to the bottle was a letter-like bundle of something. I didn't care about letters; I wanted a drink. So, I felt for the neck of the bottle and pulled it out. There was no more than a few drinks left. I swished it around, to see if it would multiply, but when the liquid settled there was always the same amount.

I pulled the cork and drained it in two drinks. I dammed the bottle's neck and put it back into the saddlebags. A fellow never knew when he might run upon a keg of whiskey and needed to carry some away. My fingers brushed by the bundle again. I got hold of it and hauled it out. The light had faded, but I didn't need much light to know it was cash. It was probably his cut from the bank robbery. Why hadn't I thought of it before? I thumbed through it. Better than five hundred dollars in that bundle alone. I dug through the saddlebags. That was all. Either he didn't get much, or he had spent the better part of his share.

I flipped the edges of the bundle as I thought over the situation. I raised some dried beef to my mouth and tore off a piece. Chewing slowly, I thought.

The sky grew ever darker and began to fill with insect sounds of chirping, buzzing, and clicking. I put the bundle of notes back into the saddlebags and removed the saddles from the horses, piling them and the saddlebags near my bedroll.

I lay along the river bottom in the marshy grass. The horses ravished the vegetation with sharp snaps of their heads.

So, what was it that took me back to the marshal when I should have just cut and run? To maintain a degree of pride in the fact that I did not run away? Was it some sort of misplaced loyalty? Or, was it worse? Was I becoming a man like the marshal? Was the excitement drawing me helplessly toward a fate similar to his? Did I like the brutality of it all? I did not like the thought of that.

"Well, just cut and run then," I said aloud. I knew I would not. What little I remember of my father could be summed up into one sentence: "See it through, boy." When I was young, he taught me to ride a horse by making me get back up whenever it threw me. He urged me on with that sentence and I could hear his voice again as I sat there.

I went to sleep then and woke several times during the night. Always, the star-filled sky stood above and the sounds of the resting horses.

Then came the light. It spread red fingers across the pale blue of the eastern sky. I woke to it and lay there watching the clouds change colors and drift slowly by. I enjoyed the short respite from the whirlwind that gathered strength and moved closer to Nevada.

I rode out from camp that morning trailing the dead man's horse. I followed the small river in a westerly direction. I knew we would meet up with the Rio Grande del Norte before long. Keeping the horses at a gait designed to overtake a walking horse, I switched from one to the other to keep them from getting too tired to run. In following the marshal, I had noticed that it served a man to have a fresh horse under him as often as possible. Two were bound to be better, yet.

I crossed a small stream at a favorable place to the south of the small river. After I had crossed, I went north, searching for the marshal's crossing. Presently, I came upon another river and followed it west.

I rode west for several miles and then saw a structure of wood standing desolate to the south. It looked like a good place to put up, if I were the marshal, so I directed my horse toward it.

The heat poured down on me from the sky. It beat down on my shoulders and revived the odors of rank clothing. The grass stood tall across the prairie approach to the structure. I looked for signs of the marshal's trail. Instead of riding straight in, I took a circular route looking for a path. I was feeling a bit foolish by then. Ahead, Jimmy Carroll was finding trail that an Indian would miss, yet I couldn't see a path through high grass. Even in my solitude, I blushed at the thought.

As I closed in on the structure, I got a strange feeling, as if being watched. I narrowed my eyes and pulled up on the reins.

"Hello, the fort," I said. I did not know what else to call it. I got no answer. I kicked the horse into a lope, then stopped. Off I went again, slower than before. I kicked the horse into a run, pulling the dallied reins tight against my leg as the dead man's horse lagged for a second.

I came around the back of the structure. Two paths revealed themselves at forty-five-degree angles to each other. I followed one in. There was a gaping hole in one of the walls. There had once been a gate across it, but it lay in a heap on the ground.

Approaching cautiously, I got down from the horse and tied both sets of reins to the downed gate. I pulled the Colt from my waistband and entered slowly, looking around. The back corner had been boxed off with walls, making a shed, or small room. I neared, breathless. I felt like shooting a hole through the door, but didn't want to attract the attention of whoever might be crawling around in the high grass.

"Come on outta there," I said, to the door. "I ain't gonna kill no one lest I have to."

I looked around for something to throw at the door. If there was someone inside, they would reveal their presence if they thought someone was banging on the door. There was not much lying around to throw.

I went back to the horses and got the empty whiskey bottle. I stood back, cocked the Colt, and tossed the bottle. "Clink," it went, and bounced off. It did not break. I thought that was a good sign.

"All right, damnit," I said, striding toward the door. A piece of leather was nailed up for a handle and I grabbed it and jerked the door open. Darkness greeted my eyes and a horrible stench filled my lungs. I bent away from the opening and covered my nostrils. Flies poured out of the opening, buzzing loud in the still, repulsive air.

Looking in from a distance, I saw something move and shot at it. The sound of the .44 was loud and seemed to echo again and again. I looked over my shoulder and proceeded toward the dark doorway. Whatever it was, it continued to move slowly, swaying, it seemed.

I winced against the smell of death emanating from within. The sun's heat reflected off the flat boards. It felt like a nightmare, where something horrible exists just out of sight. With my hand up against the reflected sun and peering into the depths of the room, I saw an outline of a man showing itself against the background of vertical shafts of light streaming through the boards.

The body of a man hung from the one horizontal beam. A rope was slung under his arms. He was split from throat to privates. Flies darkened the innards dangling from the wound. I hunched my shoulders, fighting off a shiver. How long had he been hanging there? It looked like the marshal's work, sure enough.

Looking up at the back of the man, I saw a wanted poster

sticking out of his collar. This one was worth one hundred and fifty dollars. Well, I would be damned if I would ride the fellow back to the fort just to argue with the captain. No, sir. For the first time in my life I felt I had enough money. What I wanted was peace of mind and the time to spend it.

I took out my knife and cut the man down. Coyotes and wolves have to eat like everyone else.

I left then. If someone wanted the reward money, they would have to beat the worms to him.

I followed the second trail until it joined with the small river. I kept to the river. It was early afternoon by the time the little river split in two, one fork heading southwest, the other keeping on a westerly route.

I had to be getting close to the others. Someone had to be out there. I just hoped I found the right bunch. I studied the ground around the fork and picked up a trail bearing southwest along the divided river.

The distance offered more low hills that would surely build themselves into peaks before I could get there. I enjoyed the wide prairie I traveled through, knowing it wouldn't last. No landscape ever lasted in Colorado. As soon as a man thought he found a level piece, it jumped up into sheer cliffs all around.

For the moment, I rode in the comfort of distance. I could see for miles ahead and behind. I could have used some whiskey on that piece of ground. I could have used a partner like Pete to talk to, as well. It was deathly quiet, but it was a refreshing break from the hectic noise and pace set by the marshal and Dandy Jim.

I saw them in my mind, chasing one another over the vast distances; each one playing some advantage for a life. Dandy Jim took Pete with the ambush. The marshal took that other fellow with his own ambush. It occurred to me that they would run out of lives to throw at each other. I hoped I had enough sense to abandon the party before it got down to those two and me.

CHAPTER SIXTEEN

I followed the river to a valley surrounded by high, wooded peaks. There was nowhere to go but up, and I did not feel like making the climb in the darkness that threatened. So, I set about to make camp. I had access to fresh water for the horses and coffee.

To avoid the exposure of camping out in the open, I got up close to the base of the hill. From that angle, I felt safe enough to build a fire. I prepared camp and unsaddled the horses, then led them over for a drink. I filled a canteen and let them graze on the tall grass. On the way back, I gathered firewood that lay dead along the bank.

The trail I had been following led straight up into the hills and I felt sure that the others were camped up high. Perhaps, they could see me from up there, could watch every move I made. So, what? As long as Dandy Jim did not have someone who could shoot that far, it didn't matter what any of them saw. I bet Will could hit me, that man could shoot the eye out of a fly at a hundred yards.

Thinking about it, I felt a bit self-conscious and looked up at the hills, as if to say: "Yeah, I'm gonna make a fire. I'm gonna have coffee. Now, who's the smartest one of the bunch?"

I hobbled the horses and let them graze close by. The area was dark with shadows and the cool air settled into the lower valley. The air smelled clean and pure, as if untouched by the acrid smell of a campfire. I would soon fix that.

When the fire was licking up in tall flames and I had prepared a place to set a pot of coffee, I dug in my saddlebags for some of the dried beef and hardtack. I looked about the area. For God's sake, there ought to be some fresh meat about; a deer, an elk, or something. I would have eaten a skunk by then.

I had grown soft from long trail drives where fresh meat was abundant. I had even been known to curse a fresh steak for its commonality, but I did not recall the last good meal I had. The business of chasing men was rife with inconveniences: no fires, no hunting, no raucous laughter. The fact is, it wasn't much fun at all.

I grew tired of thinking about it and wandered out away from the fire with my rifle to seek out some fresh meat. I took the hobble off my horse and took her along in case I had to drag a deer back to the fire for skinning.

There was still a bit of light to the sky, but the horizon was too high to be of any help in spotting game. Instead, I used patches of white-barked trees as a background and moved in circles to get as much use of angles as I could.

While I was so engaged, the dun started to stomp and blow air through its nostrils. I soothed the animal with my free hand and spoke to it in a calm voice. My efforts to calm it did not help. There was something out there and she didn't like it. I looked about, but was unable to see a thing.

I heard a rumble, like the sound of distant thunder. Holding tight to the reins, I turned around. The mare rose up, pulling me off balance and backward. I cursed the animal and stood staring blindly toward the sound. I tried to aim the rifle, but every time I brought the barrel level, the dun would throw her head and pull my aim off.

What was it? What lurked out in the void that so terrified the horse? Whatever it was, it got wind of us and reared up huge before my blinking eyes. The immensity of the beast blotted out the stars behind it. I let go of the reins and ratcheted a round into the chamber. A huge roar issued from the shadow and I nearly wet myself. A damn bear!

"Boom, boom, boom, boom, boom, boom," went the rifle in my hand, firing as fast as I could pump another round into the chamber and pull the trigger. When the dry, hollow clicking of the hammer landed a few times, I turned and ran after my horse.

I made it back to the camp before I stopped running. Had it not been for the light of the fire I might have run in circles for hours before I found it. I got back breathless and scared. The first thing I did was stuff that Winchester full of cartridges and pour myself a cup of coffee to bring me to my senses.

I had heard stories of bears taking several rounds before running off, much less dying. I didn't trust any weapon to kill one, especially not when I could not even see if the rounds were finding their mark. Likely as not, I only hit him once.

Sitting on my heels at the fire with the Winchester across my knees and a cup of coffee in my hand, I trembled. Then, I started thinking of the meat lying out there in the darkness. Good meat, maybe. My mouth began to water at the thought of it.

If I took a torch to light my way, I might be able to see something. I looked over at the remaining horse. If the bear was not dead, I could lose that one, too. I spit into the fire and listened to it sizzle.

Ultimately, I decided to leave the horse, scout the bear, and return for the horse if I needed it. There was nothing inviting about the darkness, especially knowing there was a bear in it. I walked on with my rifle cocked and ready. I held the torch in my left hand, a couple fingers of which supported the weight of the rifle barrel. Thus, I tromped along in fear for my life.

For all of my careful plodding, I wound up tripping over the outstretched leg of the bear. The torch went sailing into the air and the rifle discharged into the night. I pawed at the ground, trying to gain my feet, while keeping the muzzle of the rifle trained on the bear.

I staggered upright with my chest heaving and sweat drenching my face. I picked up the smoking torch. My eyes adjusted to the darkness and I found the head of the bear resting gently on its woolly forearm. I cocked the rifle and fired one shot into the fuzzy skull, just to be sure.

"Damn bear about killed me twice," I said to the night, feeling the pounding of my overworked heart.

I located the fire this time without the panicked frenzy of terror clouding my senses. I went back to the fire carrying the smoking torch. I looked over my shoulder more than once to be sure the bear wasn't after me. Ever since they nearly buried my grandfather alive, I had never been quite sure anything was completely dead.

As I neared the fire, I saw my horse standing next to the other. It was trembling and jerking its head up and down. Her eyes spoke of her terror; the flared nostrils retained the smell. She looked like she'd just been thrown from the gates of hell. To the horse, I must have looked the same.

"Damned if you . . ." came halting words from the depth of night and I screamed, throwing the torch at the voice. I cocked and levelled the rifle in the direction of the sound. I heard a smothered laugh from behind a tree.

"Don't . . . shoot," the voice said, between chuckles. I recognized it as Jimmy Carroll's voice. He stepped out from behind the tree.

"You'll get kilt one day, sneakin' up on folks the way you do."

"More likely to get kilt not sneakin' up," he countered.

"The hell you doin' here, anyway?"

"Came to lead you up to camp. We're gettin' an early start.

Prolly catch ol' Leonard tomorrow." Jimmy kept a distance from the fire. He stayed in the shadows where he was more comfortable. "Brought yur horse back," he said, nodding in the direction of the mare.

I noticed Jimmy took time to hobble her.

"Thanks."

"You ready?"

"Hell, no," I said. I had my mind set on some meat and I was not about to go up the hill without having a taste of bear. "I killed a bear and I aim to eat him. You're welcome to some of it, but I ain't goin' a step up that hill, 'til I eat some hot, fresh meat."

Jimmy nodded.

I saddled the spare horse and went to drag the bear back. It took a few minutes to find the beast in the dark, but when I did, I tossed a loop over one of the dead legs and dallied the rope to the saddle horn. The damn thing must have weighed nine hundred pounds. More than a yearling steer, I knew that.

We ate and cooked plenty for later. Jimmy stayed to the shadows while he ate. I went toward him, but never so close that a person watching could fix his position. He warned me against it right off and I obeyed his instructions. He was a wily one. He knew things it would take a man a lifetime to learn. I had neither the time nor the inclination to learn much of it, but I respected his knowledge and did as I was told.

"I suppose it'd be stupid to ask how you knew I was here."

He chuckled, pulled some gristle from his teeth, and nodded.

Later, we smothered the fire with the remnants of the coffee and trailed our horses into the dense forest. Jimmy Carroll was the best trail man in the business. He chose an easy trail up the side of a steep grade. We came upon clearing after clearing that did not seem possible given the nature of the terrain, but Jimmy readily found them.

It was a long way to the camp. Every now and then, Jimmy would stop and survey the woods, then he would start off in a different direction. Jimmy Carroll could breathe in landscape and spit out trail. A man had to admire that.

When we got to camp, Jimmy showed the way in and went about on his own private journey. He would probably sleep several hundred yards from the rest of us. Not that there was much sleep to be had. The light to the east was already growing when we arrived. My legs burnt from straining against the worst parts of the trail. My horses were tired and needed some rest before we pushed on, so I don't know what good it did to make the midnight climb to the marshal's camp.

I tied the horses with the rest and threw out my bedroll. Sleep came over me so quick, it seemed that I had just shut my eyes when George woke me with a nudge of his boot.

"Ain't got all day," he said.

I rolled over to get away from him. That worked for another moment's sleep, but soon I was greeted with a rougher nudge, a kick, I would call it.

"Yeah, yeah," I said, sitting up.

"Well, now," the marshal said, staring at me from a distance. "You made it in time for the excitement. I thought sure you'd haul that other'n off to the fort."

"To hell with him." I'd hauled enough stinkin' corpses by then. Damn magpies chasing me across the world and all.

The marshal gave me a strange smirk. He knew something. I felt I had been had, that I had failed some test and taught him something about myself. I ducked my head from his knowing gaze and rose to gather my things. When I looked at the others, I could tell they were in on it.

"What?" I asked.

"How much was in the saddlebags?" the marshal asked.

"Now, look here, Marshal. I hauled that body. I done the

work," I said, trying to stave off having to forfeit the cash.

The marshal shook his head.

"We're honor bound to return the stolen money if we can."

"Well, you can't," I said, sullenly, feeling cheated.

"You best think about it, son. I know you'll do the right thing."

Like hell, I thought. Who was he to say something like that? He didn't know me if he thought I would just turn loose of five hundred dollars without a fight. No, sir, he would just see what kind of man I was.

But the marshal didn't put up a fight. He tried to use guilt on me. It would not work, because I didn't feel guilty about keeping money that was stolen fair and square by someone else. I found it as surely as I had found the twenty under the mare's hoof the first day. I would not return any of it. If he wanted it, he would have to beat me senseless to get it.

Chapter Seventeen

There was a sense of excitement in the men as we started out. They could smell victory and were anxious to have a taste. Even I could feel the blood pumping through my veins at a speed rarely encountered.

We had just come out of a line of trees that broke onto a wide meadow and led down to a small river at the bottom. I could see Little Jimmy Carroll working his way through the trees at the edge of the open ground. He moved into and out of the foliage.

Then, he stopped and whirled the horse around. He took out his pistol and fired a shot of warning into the air. That was immediately followed by a shot that rang out from behind him and he pitched forward into the grassy slope.

"Can ya see 'em, Will?" the marshal asked.

Will didn't answer. He slid off his horse and knelt on the ground, raising the Schuetzen. "Boom," it echoed off the surrounding walls of rock.

"Get 'em?"

"Naw," he said.

"See if you can get to Jimmy," the marshal said, looking at me.

I kicked the dun. It leapt forward and we dashed out into the open. It was foolish to let myself get used as bait, but I felt a duty to Jimmy. I rode hard to his position and slipped out of the saddle at a run.

When I reached the dying man, I dropped beside him. He was staring up into the clouds with stony eyes. Occasionally, a painful grimace would flash over his face. His eyes would enliven and then settle down to a stare. I eased back to my horse and got a canteen.

I sat down next to Jimmy and slipped my right thigh under his head. I poured the water into his greedy mouth. He gulped weakly and whispered his thanks.

Behind us, I heard the sound of the gun and the whizzing of a bullet overhead. Blood welled up under Jimmy's shirt, pushing forth and soaking the cloth in regular rhythms. His face grew paler with each surge. Death hung close, waiting to rush into his empty veins.

I watched his hand search the ground until it ran into the puddle growing around him. He looked up into my eyes with distant confusion.

"Can't you put it back?" he asked, whispering.

My guts welled up and pushed at my throat, choking me with a sudden wave of emotion. I shook my head.

"I'll run out."

I nodded.

"Goddamn," he said, and died.

I slipped my leg out from under his head. I thought the proper thing to do was to close his lids, but it seemed right that he ought to be able to gaze up at the blue sky of day and the starlit night. He had chosen to live in the vast, open world and ought to be able to enjoy it.

Anger filled me. What right did they have to kill Jimmy? What right did they have to kill Pete? Why did they pick on the gentle ones? What about Will? He killed a crazy man for the hell of it. What about George, who killed a couple negro soldiers for no better reason? What about the marshal, who seemed to gut everyone he came across? Why was it always the good ones, the pleasant ones?

I stood up and looked into the direction of the shot that killed Jimmy.

"Come on, goddamnit," I said, inviting them to take a shot at me. If I could draw them out, Will could get a shot. Maybe, I could get a shot. I went to my horse and withdrew the Winchester. I levered a shell into the breech. I drew down on the line of trees searching for any sign of movement, any target.

I heard hooves beating the ground behind me. The others were bearing down on my position with the extra horses: Pete's and Jimmy's abandoned stud. I glanced over my shoulder at them and eased the hammer back on the Winchester.

"They've moved out," the marshal shouted to me.

I got aboard the dun and kicked her to meet up with the others as they raced by. Will handed me the reins to my spare horse. We kept a fast pace for quite a while. There was good footing and we made use of it as long as we could.

Up ahead, we caught glimpses of the two remaining men. They would pop out of a tree line, or out of a draw, and race on ahead. It seemed futile to run. We would catch them. No army to save them, no cover strong enough to hide in. In moving fast, they were leaving a trail broad as a railroad. The only chance they had was darkness. I suppose they thought if they could stay ahead until dark, they could escape. But they had no spare horses and we did. We used them properly and gained on them with every step.

Dandy Jim and his follower knew it was up when Will stood in his saddle, absorbing the stride of the horse through his bent knees, and let off a shot that took one of the horses down. Dandy Jim kept up his pace, riding straight on, but the other staggered, limping away from the downed animal. He scrambled about, searching frantically for cover.

We were seventy yards from him and coming fast. Will stood

in his saddle for another shot. Before he could let it off, the man raised his revolver and shot Will in the forehead. The rifleman fell backwards off his mount. In a second, George plugged the outlaw in the gut with two shots from his Whitney. The marshal didn't even slow, but kept right on the trail of Dandy Jim.

George and I rode on. We followed the marshal on a fevered dash across the landscape. Further ahead, we saw Dandy Jim playing out his last hand. He tried to jump a small gully, but his beautiful horse, worn out from the treacherous hills, the long run, and the desperate last dash, failed him. In a spray of dirt and mud, the two collided with the earth and rolled.

The marshal drew back on the reins, sliding his horse to a halt. He drew his revolver and pointed it at Dandy Jim.

"Finish it," I heard myself whisper.

But the marshal didn't finish it. He held Dandy Jim in his sights and waited for us to arrive. Dandy Jim was breathing heavily, raggedly when we got there. He looked frazzled, defeated, and weak. All of his pretense had lifted, leaving him pathetic and ordinary; his fine suit was dusty and stained; his long, greased-back hair hung across his face in disgusting strands. He stared at the ground.

"Disarm this man," the marshal said, as we pulled our horses to a stop and dismounted.

George, still clutching the revolver, swung down and whirled the weapon in a fancy gesture of triumph and holstered it. He walked up to Dandy Jim and busted him in the jaw. Dandy Jim reeled back and flopped to the ground. George stood on his wrists.

"Git everythin'," he said to me.

I removed Dandy Jim's revolver from the holster, then pulled a small knuckle-duster out of his vest pocket and a knife from his boot. I looked for other secret places a man could hide a weapon and found none. George stepped off his wrists and jerked him to his feet.

"Well, Leonard," the marshal said, grinning. "You've cost me some good men, a few months, and a lot of sleep, but I've got ya. What do ya think about that?"

Dandy Jim said nothing. He stood slumped and staring at the ground.

"This is the man you saw in Santa Fe?"

"It's him," I replied.

Dandy Jim looked up from the ground with red eyes of hate that bored through my flesh. Again, I saw the ferocity of his gaze and couldn't bear it. I looked down, but nodded.

"I'll kill you, I swear it," he said, the words coming out as a hiss, his head shaking with anger.

I believed him and I started to think of all the ways Dandy Jim might be able to do just that on the way back to Santa Fe.

"Maybe it would be better just to hang him out here or something," I suggested.

"Naw," the marshal replied, grinning. "The folks need a hanging, young'uns need to see what happens to murderers and thieves, especially famous ones. Tie him up, boys."

We tied Dandy Jim's hands together and put him in the saddle of one of the spare horses, then we tied his bound hands to the saddle horn. The marshal raised his revolver and shot the black horse with relish.

"There," he said to Dandy Jim, as if it were a declaration to the righteousness of the law.

We got the rest of the money out of each man's saddlebags and put it all together, except for the five hundred I carried. The marshal made a point of saying it was still five hundred short, but he had confidence in me. I rolled my eyes in response.

With that, we retraced our steps, picking up the dead and burying them next to each other. Dandy Jim was called on to do the digging for his man. The outlaw, a man called "Black Jack" Roberts, was buried opposite the others to separate them in death as they had been separate in life.

"Don't want the good ones getting mixed up with the bad," the marshal said, giving us the order.

We made camp a little further on where trees offered a sufficient anchor for our prisoner. The marshal respected Dandy Jim for his elusiveness, cunning, and outrageous luck. He allowed no margin for error. Even though Dandy Jim was sufficiently tied to a tree, we kept watch on his every move throughout the night. My turn came toward morning.

"Yur turn," George said, kicking my feet on his way to bed. He collapsed on his bedroll and slept with his rifle across his chest.

I woke slowly. I was terrified of Dandy Jim, more so after his capture than before. He lay next to the tree, silently threatening.

I had heard once of a man capturing a bobcat in a carpetbag. Possessing a cruel sense of humor, the man placed the bag on a railroad platform. When the train pulled out and it seemed that the bag had been abandoned, some thief snatched it up and carried it to a privy. He locked himself inside to rummage through the articles for something of value. The man followed stealthily along to watch the result of his morbid plan.

The man laughed so hard in the telling that he had to stop several times and guffaw.

The opportunist opened the bag and all hell broke loose in the privy. Fur and flesh filled the confined atmosphere and burst through the door ahead of the crazed thief as he made his escape.

Looking at Dandy Jim, I felt we had bagged a bobcat and I had been elected to open it. I couldn't shake the uneasiness I felt when I looked at him, so I didn't. I found innumerable other things to study: the trees, the ground, the sky, bugs and critters of all kinds, anything but the sleeping, captured gambler.

The next morning, we had breakfast. I reheated some of the bear meat and we boiled coffee. It was the best meal any of them had in days. Even Dandy Jim thanked me for the fresh meat. Then, we got ready. We had four extra horses as we; we hadn't kept them all. We started the long journey through the mountains. Our first destination was the town of Cimarron, where George had to stand trial for killing the soldiers. He tried to talk the marshal out of it.

"To hell with them damn niggers, anyway. Christ almighty, they drawed down on me an' you know it, Dayton."

"Don't matter what I know," the marshal said. "The town has to know it. The Army has to know it. It does no good to run. Ask Mr. Braswell here, if you don't believe me."

Dandy Jim shot a look of contempt at the marshal.

I rode ahead of the little group, doing my best to pick a trail. It wasn't too hard. All we had to do was follow the little valley that blessed us with several meadows and an occasional hill for scenery's sake. For the time being, we had it pretty good.

I could feel Dandy Jim's stare always on my neck. Whenever I looked back to check, his eyes were fixed on me, studying me, as if picking at a loose thread that would unravel his snare. It was unnerving to know it. I tried my hardest to take my mind off it, but his eyes always watched.

CHAPTER EIGHTEEN

Once again on level ground, we found a small group of adobe buildings gathered along the river. There was no name for the place, just a gathering of people who thrived on local game and some trade with Indians.

We rode through the middle of the buildings, causing a bit of a stir. The Mexican children gazed up at us with brown, inquisitive eyes. They studied Dandy Jim. They pointed at him with dirty little fingers and said, *"Cautivo"* in hushed reverence.

After we passed through the village, with only a thin whisper of dust as evidence, I pulled up to let my horse have a drink of cool water from the mountain stream. The marshal pulled up next to me.

"South seems the only way out of these hills," he remarked.

I looked the landscape over and saw low hills lying on the distant, left horizon. It looked like an easy path to the east, but I had seen low hills turn into huge peaks as I neared. I scratched my cheek in thought.

"Let's hope so," I replied.

The marshal nodded, confident in his ability to judge terrain.

"Liable to be Injuns about," I said. "There was some Injun things back there."

"Damn the Injuns, let's get a move on."

The rest of the day we marked progress along the widening valley as it turned to open ground spanning the distance between one range of mountains and the next. I had heard stories of Kit Carson passing through this country with Fremont, or on his own. Those must have been some times. First white men to see it, I heard. There had been few since.

As we rode, the thought of Indians bothered me more and more. Utahs, I thought, or Navajos. I was not anxious to meet up with either. In Nuevo Méjico, the Indian problem had been pretty well solved for a while, except for the odd, whiskey-crazed band of Mescalero Apaches. Of course, we had plenty to fear from odd, whiskey-crazed white men, too. But a man never knew. Anything could flare up a dispute between Indians and the government. Then a bunch of them would come out looking for a party, just like ours, to scalp and kill in search of vengeance.

It felt good to be out in the open, though. I could see an attack coming and prepare for it. In the mountains, I felt crowded and could sense the multitude of vicious eyes peering out from cover, deciding my fate as I passed.

Self-consciously I glanced behind me. The marshal and George had drifted further back. That left Dandy Jim and me somewhat alone. He moved easily with the rhythm of the horse. He was looking straight down. He might've been asleep. The reins of his horse were tied to the tail of mine to keep him from trying to escape.

Further back, the marshal and George were talking over some subject with calm deliberation. The whole bunch of lawmen were secretive to the core. I turned back to the trail ahead.

"Snake," Dandy Jim whispered, so low it sounded like a hiss. "Don't look around."

"I ain't gonna do nothin' to get myself hung, so keep to yourself," I said, whispering back.

"I don't hold you responsible for lying to me back in Trinidad," he said.

"I don't give a damn."

"I don't know why you're working with these men, but I

know you're not like them."

"Shut up, damn you," I replied, getting nervous. I knew the marshal would not kill Dandy Jim before reaching Santa Fe, but he would kill me if he feared betrayal. Suspicion was all he needed to shoot me for conspiracy, and I was not about to let Dandy Jim raise it.

For a moment, silence prevailed. Then the marshal and George rode up behind the prisoner and stayed back there, watching him. Old George was forever pestering the man. He told stupid jokes to aggravate him. As soon as George was within earshot, he started in again.

"Hey, Leonard," he said. "What's the difference between a live gambler and a dead one?" No answer. "A three-foot drop," he said, and roared with laughter. No one else laughed.

In all the hours I had spent on the trail with George Brimson, the only good thing I could say about him was he could handle a six-shooter. It seemed a small bit of redemption for the otherwise cruel, vicious, antagonizing, bigoted murderer with a badge.

"Why ain't ya laughin'?" he asked Dandy Jim. "Hell, if ya can't have a sense of humor about it, what's the point?"

Though a sharp retort must have risen to Dandy Jim's lips often, he never let it out. He knew George or his kind well enough to know that he reveled in his brutality. Any excuse and he would bring his iron fists down on the aging gambler. He would beat the man with relish and kick him a time or two for any perceived slight.

"The hell's the matter with you, Leonard? You think I ain't funny? I'm funny. Ask Dayton, here. Ain't I funny?" he asked, looking at the marshal. "See, there?" he said, knowing the marshal failed to confirm the fact.

"Right funny sonofabitch," I said over my shoulder, taking George's side to prove to Dandy Jim that he couldn't play me against them.

"Damn right!" George said, slapping his leathered thigh. A little puff of dust rose from the leather.

The sun bore down on us all. Dust powdered our faces and perspiration rolled down our jaws, leaving paths of mud behind. We were a melancholy band, sure enough.

Late in the day, we pulled up to make camp. We had ridden a long way over the course of the day and stopped at the entrance to the low passage between the hills. As always before, what seemed like mere humps in the horizon rose to a formidable barrier by the time we got there. But there was a low, small creek that was fed by a shallow water table. All around were scorched hills. Along the bottom, two hundred feet of soggy ground fed tall, lush grass. We camped at the dry edge of it.

The marshal decided I should go out and scout our back trail and up ahead, to see if I cut anyone's sign. What did he send me for? I could hardly find a trail to save my life. Even if I happened to cut someone's trail, I wouldn't be able to cipher it worth a damn. He had lost Little Jimmy Carroll and he couldn't make another one out of me. I didn't see the point, but I went.

Spooky, is the best way to describe the walk through the gently rising hills. Trees stood all around and swayed in the breeze. It was not much different from any other night, except that Indians were fresh on my mind and I thought I could see evidence of them everywhere. A strange sensation crawled at the back of my neck. My eyes were strained wide to the darkness.

I pushed branches and bushes out of my way. I had been through so much brush in recent times, my boots were nearly wore out at the toe and outside edges. For that reason alone, I deserved to keep the wad of bills found in the dead man's saddlebags.

While making my way in a wide circle about the camp, looking over the edges of hills and into further valleys, I started to hear bugs chirping louder, closer. Their noise grew steadily and with greater volume as I moved faster through the brush, beating at the gnarled, clawing stems.

I was in a near panic by the time I burst into a small clearing, just above the camp. I felt pursued by the noise and stumbled along the rocky ground. As the insect sounds grew to a crescendo, I came face to face with an Indian. I pumped six bullets into him before my brain could understand the image of his painted face. It happened so fast, I stood staring down at the smoking Colt in my hand. I did not recall laying a hand to the revolver, yet there it was.

I looked up at the face of the Indian, unchanged, unhurt, and staring glassy-eyed at me. It was only then that I realized he was long dead. The smell should have attested to it earlier. Two or three days had passed since he blew his last breath. An arrow, hardly visible in the darkness, protruded from his chest. It had the lifeless body pinned to a tree. Some old quarrel within the band, or something of that nature.

George rushed up, revolver in hand to lend assistance. I met him a few hundred yards from the Indian.

"The hell's all the shootin'?"

"Shot an Indian," I said, casually.

His gaze flashed over the surrounding terrain.

"Where?"

"Up there," I replied, turning and pointing to the place.

"Any more of 'em?"

"Naw."

"Well, there's liable to be."

"I doubt it," I said, regretting the story I had to tell. "He's been dead a few days."

George smirked. "Kilt yur first dead Injun, have ya?"

"I reckon."

George backed off away from me to inspect me in the scant moonlight.

"That was just you firin' then?"

How long was he going to drag it out? Wasn't it bad enough that I had to admit shooting a dead Indian without having to admit that I did it six times?

I nodded shamefully.

"Fannin'?" he asked.

"I ain't no fancy hand with a Colt."

"You did all that without fannin'?"

I nodded.

"Goddamn, boy. What was it like?"

"It was like shootin' a dead Injun six times, George, all right? Christ, what do you want to know?"

"No, boy. Ya got me all wrong. Ya have to draw, or was ya carryin' the Colt in yur hand?"

"Had to pull," I said, wondering what he was getting at.

"Remember pullin'?"

"No," I said, knowing the fact would prove my inability as a quick-draw artist. So what? I never claimed to be.

George shook his head, pleased as hell.

"Ya got it, boy! Don't ya understand? Ya got the knack. I knew it the first time ya grabbed that damn snake. Ain't ya never tried ta do the quick pull?"

"No."

"Goddamn," he said, slapping me on the back, welcoming me into a brotherhood I had no interest in joining. I could see his rotting teeth in the dim, blue light. "Yur one o' us! Goddamn, I knew it."

On the way down the hill, George told me a few things. He talked about the art of it, the beauty of the draw. Though it came out in crude railings, George spoke of "the gift" as if it were something to be proud of and marveled at. We belonged to a secret society of quick pullers, as he saw it, and he felt it was his duty to welcome me into it. When he got around to the outcome of all of this fancy pistoleering, he looked at the ground for a moment in silent reverence.

"Course, some fella's dead at the end of it, but ain't it somethin' to pull that quick? To rattle off them shots so fast most folks don't know ya shot more'n once! Ahhhhh," he said, relishing the memories and shaking his head.

I was a reluctant brother to George for a while. Worst of all, he thought it made us friends, amigos in a dirty business. I didn't have the heart to tell him I had no interest in learning the finer aspects of killing men.

So, I let him ramble and listened to his dissertation on the mechanics and reasoning of the quick draw. It all made sense to him in a mathematical way. This way takes longer than that way. If I did this thing, I would get a jump by the slightest sliver of time and beat even a brother in the collective world of quick-draw artists.

The worst part of it all was that I didn't think I could repeat the act. Before, I was scared out of my wits, driven nearly insane by the loud clamoring of insects chirping madly in the darkness. George tried to goad me into practicing, but I put him off. Strangely, he accepted my reluctance with a wry grin.

"Aw, they're all that way at first," he said.

CHAPTER NINETEEN

I watched the prisoner in the evening and gave my duties over to George in the early morning hours. He grumbled, rose, and shook his head as he moved to stoke the fire for coffee. I went to my bedroll and lay down.

I slept fitfully. Images of Indians stalking me in the darkness and visions of saloon confrontations floated in my dreams. I woke several times to stare out at the green, lush streambed. I had to force myself back to sleep.

Then, the camp erupted in confused shouting and I woke to the sound of George's Whitney revolver booming. I leapt to my feet and grabbed for the Colt lying next to the saddle. I looked around bleary-eyed at the scene.

"There he goes!" George screamed, charging for his horse and lifting the rifle out of the scabbard on his way past the saddle lying at the head of his bedroll. He slung the bit into the horse's mouth and mounted quickly onto the bare back of the horse. I gathered my thoughts and untied the rope from my saddle. I threw the coiled rope over my head and joined in the chase atop my unsaddled horse.

I left the marshal behind as he struggled to get his horse properly saddled before taking after the escaped prisoner. I knew he had a reason for it, a calm, cool reason that I couldn't think of in the confusion and excitement of the moment. Instead, I charged headlong into the chase, plowing across the soggy ground and through the shallow stream.

George rode ahead and dove into the first line of trees. The landscape seemed to swallow him, gulping horse and rider in a single bite. But I saw fragments of him emerge on the other side behind branches. He pulled up on the reins, glanced about, and then sprang forward in a new direction.

I rode hard into the spot George had. The branches came fast and I held my breath in preparation of piercing the barrier. Then, I was through and looked about for signs of George. The hollow sound of his Whitney popped to my left. I kicked the horse into that direction.

An incredible thrashing took place in some thick brush and I rode to the sound. As I turned in, I caught a flash of something moving behind me. I whirled around and saw Dandy Jim making his way across the clearing I had just come through. I shoved the pistol into my belt and unslung my rope.

Shaking out a good loop, I chased the man down. He was halfway across the clearing when I saw him. He had no recourse but to run for the nearest line of trees. The old blood of a cowpuncher filled my chest and I grinned, grateful for the opportunity to use my skill.

"Whoop, whoop," went the sound of the rope as it spun above my head. I bent forward in the saddle. The horse bore down on the running man. Dandy Jim dodged to his right, but the mare kept with him. I let go with a loop floating through the air, descending slowly over his head. I dallied the end of the rope around my waist and pulled back on the reins. Dandy Jim threw his arms up to his head and tried to bend out of the loop, but it was too late.

The rope slid down over his shoulders and the dun pulled back, drawing against the slack. When the rope pulled taut, it vibrated for a second and pulled Dandy Jim to the ground.

George rode up behind me and slapped me on the back.

"Good job!" he said.

By then, the marshal had gotten his things together and arrived on the scene. Every time Dandy Jim tried to rise, or to loosen the loop, my horse stepped back, pulling him to the ground until he lay immobile.

The marshal stepped to the ground and walked up to Dandy Jim.

"Look here, Leonard. You just made your life miserable," he said, and kicked Dandy Jim in the head. He looked over his shoulder and motioned for me to give the rope some slack. I did and he removed it. I coiled it up and stuck one arm and my head through the center.

The marshal gave Dandy Jim a few more kicks and pulled him to his feet. He pushed him toward the camp and kicked him in the pants.

With all of us up, we decided to have breakfast and start out on the next leg of the journey. We tied Dandy Jim's hands with strips of rawhide, again. But this time he had to pay for his escape attempt and the marshal had us tie his feet together with enough rawhide between to let him walk.

"You wanna run?" the marshal said. "You can run now."

I was told to put a rope around Dandy Jim's neck and lead him with my horse. If he fell, I was to drag him. It seemed cruel, but then everything the marshal did seemed cruel. Sadly, I was growing accustomed to his style of law enforcement.

"Don't make the marshal mad," I said, slipping the loop over Dandy Jim's head. "He's a serious man."

Moving on, we traveled most of the day through the low pass, encountering only one rise of any consequence. Then, we were thrown out onto a long flat plain dotted with clumps of grass and soapweed. The sun reflected off the sandy ground and smothered us in a blanket of heat.

After ten miles of the arid stretch, I could feel the rope trailing back to Dandy Jim tighten with a quick snap as it pulled him forward and made him run a few steps to keep from falling on his face. I looked back. He was sweating profusely.

"Water," he whispered.

I pulled up on the reins and swung down with one of the canteens in my hand. Dandy Jim seemed shrunken and shriveled within his gaudy gambler clothes. Whatever had been fancy about them was no longer.

"Can you remove my jacket?" he asked, as I handed him the canteen.

The marshal and George came up quickly. Dust followed them and overtook us. I waved at the cloud with my hat. The marshal swung down and stepped up to me with prompt arrogance. He pulled the canteen away from Dandy Jim's mouth, spilling some of the precious liquid onto the parched, sandy ground.

"No water," he said, thrusting the canteen into my chest.

I took the canteen and shoved the marshal away. I handed the canteen back to Dandy Jim. I stood between the marshal and his prisoner while he drank. The marshal's eyes burned with hatred.

"You sidin' with this piece of shit?" he asked, his eyes narrowing.

"Hell, no."

"Then, what's the meaning of this?"

"Ya ain't gotta kill everything, Marshal," I said, feeling the words catch in my throat. The last thing I wanted to do was interfere with him, but someone had to stand up for what was due a man, even one like Dandy Jim.

"Seems to me, you're gettin' killers mixed up with lawmen. Everything I done, I done in interest of the law. The feller drinkin' from your canteen is the one that killed folks in cold blood."

"I just aim to give him water, not a pardon," I said, taking the canteen back and ramming the cork into the hole. "I'm takin' his jacket off, too."

Dandy Jim grinned at the discussion and received a back-handed blow from the marshal.

"Goddamn, you! Don't smirk at me, boy!" he said, pointing his finger into Dandy Jim's chest. Then, he turned on me. "Don't let all that talk of being quick on the pull go to your head. Got me?"

"I ain't," I said, though I don't know if it was true, or not. I hoped I had enough common decency to give Dandy Jim a drink in any case. But somewhere in the back of my mind, I knew I could out-pull the marshal. He knew it, too. It was a bit of an edge in an argument.

The marshal oversaw the whole process of untying Dandy Jim's hands, removing the jacket, and re-tying his hands. When he was satisfied, he spun on his heel and went back to his horse.

I didn't bother to look up at George. I could imagine him working his jaw through it all. George was a loyal man and a bit more brutal than the marshal. I knew he considered my impertinence a disloyal act. I also knew I would have to hear about it before long.

The marshal went back to George, who had taken the reins of the spare horses. The marshal took one set from him and swung around to follow me. As soon as we had started to move, George leapt in with some lame joke about gamblers and death.

The afternoon slipped by in drowsy heat. Our little group progressed across the desert-like landscape. All around us were cool, high mountains, but before us lay only miles of endless horizon and scorching sand. Heat waves danced and small twist-ers lifted up from the floor of the basin, like a great buffalo lay just under the surface of the soil, his nostrils blowing sand up from the ground. I was so convinced of this I came to listen for its coarse, rumbling growl and expected its immense head to poke up out of the heat waves and devour us whole. Maybe, I just hoped it would.

When we thought we had made it through the worst of it, the earth revealed a cruel punishment for our optimism. We rode slowly up to a huge gash in the land. Some two hundred feet below raged the Rio Grande del Norte. A half mile away, across the great expanse of emptiness, was the other half of the earth we needed to continue on our path.

We had made slow progress that day, not more than twenty miles with Dandy Jim's walking pace. The sun hovering above the horizon was growing large and forgiving as the minutes passed. We sat looking from one to the other for inspiration.

"Goddamnit!" the marshal shouted, realizing there was nothing to do but follow the canyon until it played out. "Get that man aboard a horse and let's see if we can't find the end to this damned thing."

We wound up riding several miles to the south, sliding down the steep bank that remained of the canyon and crossing the wide Rio Grande. Once on the other side, we ran our horses a bit to dry things and made camp by a small river that led back northeast toward what looked like another small pass.

The way I had it figured, Taos had to be somewhere along the river. The streambed supported enough sturdy trees to supply us with an anchor for our prisoner and firewood for coffee. We made a nice fire, tied up Dandy Jim, and set coffee to brewing.

The marshal wasn't about to let my little rebellion go unmentioned. He stared at me across the fire. I tried to avoid his gaze. An argument could be the only result of acknowledgment and I preferred not to spend my time that way.

"You better get your heart straight, mister," he said.

"My heart's plenty straight. Ya can capture a man and lead him to justice. You can make him walk twenty miles through the broilin' sand. I don't give a damn about none o' that, but when you deny a thirsty man a drink of water, I draw the line."

"You want to throw in with the likes of him and you're welcome to the same rope as far as I care, but if you double-cross me, boy, I'll hunt you down."

I shook my head and spit into the dust. There was nothing further from my mind than throwing in with a man about to hang.

"It starts and stops at the water," I said.

"It had better."

I hoped that would settle it. The marshal had his say and I had mine. Unfortunately, George had not had his, yet. His came toward midnight when he woke me to stand watch over the prisoner.

"Get up, goddamn ya!"

I squinted up at him and struggled to my feet. He grabbed me roughly by the shoulder.

"Come here a minute."

I pulled away from his grasp and walked with him, staring insolently at his rigid cheek. Several yards from the others, George turned on me.

"I ain't never seen such disrespect. If I was Dayton, I'd have whupped yur ass."

"All I done was give the man a drink. The marshal took it to mean a lot more. That's his mistake, not mine."

"By God, I swear yur an ungrateful sonofabitch."

"Grateful? What the hell have I got to be grateful for? I was hired to do a job, that's all. I'm doin' it. Y'all ought to be grateful I came along. You'd have never gone to Cimarron. Likely as not, you'd still be trackin' dust in the Santa Fe Mountains."

"What about that man he give ya? He was worth some money. More than you was owed, I reckon. Ya can't be grateful fur that, even?"

"I drug him along, didn't I? I had to argue with the captain for my money, didn't I? Hell, knowin' the marshal, he probably sent me off with that man to see if Dandy Jim would follow me. No, sir, I don't owe him no debt for that trip."

"By God, I ought to slap yur insolent mouth!"

"Try it, George," I said, with a resolve that surprised him. "Ya know, the damn thing of it? You fellas been actin' like I'm some kid, but let me tell you one thing: I've been facin' Injuns and snakes and bad weather all my life. I been trackin' cattle over harsh and unforgivin' country. If you fellers with badges think you're the only men in this country, you got another think comin'. You've done mistaken peaceableness for timidity too damn long.

"I'll ride with ya, help ya all I can. I'll take Dandy Jim in for ya, pull him along the ground if I have to, but it ain't 'cause I'm scared of none of ya. I ain't never been. You fellers know yur business, I respect it and stay outta yur way. I do what I'm told, 'cause that's what a good man does, but ya go to runnin' roughshod over me and you'll get my back up in a hurry. Even a criminal like Dandy Jim deserves a drink and some rest. A damned pig deserves that much and if he don't get it, I'll stand up to make sure he does. Understand?"

George wasn't used to being lit into like that, not by someone he could outdraw, outfight, and probably outrun. He stood stunned to white-faced perplexity by what he had heard. George understood fear and intimidation as the motivation in a man's life. My devotion to principles of decency confounded him, surprised him.

"I could whup yur ass," he said, grasping for some shred of clarity.

I snorted my response and went back to the campfire. Let him brood on the conversation, I thought. I had little confidence that he would be able to understand what drove a man like me. He couldn't fathom a man who was peaceful by nature, decent by instinct. His world was one of force and might. He worried about who was stronger, faster, meaner; everything I understood was lost on him, but I had given him a piece of it.

CHAPTER TWENTY

The next morning, I had a fire built and coffee ready by the time the others woke up. I cut Dandy Jim loose from the tree as soon as the marshal rose. Anticipating a good meal in Taos, we had a cup of coffee and decided to get a move on.

Before we left, the marshal walked over to Dandy Jim and cuffed him to the ground. He kicked him a time or two and bent over his body to land a few more punches on his face. I thought I would have to intervene and was not looking forward to it, but the marshal straightened up and slapped his hands together as if completing some necessary, but distasteful chore.

"That ought to keep him thinkin' about pains instead of plans," he said, looking at me. He either said it to quell my instinct for rescue, or to prove there was a purpose to his brutality. I suppose I should have felt honored that he bothered to explain a damn thing.

We followed the small river northwest. It seemed like pleasant going, except for the new jokes George thought up overnight. He told them to Dandy Jim, but we all had to endure the ritual with grim acceptance of routine. I expected the marshal to put a stop to it sooner or later, but he didn't. Maybe he felt the torture had a greater effect on Dandy Jim, or that he was more annoyed by it than we were. I didn't see how he could be.

I led the way, pulling Dandy Jim's mount along. The other two stayed to the rear, where they could watch everything.

About midmorning, I noticed the dun sniffing the air and whipping its head from side to side. I narrowed my eyes and peered into the distance. Then, the earth opened up and spit out Indians. Twenty of the finely muscled braves pulled their horses into a line in front of us. I jerked back on the reins and waited for the marshal to come abreast.

"Savage sonsabitches," George muttered, pulling up next to me.

"What tribe?" the marshal asked.

"Hell if I know," I replied. "Utahs, or Navajo. Apaches would probably be killin' us."

"Friendly?"

"Depends on whether or not they've been fed maggot beef by the reservation agent."

"Goddamn red bastards," George said.

"Twenty goddamn red bastards," I corrected.

He screwed up his face and spit black tobacco juice past the nose of my horse. The dun threw its head back and stomped.

"Stay here," the marshal said, and handed George the reins of the horse he trailed. He kicked his horse ahead.

"What do we do if they kill him?" I asked George.

"Shoot Leonard and run like hell," he replied.

I looked back at Dandy Jim. He rolled his eyes and looked past my shoulder at the Indians.

"Everything starts with killing me," Dandy Jim muttered.

George twisted around in his saddle and thrust a stubby finger out at the captive.

"You just shut yur damn mouth, gambler."

"Or, what?"

"Or, I'll put a piece of lead through ya so damn fast, you won't know yur dead 'til sundown!"

I chuckled at the saying. It seemed rather quick for George. I figured he must've heard it somewhere. George looked at me solemn and offended for a moment, then he let out a little laugh of his own.

"Ain't that right?" he said, pleased with himself.

"Wouldn't surprise me none."

Ahead, we saw the leader of the Indians detach himself from the others and move toward the marshal.

"Get ready, now," George said.

We adjusted our revolvers and kept a strict eye on the proceedings. The Indian raised his hand in greeting. The marshal mimicked the move and they came together to talk.

"Does the marshal know Injun?" I asked.

"Don't hardly know Mex'n," George replied.

The Indian pointed toward us and made grand gestures to the marshal. The marshal looked back at us and shook his head. To that, the Indian pointed at the marshal and brought his hand down in a stiff motion.

"This ain't lookin' good," George said, fidgeting.

We could hear the faint voice of the Indian. It was a guttural language that sounded like an ass-chewing from beginning to end. More gestures were made, none looked too friendly. My hopes for a peaceful settlement of the conversation were growing dim.

The marshal turned around and rode slowly toward us. He held a stern look on his face. I wanted to call out to him to find out what he knew. It was agonizing waiting for him to approach. The marshal pulled up to us and bent over to lean his forearm on the saddle horn.

"Any of you got tobacco?" he asked.

"Chaw," George replied.

"Smokin' tobacco."

"Hell, dry it out. Try that."

"I think they want something for passing through their land," the marshal said. "That, or they want to do some unnatural things to George."

George's face went white and he thrust his chest out.

"By God, I'll kill every one o' them red sonsabitches for thinkin' it."

"Relax, George. I'm sure they were talking about the horses you're holdin'."

"Good thing for them," he said, spitting.

"I want to offer some tobacco, first," the marshal said. "It ain't smart to give up a horse too easy."

"Offer 'em one horse, the poorest one," I suggested.

"Then what will George do for a horse?" Dandy Jim asked. George backed his horse closer to Dandy Jim and smacked him upside the head.

"Mister," the marshal said, glaring with flaming eyes at Dandy Jim, "don't start usin' that mouth. I could bring ya in dead and cheat the citizens of Santa Fe of the pleasure of watchin' you hang. Don't think I won't."

Dandy Jim settled back into himself, like a turtle crawling back into its shell.

"Give me Will's horse," the marshal said. He took the reins and led it toward the Indian. The Indian was not pleased with the prospect of just one horse. He started his tirade of sharp exclamations, long before the marshal reached his position and continued well after. The Indian moved out from behind the marshal and pranced his mount back and forth, pointing at the other three horses.

"That bastard's pointin' at me!" George said, feeling as if he were the object of the Indian leader's desire. It took all I could to keep from laughing out loud. "Goddamn him. I'll kill him first."

There were some tense minutes to be had on the open meadow, but in the end, the Indians went away peacefully with two horses and a few provisions that we had in our saddlebags.

Toward the end of the negotiation, both groups moved together and traded articles. I got a nice necklace of bear claws for the shiny deputy's badge I pulled out of my hip pocket.

As soon as we moved toward Taos, I heard about it.

"Mister, that wasn't yur badge to trade," the marshal said.

I pulled the necklace over my head and offered it to him. He shook his head.

"That ain't the point. I gave you that badge to keep you out of trouble, not to go tradin' for Indian trinkets."

I shrugged and replaced the necklace. It seemed like a good trade to me.

We rode up to Taos in good spirits. There was a small army barracks about ten miles out of town. It had been abandoned for several years. We sniffed around for a bit and rode for the town. After the days of watching Dandy Jim, I think we all wanted to lock him up for the night and have a bit of whiskey. I did.

There were scant accommodations, but we found the jail on the first trip through. We went inside the little adobe building thrusting Dandy Jim ahead of us, like herding a prize bull into the auction arena.

A startled Mexican man stood up from behind a shabby desk. He looked angry.

"United States Marshal Dayton Howard," the marshal said, identifying himself. "This here's Deputy Marshal George Brimson."

The constable lurched backward, his hand searching for the butt of his revolver. To say George beat him to the draw would be to say the sun was a little warm in Nuevo Méjico. Fact is, George beat him to the draw twice. The first time, he froze the man in his sights and whipped the Whitney revolver around on his finger. He offered the butt of the weapon to the constable, but before he could reach up to it, he whipped it back around and holstered it. When the constable thought he could get his pistol out, George jerked his up a second time, cocked it, and pressed the muzzle against the man's nose.

"I think that settles that," the marshal drawled in pure Texas fashion. "Look here, officer, I know about all that trouble in Cimarron. Fact is, we're just on our way to turn the deputy here in to Mr. Bowman.

"Now, for the business at hand. This here, is Leonard Braswell, better known as Dandy Jim Beudreaux. He's the man we were after when the ruckus with Deputy Brimson came about. Now that we have our man, we aim to settle things proper with the Cimarron authorities. Until then, the deputy is in my custody."

"No! *Es no bueno.* I must take him into custody *muy pronto.* The army commands this."

"By God, you little greaser, you ain't takin' me into custody. I'll kill ya first."

"Now, George," the marshal said. "You wait outside, while I deal with this gentleman."

"He ain't no goddamned gentleman," George said, on his way out. As if George had a clear idea of what a gentleman was.

As soon as the door slapped shut, the marshal started in with his calm reasoning.

"I understand your devotion to duty . . ." he began and droned on about the exemplary fashion of law enforcement in Taos. It was widely held, he said, that Taos was a town of proper order and law-abiding citizens and that it all stemmed from the conscientiousness of the local constable, namely, the man standing before him.

It was an untidy sum of oily rubbish designed to placate the man. I found it hard to tolerate such greasy words coming from the man I knew had gutted a person for the hell of it. At the tail end of it, his exaggeration got so wild I literally had to turn away to keep from laughing out loud.

"By God," he said, "it's a travesty that this fine city hasn't yet found sense enough to erect a proper monument to your service. I'll take it up with the governor myself, when I turn this piece of filth," he flipped a thumb at Dandy Jim, "in at Santa Fe.

"Furthermore," he continued, "I'll take all responsibility for Deputy Brimson. If a hair should be harmed on your head for letting the deputy accompany me to Cimarron, I'll threaten to resign unless all injustices are corrected."

The constable had a nose for horseshit the same as I did, but he could not argue with the sincerity of the marshal. The finer edge of what the marshal was saying was simply that the constable ran his town with great effectiveness, but the marshal was a man of consequence. He was a man who spoke personally with the governor, with senators and the like. That he had the power to speak personally with generals and get the proper outcome, if he desired. More importantly, he had the power to persecute a minor official that stood in his way.

The constable was a savvy man and reluctantly agreed to imprison Dandy Jim for the night and to leave George alone during his stay. Provided, of course, that the stay did not extend beyond sunrise. Everyone was in agreement and we went out to the saloon free of our prisoner, for a time.

"I've never seen a slicker tongue, nor a quicker blade than you have, Marshal."

"Whichever serves the purpose," the marshal said.

CHAPTER TWENTY-ONE

The marshal, George, and I went to a small cantina on the main street. A few Mexicans sat on the benches out front discussing events of the day.

Inside, there were three tables and a short bar with two stools in front of it. We took up a table in a corner flanked on one side by a wall of adobe. On the other side, a small window faced out onto the street.

George was growing edgy at the prospect of turning himself in at Cimarron and fidgeted around for an excuse not to do so.

"Ya know," he said, after draining his first cup of whiskey. "I oughta just foller you fellas to Santa Fe. That thar gambler's a sneaky one. Ya never know what he'd pull if'n he got a chance."

"There's no doubt about that," the marshal replied. "But, Frank here's willing to go with me, ain't you, Frank?"

"Nothin' better to do, I reckon."

"Well, I don't know." George paused thoughtfully. "Frank, I don't mean to talk ya down none, but you ain't a proper deputy. Ya ain't even got no badge no more."

"He'll do fine," the marshal said.

George rubbed his cheek and held his cup out for more whiskey. The marshal poured it full. George kicked back in his chair, balancing it on the two rear legs. He adjusted his revolver so he could reach it easier from a sitting position.

Two Mexicans strolled in laughing. They rattled off some Mexican too quickly for me to understand, but I got the gist of it. It was just small talk to the bartender. The marshal and George followed the men with narrowed eyes.

The two gathered at the bar and passed a single bottle from mouth to mouth. One of the men pulled his revolver and shot into the ceiling. The abruptness of the shot startled George and he fell over backward in the chair. He made a good show of it by rolling over into a somersault and coming to his feet with the six-shooter in his hand. He shot into the ceiling himself and grinned a maniac's grin.

The men at the bar whirled around to stare at the crazed gringo. Slowly, the apparent leader smiled a malevolent, mustached smile at George.

"Now, George," the marshal said. "You're barely tolerated in this town as it is. Don't go pushin' your welcome."

"Hell, these boys are pistoleros, by God," George said, welcoming them as brothers in a common understanding. He fired another shot into the ceiling and gestured for them to do the same. Then, one of the men understood and shot his revolver timidly into the ceiling.

"There ya go!" George said, encouraging him to do some more. *"Muy bueno."*

I heard the marshal cuss and mutter under his breath. I stared at him for some explanation. Instead, he watched George with wary eyes.

"Stop it, George," he said.

George turned with a smile frozen on his face and stared with distant, vacant eyes. He was a man obsessed with the use of firearms, wrapped completely in the heart-thudding excitement of it all.

The other Mexican slowly pulled his pistol from the worn holster at his side.

"Sí, sí," George said, and went over to buy the men a bottle. He tried to win them over with drinks and encouragement to fire their weapons. He showed them the way it was supposed to go by firing a few more times into the ceiling, then he broke his Whitney open to reload.

The marshal wagged his head in weary tolerance.

"Goddamnit, George!" he said.

George looked at him and tried to quiet his anxiety by waving a hand for him to await the wonderful outcome.

By then, shooting was slowing. Behind the bar, the bartender started getting nervous and tried to escape. One of the men grabbed him by his shirt and insisted he give them the bottle George paid for. The bartender pulled a bottle up and set it on the bar.

Then George, lost in some world of his own making, raised his revolver and shot the bartender between the eyes. Blood sprayed out across the wall. The bartender's face registered surprise as he slipped down below the bar. I leapt to my feet and looked at the marshal, who buried his face into his palms.

There was a moment when the ringing of the last shot reverberated in the hollowness of the room. All else was quiet. Then, a shrieking of horror came from the back room as a woman rushed in and bent over the dead man. She wept and irrationally tried to gather his skull together.

The Mexicans stared at George, angry, confused, but cognizant that they had no shots left in their weapons. George revealed his badge pinned to his vest and the Mexicans realized they had been tricked.

Understanding the gist of the situation, I sat down and searched my mind for the proper thing to do.

The woman stood up from behind the bar, looked from George to the others, and began to scream at them in rapid, indecipherable Spanish. She beat on the bar with her open palm and spit sprayed from her foaming mouth. She tried to get at them over the bar, but she was too short and too round to accomplish it.

"*Abandonar* your *armas*," George said, using what Spanish he had and then whispered some consoling words to the woman and started pushing the men toward the door. The pistols dropped heavily to the floor in their wake.

There was a surprising lack of argument from George's prisoners. It astounded me to watch him gather them up without protest and herd them off to their doom. I stared at the marshal in gape-mouthed fashion. He pulled his face from his hands and looked back up at me with misery and shame in his eyes.

"George, well, he gets a little out of control now and again."

"By God, Marshal, you may call that 'a little out of control,' I call it downright murder." I shook my head, as if to wipe the incident from my mind. "That man shouldn't be runnin' loose." I put my hands on my hips.

"I know it, but he's never killed anyone important."

"Not important to you, maybe." I blew air through my nostrils and tried to get a handle on what needed to be done. "Ya can't keep coverin' for him."

"What the hell am I supposed to do about it? You know how fast he is with that Whitney."

"Hell, yur a lawman, ain't ya? Do what's right."

The marshal sat there for a moment. He poured himself another cup of whiskey and took a sip. He was miserable about the killing. I could see it in his tired face; deep, weary lines crisscrossed his leathery skin marking time like rings in a tree trunk. Every line representing another year of chasing outlaws through the West.

At the moment, he looked like a man forced to kill a favorite hound for some medical malady for which there was no cure. George had rabies, or the human equivalent. He had grown mad with a lust for blood. Perhaps the marshal had seen the signs, tried to ignore them until it was no longer possible.

He drained the cup of whiskey and came to grips with the inevitable. He had to put George to sleep. Worst of all, George was unlike a dog in one important aspect: he could shoot back.

"I don't have the heart," he muttered so softly I could barely hear him.

I cocked my head a little to catch the words as some of the townsfolk gathered about the saloon and some men came in and hauled the body away. The fat Mexican woman followed, wailing.

I glanced over my shoulder to make sure George wasn't standing outside, listening.

"Goddamnit, Marshal," I said, but didn't finish. He knew what I meant.

"I can't do it. I nearly raised him from a boy. He was fifteen years old when he first started beggin' me for a job. He spent his whole youth working with a revolver to prove he was worth a try."

"I don't give a good goddamn if you hatched the murderin' sonofabitch."

"He don't understand. He thinks he put a bunch of bad men in jail. He thinks he done the right thing."

"I guess he learns today."

The marshal nodded, but his nod lacked the force of conviction.

A moment later, George arrived. He lurched into the doorway, grinning.

"Goddamn, them Mex'ns don't even know who shot the old boy. They's so damn drunk! Hah hah," he laughed and plopped down in one of the chairs. He looked at both of us, grinning, too caught up in his own pleasure to recognize that something bad was brewing. He poured himself a cup of whiskey.

"Hell, sit down, Frank."

"What'd you do with 'em?" I asked.

"Took 'em over to the jail. Didn't want ol' Leonard to get lonesome."

"You can't go around killin' innocent folks, George," the marshal croaked, his voice trailing thin in the silent room.

"Innocent?" George seemed confused. "He was just some old Mex'n. Prolly happy to be dead than here, anyways. Goddamn little greaser town."

The marshal slapped his hand on the top of the table.

"Innocent, George. He didn't do a damned thing wrong. There ain't no poster on him. He wasn't wanted for nothin'. That's what innocent is."

George blinked, sensing a confrontation that he wanted to avoid.

"Don't ya get it?" George asked. "I got them ol' boys in jail for it. They was surely wanted for somethin'. I could see in their faces they was."

"They were vaqueros, George. Just some old 'punchers in from trailing a herd," I said, helping to prop up the marshal. "You had no right to shoot that bartender and no right to arrest them innocent workin' men for it."

He brushed me off with a wave of his hand and leaned across the table toward the marshal.

"They got another little drinkin' place up the street," he said.

The marshal reached out and slapped George across the face. George snapped back, stunned, and finally realized the situation for its seriousness.

"I got to turn you into the constable. Don't you see that? It's the law."

George let out an unbelieving chuckle and leaned back in the chair. He glanced up at me, but quickly turned away from my stern look.

"Hey, what's goin' on here? You fellers turnin' on me?"

"Ya broke the law, George. You murdered an innocent man."

"Like hell, he was just a Mex'n," he said, a tight grin spread across his face. "That it, Marshal? Ya turnin' on me? You and this here feller?"

"I've got no choice. I'm sworn to uphold the law."

"What about Will? That time he shot that crazy man? You didn't turn him into the law."

"No, I didn't. It ain't the same."

"It's the same to me," George said, becoming belligerent. I could see his jaw starting to work. He looked up at me with a stare that was part hurt, part hate.

"Thinkin' you can take me on the draw?" he asked.

"No," I replied.

"Damn right, you can't. Neither can you, Marshal, and I know damn well that old man at the jail can't." He searched the room for a moment and looked outside at the sunlight fading in the west and coloring the street an eerie orange.

There it was, the predicament we all faced. George needed to be arrested, but no one could do it. We sat there for a time, letting the challenge sink in. George poured himself another whiskey and sipped at it.

Before there could be a settlement of the situation, another rose up in the street. Apparently, when they put the stories together in the same language, it came out that George killed the bartender. Proof of the assumption was filling the streets in the form of a mob determined to get the gringos that had killed the local man.

A bullet ripped through the window and buried itself into the bar. We all hugged the dirt floor and maneuvered around to see what was going on. I looked out from the corner of the window and saw a large group of men gathering quickly in front of the building. Some were armed only with pitchforks.

"*Asesinos Norteamericanos!*" was heard from the mob and bullets started picking the saloon to pieces.

"Jesus Christ, George, you see what happens?" the marshal scolded.

"I'm sorry," George said.

"Shut up and shoot back," I demanded, firing into the crowd for the second time.

"Frank, see if you can't slip out the back and get the horses."

I didn't need any coaxing on that score and threw myself to it. I scrambled out through the small kitchen and living quarters behind the bar. There were only two rooms and I dove through one of the open windows. I got to my feet and went in search of some saddled horses. I knew where ours were. They were tied in front of the constable's office.

In the confusion of the moment, I found three at the livery. I had to wait for the stable boy to become curious about the firing and wander off, but I got the horses. By the time I got back, there were two men sneaking around back of the saloon. I had never killed a man before, but I had no choice.

I drew the Colt from my waistband and fired twice. I took the first man in the chest and the second in the head.

"Jesus Christ," I whispered to myself. It seemed as if I were in a whiskey dream, doing things I didn't understand, but too busy to cipher it out.

"Come on," I screamed into the saloon.

In a second, I saw George running through the building carrying the marshal over his shoulder. Bullets whipped all around him, blowing chunks of adobe out of the walls, as if the saloon itself were trying to reach out to them as they passed.

George threw the marshal onto one of the horses. The marshal struggled to right himself with a bullet wound in his left shoulder. When we were seated, we bolted down a little slope and through a river. Once on the other side, I stopped to take a few shots at those following us. I plugged one man in the gut and another fired at me, skinning a branch beside my head.

That was enough for me and I took after the others.

We rode up the slope and wound ourselves through the trees and then back across the river a few miles away from town. We took up a position directly across from where we had vanished into the foliage. We hoped by sticking close to the town we would be able to see anyone following us.

There wasn't much of a chase in the end and we felt comfortable enough to go ahead and make camp. To our great disappointment, there was not much in the way of supplies in the saddlebags, just some ranching gear and a little jerked beef. Not enough to feed any of us a proper meal.

I stood out on a rock, in the silence of night, and stared down at the buzzing streets of town. Dim lantern lights burned in the windows. People milled about and got drunk. There they were, I thought, the innocent. And here I am, the guilty. What an awful turn of events I had been through since the day I saw Dandy Jim in that saloon in Santa Fe.

I felt tricked and betrayed. All I ever wanted to do was have a drink in Santa Fe before I looked up another ranch job. In a few short weeks, I had traded places with Dandy Jim and it was I, who had been chased out of town by rifle fire—and pitchforks, I added, to my dry amusement.

CHAPTER TWENTY-TWO

I was a long way from home. I was even further away from the people and life I understood. Stranded on that rock high above Taos, I thought of just how far I had drifted from what my life was supposed to be.

Ever since I settled down to punching cows for a living, I had pretty well accepted that my life would be spent tending cows and riding the range. Every year I could count on a trail drive and a high time at the end of it. Aside from that and an occasional bunkhouse tiff, my days were supposed to slowly wander off toward a setting sun. Then, they would lay me into the ground and scatter what little I owned amongst the other hands. All I ever asked of anyone was to give my horse to a good man.

It was a disappointment to find that I would be harboring a murderer at the end, that I would be hung alongside him for his treacherous acts. I could hear voices from my past bemoaning my ultimate fate.

Skinny Jacobsen: "Well, that boy always had a wild streak." Then, Skinny would shake his head and mutter something about not knowing I would hurt someone, that I would fall in with the likes of Dandy Jim.

My mother: "Never did have much a mind of his own, that one. I warned him. I sure did. I sat him down and scolded him proper for his willingness to go along with the crowd. 'If those fellows jumped off a cliff you'd be right behind them,' I told him. Oh Lord, what will become of his soul?"

Others would never believe it. My friend and partner Hank Duggins would be one. "Aw, he ain't the kind," he would say of me. Even when they brought the newspaper to show him, he would say: "Don't trust no man's ink!" and stalk off.

Just as I was feeling right sorry for myself, I heard the marshal moan. George was tending to his wound. I looked over my shoulder at the two dim figures huddled in the darkness. I could see the bare chest of the marshal and the fuzzy bandage against his smooth skin.

There was no one more deserving of a hanging than George Brimson, but there was no way to do it. We needed him if we planned to make it out alive.

The thought flashed through my mind to just kill them both, right there, but I was no cold-blooded killer. I couldn't do it the way they could. It bothered my conscience too much, but they were becoming a load to bear.

I sucked my teeth in resignation and backed away from the rock. The town had settled down and most of the citizens had gone to bed. I watched the posse come in an hour after it set out for us. That was the sort of posse I wanted to be a part of, not the death ride I had been on.

"He gonna live?" I asked, taking a seat on a rock.

"Dayton's tougher than a keg o' nails," George said, easing the marshal's back against a tree. The marshal winced.

"I have it figured," the marshal said.

"What?"

"How we're gonna break Leonard out of jail."

"What?" I asked, shaking my head. "No, no. It's best if we get outta here without a hangin', ours."

"We're gonna pretend to turn George over for the killin'," the marshal said, as if he had not heard my protest. "We'll come through the door with him in front of us. We'll come in unarmed, so they believe that we're playing straight. When I give the nod, George's gonna grab the constable's pistol and we'll make him open Leonard's cell. We'll grab our horses and git."

"I don't want no more killin'," I said. "There's been too much of it already and if we do something now, it'll only be to save our own skins. There ain't no law that's gonna overlook killin' the constable or one of his deputies."

"Hell, Frank, you think I'd kill another lawman?"

"I don't know what you'd do, Marshal. And I damn sure don't know what George wouldn't do."

He shook his head, as if disappointed in me for the thought. George tried a look of incredulity, but couldn't pull it off. He was ankle deep in killin' and he knew it.

I helped the marshal to his feet and we prepared to leave. We made a decision to leave the horses where they were and make our way down the hill on foot. We were less likely to be seen and we could keep control of the noise. A man never knew when a strange horse would let out a neighing that could raise the dead.

When the marshal got to his feet, he tottered for a moment and had to put his hands out to steady himself.

"You gonna make it?" I asked.

He nodded, but the pain showed deep in his face.

"If we had an ounce of sense in our heads, we would just chuck this whole idea and get outta here," I said. "What's so damned important about bringin' Dandy Jim back anyways?"

"He's the only proof we have that we were doing our duty. If we leave without him, if we don't bring him back to Santa Fe now, everything we've done will look criminal. We're stuck now."

"I swear to God, George," I said, "you ever pull down on a man with me around again, I'll shoot ya in the back of the head if I have to."

I went down the hill first to find a path. George stayed to help support the marshal.

"Don't forget to grab the saddlebags," the marshal said from behind me.

I could feel my brow wrinkle at the words. What difference could the saddlebags make? We would be lucky as hell to get Dandy Jim, much less our horses, much less the saddlebags. I thought about the five hundred dollars in my saddlebags and the rest of the bear meat. I sure didn't want to lose them, but I would not spend an extra second trying to find them.

Maybe the marshal was just trying to be thorough. Maybe he thought he could buy his way out of trouble. Maybe he thought if he brought Dandy Jim and the money back to Santa Fe, the governor wouldn't care how he did it. Well, that was going to have to be their burden. I wouldn't make it mine.

It was a treacherous trail to the bottom. I slipped in the darkness and had visions of sliding right into the side of the jail. I caught a tree on the way down and got my feet under me again.

"Watch that step," I yelled back, waiting to catch the others as they went by. They kept their footing and met me at the tree.

We were only a few hundred feet above the jail at that point. We could see our horses still tied to the rail, still saddled. Hopefully, the saddlebags remained in place. It was too dark to tell for sure.

The marshal was still bleeding from the hole in his shoulder, or he had started bleeding again. Even in the dim light, it was easy to see the pale, drained look on his face. He winced from pain and bit his lip.

"Maybe you ought to cover us from here," I suggested.

"I can make it," he said.

"Then follow me."

I went down the rest of the way and waited behind the jail. While I waited for the others, I eased my way to the street and checked to see that the front door was unguarded. On that side of the building there was a small window. It was too high to see through without something to stand on. I looked for something handy.

I wasn't able to find anything that looked sturdy enough to take my weight, so I decided to wait until George could give me a lift. I worked my way to the back of the building to wait. George and the marshal came out of the trees.

"There's a window on the south side," I said. "I need a lift to see inside."

George followed me around to the window and I stepped into the stirrup he made by interlacing his fingers. I grabbed hold of the thick adobe ledge that framed the window. Looking inside, I could see the deputy at the front of the building. He faced the door over a table and sat with another man whose back was toward the window.

At the back, I could see a cell standing open. I could not see below the window. I motioned for George to lower me and I stepped to the ground. We walked back to the marshal, who was leaning against a tree. His white, drained face glowed in the darkness surrounding it. Lord, if he didn't look dead, I didn't know what did. But when we neared his eyes flickered to life. He looked up at us.

I told him what I saw. He thought for a moment and quickly summarized the situation.

"So, they've either moved him, or the deputy's playing cards with him."

"That's the way it looks," I affirmed.

"Either way, that makes them accessories to escape."

Putting what I knew of the marshal and what he had said together, I could see his mind working to envelope the constable in an air of illegality. Not too much, just enough to kill him for it. He was already justifying the murder.

It made sense in a desperate sort of way. Without the corroboration of a lawman, any charges Dandy Jim could bring against us would sound hollow. The murder of the bartender would be mere speculation. The marshal figured he could weather that storm.

Again, I was placed in a situation uncomfortable to my morals. When did I get a set of morals anyway? I had never had to deal with them this much before. Was there no end to the death, the blood? Christ, when did these men get their fill? It offended me, thinking of them scything a wide path of destruction on their way to enforcing the law. I was convinced that whatever killing Dandy Jim had done to become such a wanted man, the men I secretly huddled with behind the jail were guilty of more in tracking him down. Murder and brutality with a moral end? It wouldn't wash in my conscience.

I stood in the middle of all of it, somewhere between the greed and brutality of Dandy Jim and the cruelty and venom of the marshal. The only way to free myself of the predicament was to go along with the marshal until I could be rid of them. I would disappear into the confused web of ranches and never raise my head to a lawman again.

We revised the original plan, exchanging George's role for the marshal. He would enter the jail, ostensibly turning himself in. He said they would believe it if he demanded medical attention for his shoulder. As soon as he had gained their trust and found out where Dandy Jim was, he would make to faint, hoping they would catch him. George and I were to burst in and take them prisoners. If all went well, we would be out of town before the alarm could be raised.

We looked into one another's eyes. It seemed that we were kidding ourselves. None of us held the conviction within ourselves that the plan would work. It was our best chance of getting out of the trouble we faced and we knew it. Nothing better than that would offer itself.

"We oughta get our horses and be grateful for that," I said, stating the obvious. But I knew that didn't solve our credibility problem and we would probably all be hunted down the same as Dandy Jim. The worst part for me lay in understanding that George and the marshal knew enough about the law to stay one step ahead of it. I did not.

"Let's move," the marshal said, tiptoeing between the buildings.

George and I followed and stopped at the corner in the deepest shadows covering the marshal as he stepped up to the door.

"I'm hurt, let me in," he called to the door.

"*Que pasa?*"

"It's Marshal Dayton Howard. I've come to turn myself in if you'll get me a doctor. Please," he said, looking over his shoulder in mock pain. "It hurts."

A scraping of heavy wood sounded as the door was unbolted. The leather hinges creaked as the door was opened enough to look out.

"Please," he said, showing his wound.

"*Aja!*" the voice said in surprise.

The marshal stumbled forward, as if fainting and falling against the door, knocking it open. We could see his feet sticking out of the doorway. When the pair of feet started to move across the ground, George and I pounced on the opportunity and came around the corner.

We burst in with guns drawn. The Mexican deputy started to cry out, but George pistol-whipped the man and he crumpled to the ground. I chose the other man, who turned out to be Dandy Jim and thrust the muzzle of the Colt under his chin.

I shook my head at him as if to say: "So easily captured, yet so hard to keep hold of."

Dandy Jim wasn't armed, but he wasn't shackled either. The

marshal pulled himself up from the floor with a deep groan. I pushed Dandy Jim back to the wall.

"You cuttin' a deal for yurself?"

Dandy Jim winked at me. Winked! I nearly cuffed him for it. Before I could even think about it, I felt a hand on my shoulder. The marshal spun me away with a force that belied his delicate condition. I saw the glint of his knife as he stepped forward.

"Where's the money?" he asked. When he got no response, he added: "I've gutted men, before. Ain't no difference how I take ya back, Leonard."

"The constable's got it. Most of it anyway. I didn't tell him about Snake's five hundred dollars."

"I wish you'd quit calling me that," I said, preferring Frank.

"Where is he?"

Dandy Jim shrugged his shoulders. His insolence was met by the flash of the marshal's blade. A spurt of blood leapt from Dandy Jim's cheek. Small, red drops left bloody trails on his skin.

"I can cut you a lot before ya die, Leonard."

"Cut away, I don't know where the man is," he said, leaning his cheek against his shoulder to blot at the blood and then looked at the shoulder to see how much was there.

"The way I see it," Dandy Jim continued, "you can't be long in asking. The deputy here is due for relief any minute."

"That's a goddamn lie," George said, shoving a finger into the gambler's face.

Dandy Jim stared at him with tired, dead eyes. He shrugged and looked calmly about the building and his captors.

"We got our prisoner," I said. "That's all we need."

The marshal gave Dandy Jim a thoughtful look, then reared back. He struck the gambler with the hand holding the Bowie knife's handle and knocked Dandy Jim unconscious.

"That oughta keep him quiet," the marshal said. "Put him on

a horse and let's get going." He crumpled to the floor, exhausted. We tried to help him to a chair, but he would have none of it. "Do what I told ya," he roared.

I went outside, looked up and down the abandoned street, and gathered the horses. I led them back to the space between the buildings, where the shadows could hide our movements until it was time to ride.

I heard rustling and banging coming from inside the jail. George came out first with Dandy Jim over his shoulder. We tied him over the back of the horse he had ridden into town. When I looked up, the marshal stepped into the little alley. A second later, a whoosh sounded as the jail erupted into flames.

In a moment, we were thundering through the town. The fire was set, I imagine, as a diversion. If the townspeople were attracted to the fire, they wouldn't be chasing us. I looked back on occasion to see how Dandy Jim was faring. He bounced up and down over his saddle, banging his face on the horse's side.

Once out of town, we made our way through a narrow canyon. We encountered several switchbacks and then took up positions high on one bank to see if anyone was dumb enough to make a pursuit. If they did, we would cut them to pieces with rifles.

We took cover behind some rocks and waited. No one came and we waited for Dandy Jim to come to. We cut him loose of the horse and tied him to a tree. The time would come to get some answers and I was not looking forward to the process.

Meanwhile, the marshal's wound had started to bleed again, and George knelt over him to do the nursing.

"Ouch! Damn you, George, can't you be more careful?"

"Here, Dayton, bite this twig," George said, being helpful.

CHAPTER TWENTY-THREE

It must have been near midnight when we started down toward Cimarron. Dandy Jim had come to, but we gagged him against giving our position away in the narrow canyon. None of us thought it would hurt any to leave the gag in for a while.

We followed a winding trail of stream at the base of low hills. The trail was marred by trees and soft, muddy ground.

I rode next to the marshal, catching him when he threatened to spill from his saddle. He cursed me every time I laid a hand to him, but it was the only thing keeping him upright.

That ride was about as horrible as it could get. Unseen branches whipped leaves and twigs across our faces. Bushes blocked the easiest paths. When we thought we had found some decent ground to ride on, the earth would tilt upward and take off into the sky, sending us careening down into the swift river, or through boggy mud. The legs of the horses would sink in the soggy river bottom and make a sucking sound on pulling free.

"By God," George said, once, "this is the nastiest joke God ever played on Man."

Then, as if by prayers alone, the land opened up wide and level. We spread out away from each other and were grateful for the distance as all of us stunk from being without a bath the past weeks. Added to the general stench was the soured whiskey breath we blew on each other as we spoke.

I decided to ungag Dandy Jim. There was no pursuit and nothing ahead of us, but open ground.

181

"Make a damn sound and I'll plug ya myself," I said, removing the handkerchief from his mouth and thrusting it into his shirt pocket.

Dandy Jim was looking poorly. He still wore the scars from the beating the marshal gave him after his attempt at escape. Added to those, a large swollen lump stuck out the side of his face, closing his left eye. The other eye shone with an air of contempt and defiance. I knew from the look of him that he still had a few hands to play before he would cash in.

Dandy Jim Beudreaux, or Leonard Braswell, whoever, was a tough man. My opinion of him had not diminished from when I envisioned him as a bobcat in a carpetbag. There was an air of threat about him at all times. There was a cleverness that brought events around to his benefit. His tongue and his eyes could whip a man as surely as a lash. Worst of all, I knew I would miss him.

I can't say how I arrived at that belief. Maybe I had been thinking about it the whole time. The stories from the book came back to me and I studied the man in the darkness, putting what I knew of him up against what I had read. As broad and wild as some of his escapades were reported to be, I could see the man in the commission of such acts.

Dandy Jim was special, unique. If he had wanted to be a senator, he could have been a great success. If he had wanted to be a lawman, he would have been as good, or better, than the marshal who caught him. But he chose gambling and outlawry as a career and even in that unlikely profession, he was received with awe and respect. Now, he would swing for it. I only hoped it would be before George, or myself for that matter.

Several miles after we had come to the flat area, we were met with a rising of the horizon. Another mountain stood before us, forcing us to weave our way through. Fortunately, the sky was breaking out in a pale shade of blue to the east. It would be dawn soon and we could see where we were going. Already, the obstacles were growing more distinct.

We stayed with the river and continued in a winding direction that pointed eventually eastward. By that time, I was starting to wear down. I could not stop yawning. I told myself I wouldn't, but in the next second my mouth would strain to its widest and I would involuntarily shake my head and sigh.

Once, when my mouth was stretching out into an oval, a bug flew straight in and bounced off the back of my throat. I choked and gagged and spit. The others shot glances at me. I saw looks of curious concern, but I knew that if I had dropped out of the saddle and died, they would not bother to stop. Not even to take my horse. After all I had been through with them, I meant nothing. I was an extra hand with a gun, an added horse for the roundup of outlaws. I was as much of a burden as an asset. My account was even in that respect and not an ounce more.

It occurred to me then that I did not care for them, either. I felt closer to the prisoner than the posse. I let out a chuckle at the thought of it and they turned their tired, tolerant eyes on me. I waved them off with my hand and resumed my private thoughts.

We came down off a rise and into a huge meadow. As the sun burnt the eastern sky into a flaming orange and yellow sunrise, we saw a lake in the distance. In a land so full of rivers, there weren't but a handful of lakes in all the country we had traveled. Then, we all saw it at the same time and jerked back on the reins.

A fire glowed at the far edge of the lake, obscured by the colors of the rising sun reflecting off the shiny, placid surface. I looked back at Dandy Jim and saw a glint in his eye. I cuffed him upside the head and dug in his pocket for the handkerchief to stuff in his mouth. George was more effective by sticking the Whitney revolver to his head.

At the same time, the marshal tumbled out of his saddle and struck the ground with a thud. I quickly gagged the prisoner and rushed to the marshal. His breathing was shallow, and the wound had been bleeding again. I made him as comfortable as possible.

"You best go see who's at the fire," I said, looking up at George. He started off and I had another thought. "For God's sake don't kill the sonofabitch."

George broke all pretense at stealth and charged headlong toward the fire. It was a long way around to the eastern side of the lake and I watched as the figure of George began to recede to a dark spot as he worked around the north side of the lake. At the fire, the man recognized George as a threat and scrambled to get to his horse. Whoever it was pulled himself into the saddle. From then on, it was a race to the trees.

My attention was divided between the two mounted figures, the marshal and Dandy Jim. After the marshal was breathing a little better, I got Dandy Jim off his horse and sat him down near the marshal. Dandy Jim's cheek was a bit swollen from where I cuffed him. He sat moodily beside his hated rival.

Across the lake, the dots grew closer. I looked back at Dandy Jim and removed his gag. No reason to keep it in.

"Don't mean I want ya talkin' to me," I said, trying to hide my fear of his voice. Dandy Jim could talk a bit and connive better than most. I didn't want him gagged, but I didn't want him talking, either.

"It was George that killed the bartender, wasn't it?" Dandy Jim inquired.

"Goddamn it, now. I done told ya. Shut up or I'll put the gag back in yur mouth."

Dandy Jim shrugged and poked at the ground with a twig he had found. His wrists were tied together and he often looked as if he were praying. Somehow, it didn't seem strange enough to suit me. What kind of man was he, really?

I looked up to see how the race was coming. I guess I always knew how it would turn out. The thought of George missing a chance at brutality seemed impossible. When I had been looking up, I had just been checking to see when, not if. As they drew closer to each other there were faint, small sounds of revolvers popping in the distance.

"Damnit, George," I whispered to myself, but loud enough for anyone to hear.

Dandy Jim sighed. When I shot a look toward him, he shrugged and smiled to himself. His one open eye glinted a bit and I knew he had something to say. I didn't see how it could hurt, so I asked him about it.

"Well," he replied, "it seems unfair that I'm to be hung while there's men like George to stand about gawking."

It was a sentiment I shared. Both of them needed to swing.

"George ain't no bargain, I'll give ya that."

The marshal's face bunched into a knot and he let out a moan.

"The man's dying. You ought to just put a bullet in him and be done with it."

Dandy Jim barely got the words out, before I had my Colt trained on the gambler's face. The hammer was back, waiting for the slightest pressure of my finger to send a bit of lead into his implacable face. It took a lot of will to keep from pulling the trigger. I spit out the side of my mouth and eased the hammer back to a harmless position.

"Don't goad me," I said. "Right now, that marshal is the only one keeping you alive, who wants to keep you alive. With him dead, your life don't mean nothin' to me."

I turned back to check on George's progress; he was making his way back with the man surprisingly alive and riding up front. His hands were thrown out to his sides in a sign of

185

submission.

"Who do you suppose that is?" Dandy Jim asked.

"How the hell should I know?"

The sun poked its hot gaze over the rim of the mountains and shed bright light upon our little camp. I decided in favor of some coffee and marched my prisoner down to a grove of trees. I loaded his arms with small branches and a few larger ones.

In a few minutes, we had a fire going and coffee brewing. The two figures made their way ever closer. Certain aspects of the man in front could be made out. He was bareheaded. He must have lost his hat some time during the chase. He was a fat man, who swayed back and forth in the saddle.

George rode behind, saddlebags over his shoulder, his revolver aimed at the back of the other man.

"Lookie who I got here," he called over the distance.

I raised my hand to the sun, blotting it out to get a better look. It was the constable from Taos. I looked over my shoulder at Dandy Jim.

"The hell's goin' on here?"

Dandy Jim shrugged and picked up a twig from the pile of firewood, one hand moving to do the work and the one tied to it following like a shadow with no other purpose than to accompany the first. He flipped at the sandy ground with the twig.

The others pulled up to the camp. With the marshal unconscious, I felt I had to be in charge, somewhat. I refused to let George think he was running the show. If I paled from the role, he would surely kill the two prisoners and probably me, too. Then, when the marshal was able to ride, they would move off into a world all their own with money to live on.

"Get that feller down and tie him up," I ordered. George did not bother to think it out and promptly did as he was told.

With no one to chase and no one chasing us, we had time on

our hands. While the marshal healed up some, I thought it was time I did some fishing. I dug through my saddlebags and pulled out the five hundred dollars. I set the bundle on the ground.

I saw a surreptitious stare shoot between the constable and Dandy Jim. Then, the Mexican looked off into the distance, as if it were a casual glance he had thrown at his fellow captive. There was something there, all right, but I didn't let on I knew too much.

From the saddlebags, I removed a crude hook and some string. I replaced the money and walked off toward the lake. I stopped long enough to locate a long branch to use as a fishing pole. I dug for worms in the soggy ground at the edge of the lake.

I had hardly thrown the line into the water when my pole bent and I jerked back to set the hook. I reached up to where the string was tied to the end and fought the fish for a bit, tiring him out. Slowly, I dragged him closer to shore until I pulled his shiny, scaly body through the mud and up to my boot. I stepped on his side and dug the hook out of his grotesque lip.

Another worm went reluctantly onto the hook and sailed high into the air, hung suspended, and dropped to the calm surface of the lake. A few minutes passed, while I swatted at mosquitos. Then, another strike and I set the hook again.

I caught six good-sized fish in less than a quarter hour. A slap in the jaw would not have knocked the smile off my face as I walked up to the fire with the fish clutched to my chest.

"By God, yur a fisherman!" George boomed as I neared.

We set the fish to cooking and I sat down to doze a minute or two. It seemed like years since I had a moment's peace. I looked up into the deep blue sky and watched light clouds drift by. As my eyelids began to droop, I gave some last instructions: "Don't kill no one and wake me when the fish're done."

Chapter Twenty-Four

I woke to the grumbling, angry sound of George's voice. He was cussing one of the prisoners and I could tell he was working himself up to a killing. I shook myself awake and sat up.

"Shut up."

George looked startled. He kicked at the dust and sat down with a plop.

"How's the marshal?"

"Aw, he's about the same."

"Fish done, yet?"

"Purt near."

I stood up and stretched. When I looked down at the marshal, his face was turning red from the sun. I walked over and put his hat over his face. Next, I bent over the fire. Using the wide blade of my knife as a utensil, I turned the fish over and let them cook some more.

We ate breakfast and I washed the tin plates, scrubbing them by the lake with sand and rinsing them off. I was busy at it and thinking about what to do with the two captives. I had to take Dandy Jim back to Santa Fe and let the proper authorities do what they would with him. But the constable was a more perplexing matter. What was I to do with him? What would the marshal do? What was I going to do with the marshal?

I heard George cussing behind me. He was interrogating the constable and not liking the answers. I hurried with the plates and went back up to camp with a couple pans full of water to douse the fire.

"Hissss!" went the embers, and smoke and steam bellowed up.

"All right, let's get down to business," I said, squatting before the line of men. The constable sat on the left end with Dandy Jim in the middle and the marshal on the right. I arranged them so I could keep an eye on the prisoners and the marshal at the same time. The marshal lay at an angle, his feet pointing at those gathered next to the campfire. George roamed around behind me, pacing.

"What the hell're you doin' with all that money and why wasn't this man locked up proper?"

"Yeah," George added, kicking dust at the constable.

The constable glared back at me with intense, brown eyes overburdened by contempt for our whole ruse of law and order. He knew us as murderers.

"Now look, goddamnit. George here'd just as soon put a piece of lead in both of ya."

"Damn right," George added.

"Somebody better start tellin' me somethin', or I'm liable to let him have his fun."

The constable wavered a bit and started to speak up, but changed his mind when he caught a glimpse of Dandy Jim. Again, there were signs of a connection that I didn't understand. I decided to push it a little.

"Good lawman like yurself." I stood, to emphasize the point. "Takin' up with a no-account outlaw like Dandy Jim Beudreaux. No, sir, the governor ain't gonna think much o' that." I let the words hang for a moment. "It's his money, you know. Dandy Jim stole it from the bank. Did he tell ya that part?"

The constable looked at the ground.

"I didn't think so. Ain't like him to do such a thing. The hell were ya goin' to do with it, anyhow? Go down to Cimarron and buy a whore? Gamble some? Hell, yur a family man, ain't ya?" I shook my head in dismay. "What will they think?"

"Damn shame," George said, thinking he was adding to the sum of my argument, but greatly detracting from it in a way he could not understand.

The constable looked sharply at him, hatred of hypocrisy blooming in his expression.

"George, get outta here for a moment. Go skip rocks, or somethin'."

"You ain't my boss," he said, putting it together that I had no authority to order him. The fact was, George was the only one of us that had any authority. Even the marshal's was undercut by his condition.

"Do as I say," I snapped, hoping to bully him out of his righteous complaint.

George sulked and strolled off reluctantly. Soon, he was involved in whatever amused him down by the lake, like a child told to go to his room and finding something interesting there.

"Dandy Jim'll tell ya, I ain't like these others. I don't hold with their ways. Fact is, we were just planning to have George arrested for the murder, when that mob came after us. I'm yur best chance to straighten this out," I said, squatting and looking sincere.

He looked over at Dandy Jim, who nodded his agreement. The constable seemed to battle himself to find the best thing to do. He started to speak, then stopped. He thought for a minute, then opened up like a dam.

"Meester Beudreaux, he tells me first off how hees been taken prisoner by the marshals." He looked over at Dandy Jim a moment for support or permission. "He says you are all keelers of men. He says you have heem by mistake, that he is not the man you seek. I think he iss loco. I say, 'no ess possible.' I have seen your badges.

190

"Then the murder," he began and got choked by his words. "This man you keel, he ess me *primo*. Then, I know Meester Beudreaux iss telling me the truth, that you are keelers of men."

"Well, now," I said. "That explains everything, but why are you hauling the money off to Cimarron?"

At the mention of the money, he blanched and sought the ground for an answer. I waited patiently for him to decide what sort of admission to make. Dandy Jim threw himself backward. The constable was startled and looked up, then his eyes grew wide.

"Boom!" went the marshal's revolver.

I scrambled away. When I looked, the back of the constable's head was spread out on the ground. The front half of his head looked as normal as a head can look with a bullet hole in it, but the back half spread out in flaps of flimsy skin. Blood gushed and soaked into the sand. The rest of the constable's body shuddered and quivered as his heart fought to pump lessening quantities of blood. Then, the great release of life came to the crumpled figure, his wrists were bound together and extended toward me, as if in a plea for help.

George began to yell in ecstasy from the lake. He was dancing around and raised his revolver into the air and fired off a couple of rounds.

"Damn right!" he screamed. "That a way to go, Dayton. Kill 'em all."

My first instinct was anger. There was no need to kill the constable. It served no purpose, and it left me with a lot of unanswered questions. Then I looked at Dandy Jim and it hit me. The marshal was trying to kill Dandy Jim.

I stood up and brushed myself off. I aimed my footsteps toward the marshal, but by the time I got there, he was unconscious again. His hand loosely held the revolver and his mouth gaped open, but some of his color had returned and his

191

wound was dry. I stood over him, puzzled. I glanced at Dandy Jim still laying on his back.

"Shut the hell up, George," I called down to the lake.

"Yeeha!" he yelled back.

I set about to dig a grave, but there were no shovels. I wanted to pile stones on top of the body, but there were too few.

"Coyotes and wolves have to eat," I whispered.

By then, I was ready to leave. I just wanted to be done with this business. I was weary of traipsing about the country, worn out from the constant killings and ready for a night in a saloon.

"George, we're losin' daylight. We gotta get the marshal on a horse and down to Cimarron."

"Hell, let's not," he proposed. "Let's just head for Santa Fe and haul this murderin' gambler to his doom."

"That ain't what the marshal wants. You have to stand trial, George, or you'll be runnin' the rest of yur life and makin' criminals of anyone who helps ya."

He took the news calmly, deliberately. There was no way out of it and he knew it.

"Besides," I said. "They'll find ya innocent. I was there. I know what happened."

He brightened at that and we set about to get the marshal loaded. It was a bit of a fight to work it so he would stay aboard the horse without cutting off the circulation to his hands and feet. We improvised and wadded cloth under the rawhide strips used to secure the man in place.

"There!" I proclaimed and nodded my head.

"What? Whaaat's goin' on?" the marshal asked. "The hell am I tied up for? You cut me loose," he ordered. George responded quickly. "Sonsabitches," the marshal said, kicking at George as he came out from under the horse.

Once free, the marshal looked around and saw the constable laying on the ground with half his head shot away.

"Who the hell's that? How long have I been out? Who shot that man?"

I explained it all to the marshal as we made our way up over one last pass and started down the heavily wooded canyon that led to Cimarron. Occasionally, there would be wide meadows, but they were few. It was another tricky ride in a long string of them. The only good thing about it was it would be the last. My heart filled with anticipation at the thought of level ground all the way to Santa Fe and freedom.

When talking about it, the marshal didn't remember waking up, or shooting anyone. I found it hard to believe him, but I suppose it could happen. I had been witness to stranger things, so I gave him the benefit of the doubt. I shrugged at his protestations and said: "Well, you did it, all right."

On that long, last ride down the canyon I was bothered by the money. What was the situation? Did Dandy Jim bribe him with it? Did the constable steal it? I didn't understand and it drove me crazy that the answer lay ready for the picking, but for a bullet fired in delirium.

It all seemed too fantastic, and yet just fantastic enough to be fact. The world had revealed itself to me in just such a way. The wild claims of a man were amusing at times, but I had come to learn that some of the wildest I had heard were true. Stranger than that, some of the most conservative claims I readily believed were complete lies. It left a man helpless to judge, so I chose to believe the marshal.

The marshal started to nod with fatigue as we came out of the canyon and found Cimarron on the horizon.

"What's the difference between a live deputy and a dead one?" Dandy Jim said, turning one of George's bad jokes on him. "A three-foot drop," he finished over the loud protest of George.

"I ain't gonna hang," he said, snapping the Whitney revolver up to eye level with the prisoner.

"Both of ya, shut up," the marshal said, putting his hand to his wound.

"It won't be long now, Marshal," I said, hoping to ease his mind.

"I got eyes," he replied, staring at the distant town.

We rode into town without incident. There were no angry mobs or lines of military men waiting to take George into custody. The fact was, we had a hard time finding Mace Bowman.

"Hell, Dayton, no one cares anyways. Let's just move on," George suggested.

The marshal coughed, pressed against the wound with his free hand, and shook his head.

"We need to find you a doctor," I said.

"Later."

Mace Bowman was in the St. James having his evening meal when I caught up to him. I went into the place and walked up to his table. The spoonful of soup stopped halfway to his mouth. He stared at me for a moment.

"Where's that deputy?" he asked, slurping soup and leaving traces on the fringe ends of his mustache.

"Outside. We caught Dandy Jim Beudreaux and need to put him up in yur jail."

"I got deputies."

"Get done robbin' the hotel, did they?"

The spoon dropped and clattered off the bowl. He froze me with his sparkling, angry eyes. It seemed that life was shot into them by my comment. I waited for the explosion of his temper.

"Impertinent sonofabitch," he said, picking up his spoon. "The hell ya waitin' for? Put 'em in jail, damn ya."

"We can't put 'em in the same cell."

"Why the hell not?"

"They'll kill each other."

"So what?"

"Mr. Bowman, the marshal's outside, take it up with him. He needs a doctor, too, been shot."

"Is he bleedin' to death?"

"No."

"Then, he can wait 'til I'm done with my dinner, can't he?"

I shrugged and walked off. I wasn't going to get anything extra from him.

I stopped at the desk to inquire about a doctor. A young man stood there dressed in fine clothing chewing tobacco. As I neared, he spit into a hidden cuspidor. I told him about the marshal.

"Is the marshal staying at the hotel?"

"No."

"We have a doctor for hotel guests only."

"You got yur own doctor?"

"I didn't say that," the young man said, pulling back from the counter.

"So, there's a doctor in town?"

"Yes."

"Where is he?"

"That's none of my business unless you're a guest."

I took off my hat and scratched my head.

"Well, it ain't that big o' town," I said, deciding to have a look for myself. Before I left, I checked to see how Bowman was coming along with his meal. As I looked in, he received a full plate.

"Damnedest place I ever seen," I mumbled as I went out into the bright sunshine.

CHAPTER TWENTY-FIVE

The four of us stood in the dusty street of Cimarron. Dandy Jim remained tied at the hands, calmly waiting for events to unfold. The marshal coughed and spit into the dust. George looked around at the little town as if it were the last sight he would ever see. I kicked at the dust, waiting for Bowman to finish his dinner.

We could have gone to the jail, but we weren't sure about the deputies. We wanted Bowman along to keep things straightened out. If we presented ourselves to some deputy, we might all be arrested. Worse yet, once in jail we could not count on Bowman to let us out.

"I suppose I ought to check on the newspaper to see if they know where the doctor is," I said, looking at the others in the dim, remaining light of a low hanging sun. None bothered to nod, or acknowledge the statement in any way, so I started off.

As I walked over to the newspaper office, I saw the repaired doorway of the little building and it reminded me of Clay Allison. I looked all around hoping not to run into Allison in the midst of the other complexities of Cimarron. My thoughts turned to the morning he jerked the printing press out of the building and delivered it to the river.

It was a bit amusing to think about it. Other men might have done far worse. Yes, I told myself, but not many would hang a man's head on a pole. I decided that Mr. Allison was one to keep on the right side of, if that were possible.

I knocked on the little door and cupped my hands on each side of my face to see through the window. The place was dark, but the printing press was replaced. It looked like the same one, or one just like the other. I kicked the door in frustration and turned around to face the group by the hotel. George looked over and I threw my hands up in futility.

Bowman walked out of the hotel then. I hurried my pace to be in on whatever decisions were to be made. He crossed, sizing up the party and shooting a quick glance in my direction.

"I'll be damned," he said to the others, the words coming faintly over the distance between him and me. "I can't even tell who the criminal is. From the looks of ya, every damned one of ya might be."

"That thar's Leonard Braswell, most vicious damned gambler and killer in three territories and two states," George said, as if to diminish his own exploits.

"What about you?" Bowman asked. "You're the one that killed two soldiers a few weeks ago. I got to put you in jail, too."

"Aw hell, them's niggers. This fella kills white men, probably even women."

By then, I had reached the gathering and lent my assistance.

"It was self-defense," I said, grudgingly helping George escape the wrath of Bowman.

"So you say," he replied. "But, hell, you ain't a judge, are ya?" He looked me up and down. "Didn't think so."

"Enough o' this," the marshal blurted, his pains growing deeper, his face contorting to fight them off. "Let's get the ones in jail that need to be."

"Foller me," Bowman said, taking his leisurely strides toward the little jail. He stopped on the way there and went down the street for a moment to have a look in at a house. We stood, baffled, ten feet from the door.

"That man never does make it all the way across a street at

one time," George observed.

I nodded, trying to figure out what was pressing enough to cause the detour. Maybe it was just his way of letting us know we were nothing more than a diversion to his other duties. Whatever the reason, he went about his own routine without regard for anyone else.

Bowman came back and seemed startled to see us in the same place he had left us. He had the look of a man who had forgotten a thing and surprisingly found it in the first place he looked.

"Come along," he said, waving a hand and pushing on the door to the jail.

Once inside, we locked Dandy Jim up in the cell. He took to the bed in a hurry and lay down. He was a cool one, I had to give him credit for that. Nothing seemed to bother the man. He stared up at the ceiling and threw one leg over the other, completely relaxed.

"I'm gonna have to shackle this man to the cell," Bowman said, pulling a chair over for George to sit on while he slipped the shackles through one square in the flat-metal cage and out the other. George offered his wrists up with a doubtful, helpless look at the marshal.

Bowman reached into the holster and removed George's revolver.

"Got any more?"

"Got a rifle in the scabbard outside."

"Bill, you wanna go out an' get the man's rifle?"

"Which one's his?" he asked, stepping out of the crowd of us and moving toward the door.

"I'll show ya," I said, more to get out of the crowded little room than to offer kindness.

When everything was settled, I followed the marshal and Bowman to the hotel. I carried our saddlebags over and stood while the marshal rented a room. Bowman quickly departed, as if relieved from a month-long duty of scooping horseshit.

"Will you be staying with us as well?" the sharp-dressed man asked.

I hated like hell to pay for a room. I could sleep outside as well as anywhere, but there comes a time when a man ought to take advantage of the comforts offered to him. Besides that, the marshal looked as if he could lose consciousness at any time and I thought I should be close at hand. The final straw in my decision had to do with the money in the saddlebags. I knew of nowhere safer to keep it than a room where I had the key.

"Yeah, hell," I said, giving in. "Put me next to the marshal and call up a doctor for him, will ya?"

"Right away," he said, pointing out where I should sign the register. "Doc," he said, to a man sitting on a sofa idly reading a newspaper in the lobby. "This man needs your immediate attention."

The doctor flipped half of the paper toward himself and looked over the bend at the ragged, bloody marshal; barely conscious, barely alive. He casually laid the paper aside and took up the bag stuffed under the low table in front of him.

"How long you been sittin' there?" I asked.

He glared at me. Instead of answering the question, he started shouting orders.

"Get some water boiling and have that man taken to his room. I shall attend him there." He started to walk toward the dining hall, but stopped and turned after he passed me. "Is there a bullet?"

"Went through," I replied, taking the marshal by the arm, assisting him toward the long hall.

The doctor weighed the information and continued on.

"If I can ride half the damn way through New Mexico, I can damn sure make it to my room," he said, pulling away from my helpful grasp. I kept my hand close, just in case.

I opened the door on a large room with a huge bed sitting square in the middle of it. Off the outside corner was another smaller room with a short bed, a child's bed. That's where I could sleep, I thought. To hell with two rooms. But I had been forced to pay in advance for one night. It was supposed to be punishment for trying to get out of the bill the last time. I figured to switch the next day as long as the marshal were able to pay and if he didn't die before then.

The marshal sat down on the bed and leaned back. I swung his legs up and into the center. He lay staring at the ceiling. He winced from time to time and made to rub the wound, but thought better of it. His hand hung in midair, moving rigidly with every groan.

The door stood open and I shot worried, impatient glances at it. The funny thing was, I didn't feel a damned thing about the marshal. His fortunes were tied to mine, that's all. If he died, I would have to take Dandy Jim back to Santa Fe with George. That was bad enough, but what if George were found guilty? Then, I might have to do it alone, or hire someone I didn't know, who might turn out to throw in with Dandy Jim and cut my throat on the way.

No, sir, I did not like the way things were turning out. Where was that doctor? I walked to the door to have a look down the hall. I saw a man carrying hot water in a basin and some towels. I stepped out of his way and let him bring them into the room.

"Where's the doctor?"

"He'll be along shortly," the man said.

"I didn't ask when, I asked where."

"Not my affair," he said, standing before me with his palm out.

I looked at him, then at the pan of water. Christ almighty, was I supposed to pay for everything?

"Marshal, this man needs some money," but the marshal was unconscious. "Put it on his bill," I said.

The man turned and walked down the hall. I gave the marshal a quick glance to make sure he wasn't about to roll off the bed, and I started after the porter. When I reached the dining hall/saloon area, I looked into the room. There at the bar was the doctor, throwing down a shot of whiskey.

"Hey, goddamnit!" I yelled. The doctor hunched his shoulders like a dog sticking its tail between its legs. "Get down to doctorin' 'fore the water gets cold."

The doctor hurriedly sloshed whiskey into a glass and took one last drink. He turned away from the bar, grabbed up the little bag, and walked quickly toward me, avoiding my gaze.

I was not accustomed to yelling at people, much less refined men of honest profession, but if that's what it took to get something done in Cimarron, I would get used to it.

I followed the doctor to the room, like I would herd a steer to a set of corrals. I blocked his avenues of escape and shaded him toward the room. I chased him in and pulled the door shut behind us. I stood with arms folded and leaned against the door. I decided he would either doctor, or need doctoring.

He slowly peeled back the crusted, cloth wrapping. The marshal stirred a bit, though he remained unconscious. His jaw worked and his eyes tightened.

So encrusted were the bandages, the doctor had to clip at them with tiny scissors and leave the severed fringes stuck to the ragged edges of skin. When he lifted the center part of the wrapping, there was a sucking sound and a putrid smell rose in the room. The doctor put his knuckles to his mouth to fight off the odor. My eyes started to water.

The doctor put his hand to the marshal's forehead. He shook his head, wiped his mouth, and looked over his shoulder.

"This man hasn't long to live," he said.

Instantly, my mind sought out the benefits and drawbacks of the marshal's death. I was ashamed for it later, but all I could do at the time was assess the situation as it affected me.

"Now, what am I gonna do?" I asked, rhetorically.

The doctor raised an eyebrow.

"How long?"

"Day, maybe two."

"Well, I'll be goddamned!" I said, another thing for me to be ashamed of later. "The sonofabitch drags me all over the damn mountains and drops me in Cimarron with two prisoners to take care of." I shook my head.

"All of that is mere conjecture and speculation to me. All I know is this man is about to die." He held the haughty air for a moment and blurted out: "For an extra fee, I could arrange the funeral."

"Dig around in his pockets and see if he has some money," I suggested. "I ain't putting a nickel in. That sonofabitch ain't done nothin' since I met him, but sidestep what's rightfully owed to me. Leavin' fellers hangin' with their guts out. What for? So I could haul 'em off for him and get paid for extra work by collectin' the reward? No, sir," I said, realizing I was voicing my inner thoughts to a man I didn't know. I clamped my mouth shut and jerked the door open.

It all meant that I would have to take Dandy Jim back to Santa Fe. I would have to talk to Bowman more than I cared to. The whole damn escapade was thrust on my shoulders. Me! I wasn't even a proper deputy for heaven's sake.

Another part of my mind made a proper retort. "You're still alive," it said. "You're the only one of the bunch that got out of it with his skin and his freedom. Look at you, feeling sorry for yourself. Have a drink and think it out."

So, I went into the saloon and bellied up to the bar.

"Whiskey!"

CHAPTER TWENTY-SIX

I stood at the bar in the St. James. After downing my second glass of whiskey, I bought a bottle and went to my room. There, I hid the saddlebags and locked the door on my way out.

The part I dreaded most was talking to Bowman. He was an edgy sort of fellow and it didn't take much to get on the wrong side of him. I kicked at the dirt to celebrate my misery as I strolled across the dark street to the jail.

I gave a brief knock and entered. George was dozing on the chair and roused himself awake when I entered. He pushed forward far enough to reach his finger to the corner of his eye and dislodge a particle of sleep dust.

"How's Dayton?"

"He's dying."

George blinked and shook his head, then peered up at me to see if I were real, or made of dream stuff.

"Dyin'?"

I nodded and turned to the deputy.

"What's the chance of finding Bowman?"

"None," he replied.

A soft snore came drifting from the cell. Dandy Jim was getting a good night's sleep, damn him.

"This here's official business," I said.

"He conducts business during the day."

"The hell does he do during the night?"

"That's none of my business, mister," the deputy said. "If'n you was smart, you'd make it none of yourn, neither."

Well, I couldn't argue with that. I jerked the door inward and stepped through. I took a deep breath of clean, mountain air and stepped off the small walkway. Back to the St. James. The hotel seemed to suck the whole universe toward itself, attracting the misguided and lost from across the globe. I seemed to fit the category, so I went back to the saloon.

The hour was growing late, by then. The worst men the country had to offer were quickly gathering in the elegant saloon. I leaned on the bar, ordered a whiskey, and stared at the mural across the back wall.

"What're ye? A damn Injun?" someone said behind me. "I'm talkin' to ye."

I looked around with a scowl at the loud-mouthed drunk to see who in the world he might be accosting. I was startled to find him looking at me. He was a big man with a heavy beard and dressed in buckskins. He carried a long rifle in a buckskin sheath. A red-headed mountain man, I quickly deduced.

"Are you talkin' to me?"

"Where'd ye get them claws at?"

I'd forgotten about the necklace of bear claws hanging from my neck.

"Some Injuns up by Taos. Traded a marshal's badge for 'em."

"Coulda got more'n that, ye could."

I shrugged. What did I care about the going price for a bear-claw necklace? For that matter, what did I care about the value of a badge?

"Depends on how much store I set in that badge, don't it?"

The man spread a huge grin and pulled up a piece of bar next to me.

"Ye don't know the length of time a man can spend twixt hearin' English spoke, lest ye've been up on the sharp end of the world." Then he turned to the bartender, who happened to be the owner, Henri Lambert. "Whiskey, I said, by damn ye!" he roared.

"You didn't say a thing about whiskey, mister," Henri fumed.

"By gum, I thunk it hard enough for ye to hear in the street."

"Know where Bowman is?" I asked, taking advantage of Henri's attention.

Henri refused to answer; he didn't even make out he had heard. I took the hint and sipped at the whiskey. From then on, I talked with the mountain man to while away the hours, hoping for Bowman to show his face.

"Don't know how ya can tolerate the up and down of that country," I said to the mountain man. "I'm a flatlander."

"By gum, that's whar the trappin's is, boy."

"Damn sure trapped me," I agreed.

He let out a roar of laughter and slapped me on the back. The blow stunned me, would have sent me to my knees had my elbow not been leveraged against it.

Bowman never did show and I stumbled wildly out of the bar sometime in the early hours of morning.

When I got to my room, I checked over the saddlebags, making sure the money was still there. There was a god-awful amount of it. My little package of five hundred seemed like an acorn compared to the oak tree share of the total.

I stuffed the saddlebags between my bed and the wall. I tried to go to sleep, but the moaning and cursing of the marshal in the next room filled the night. He was dying, I thought. I hoped I would not end up that way in the end. Any death would be better than rotting myself to oblivion. If I had any decency, I would walk next door and put a bullet in his brain.

Somehow, I did fall asleep. I didn't know it until I woke to the sharp sound of a revolver. I pulled on my britches. I could hear people starting to gather at the door next to mine.

"Shootin's not allowed in the rooms!" I heard a woman say.

My first thought was that a robber was looking for the money. In a town as small as Cimarron, it was bound to get out that the marshal had recovered the loot from a bank robbery and was dying in his hotel room.

I opened the door to my room. I held the Colt out in front of me and walked into the hall. The woman turned around, squealed, and rushed on. I thought the revolver might have frightened her, that, or the sight of me stumbling half-dressed through the hall.

I grabbed the doorknob, turned it slowly, and pushed the door open. The marshal was dead by his own hand. I was surprised he had the strength and clarity to do it. I let out a breath that seemed to come from weeks of holding it. That part was over, the marshal's part. I suppose that left me in charge of taking Dandy Jim back to Santa Fe. It was coming, anyway. The death of the marshal only set it solid in my mind.

I went back to my room, cleaned up the best I could, and set out to find Bowman. I walked across the street to the jail and pushed the door open. Bowman sat behind the small desk, giving orders to his two deputies. They nodded and leaned their palms against the butts of their revolvers in almost identical fashion, the way Bowman did at times. The two of them—one, lanky and tall, the other, short and skinny—did not seem to be permanent deputies. They had to be told the most routine of duties. I suppose they were only brought on when they had prisoners, or when Bowman was unavailable.

"Get outside and wait!" Bowman yelled at me.

"I've got proper business," I replied.

"Not yet, you ain't."

I rolled my eyes and stepped out of the building. Two or three minutes later, Bowman strode out of the place. He was headed to the hotel. I fell into step with him.

"Listen, Sheriff, when's George's trial?"

"Week, maybe longer."

"What?"

"Circuit judge don't come through, but once a month," he replied. Three quarters of the way to the hotel he stopped, fumbled with his vest, and started walking along the street. I kept up with him.

"In that case, I'll be taking Mr. Beudreaux to Santa Fe."

"Suit yurself, he ain't wanted in Cimarron. I've only kept him for the marshal."

Bowman veered off and went alongside the hotel. He stopped at a window and looked in.

"Now, why the hell don't they just clean it up?" he asked himself, but looked at me, so I shrugged a reply. "Ain't hard to see he kilt hisself, is it?"

I looked at him, then, through the window. The marshal lay there, a pool of his own blood gathered around his head, gravitating toward the impression in the pillow.

"How'd you know the shot came from here?"

"A man has to know the sounds of his town," he declared and walked around to the front of the hotel. He tossed a hand toward the small jail. "Well, go get him out."

"I will, I need to get some things together first."

"Then, what the hell're ya talkin' to me for?"

I went around to the small corral and found the stable boy. I picked out our horses, mine, the marshal's, and the one Dandy Jim rode.

"Get 'em ready, will ya? Fill the canteens."

The boy nodded and I went back around to get the saddle-bags. I strode up to the hotel and walked briskly through the lobby. The door next to mine stood open. Bowman leaned across the hall from it, throwing orders into the room.

"Just wrap him in the damned sheet. Christ," he said, wagging his head.

I clicked open my door and got hold of the saddlebags. Pulling the bottle of whiskey out of one, I threw back a splash. I got my things together and went down the hall. I handed the marshal's saddlebags to Bowman. Of course, I kept the one with the money and my personal set. Then, giving one last look, I went up to the desk and dropped the key.

"That'll be ten dollars," the young man said.

"For what? I paid last night, you sorry sonofabitch," I yelled, dropping the saddlebags containing some five thousand and doing the best I could to keep my hand from the Colt.

"The doctor, the sheets, and various items used in the marshal's care."

"What the hell's that got to do with me?"

"You brought him in. You're his employee, I understand. That makes you responsible for his expenses."

"Like hell!"

I could hear Bowman's footsteps coming hard behind me.

"What's the fuss here?" he asked, moving shoulder level with me.

"This man refuses to pay his bill."

Bowman turned to stare at me.

"It ain't my bill. It's the marshal's bill."

He looked back at the clerk for his version.

"The government owes a bill. He's the only representative of the government."

Again, Bowman turned to me, figuring things on his own as the discussion progressed.

"I'm just a hired hand. I can't sign for the government. Hell, I ain't even a proper deputy."

"Then, what're you plannin' to do? Break the gambler out of my jail?"

"No, the marshal was goin' to take the man to Santa Fe. I've been in on it through hill and dale and I figured to end the job, that's all." I thought for a moment. "If you want someone responsible for the bill, George is a proper deputy."

"Where's this George?" the clerk asked.

"In jail," Bowman replied.

"Got any money?"

"He's damn well got a hand for signin'," I said.

All this time of arguing over a ten-dollar bill, I had thousands at my feet. But I was not about to let on I had a dime. Not in that town, not with unscrupulous persons of unknown quantities to hear of it. Especially not before I rode out into the wasteland of prairie between Cimarron and Santa Fe. I would rather put a bullet through my own head.

Bowman took advantage of the silence. His hand moved over his jaw in thought. Then, he turned to me.

"You best get outta town and take that damn gambler with ya."

"Mace!" the clerk said.

Bowman glared at him and he slumped back, defeated.

It seemed like the best chance I had to get out of town, so I grabbed up the saddlebags and went out. The stable boy had just brought the horses around and was tying them off at the rail when I came through the door. I tossed him a coin as I passed and kept on toward the jail.

"I'm here for the prisoner in the cell," I told the deputy.

"Ain't ya gonna wait for me?" George asked.

"Naw, the sheriff told me to git and I know what that means."

"How's the marshal?"

"Dead."

The deputy walked over to the cell with a key on a ring.

"Dead?"

"Shot himself," I said. "He was a goner and I suppose he knew it."

I saw sadness in George's eyes. An actual human emotion,

imagine that.

The iron door swung open and Dandy Jim stepped out. There was a look of amusement on his face, as if his fortunes had taken a change for the better.

"Just you and me, I reckon," he said, smiling.

"Shut up, gambler," I snapped, angry that he would assume I would be much easier on him than the others. No, I wouldn't cuff him every chance I got, like the marshal, nor would I shoot him at the slightest provocation, like George, but I was killing him with miles. The closer we got to Santa Fe, the closer he got to death.

"Reckon you can handle this hombre alone?" the deputy asked.

"You volunteerin'?"

He shook his head in a slow, deliberate manner. "You might hire someone."

"No need," I replied. "If he tries anything, I plan to kill him. If anyone else tries to break him loose, I aim to kill him. Whatever troubles I have on the way, this'n ain't liable to be one."

We started out of town with Dandy Jim leading the way, his hands tied together and to the saddle horn. Behind that, was the marshal's horse, which was tied to the first. I brought up the rear.

My figuring was this: if Dandy Jim tried to make a break, he would have to fight the riderless horse behind. That would give me a chance to catch him, or to take a shot at him. Meanwhile, I could keep an eye on whatever tricks he would try and have a chance to counter them.

Santa Fe seemed to lie somewhere ahead, like a mythical city of relief from all burdens and troubles, like heaven. The name held a sense of awe and wonder about it that other towns did, when driving cattle, railhead towns like Abilene, Dodge City, and Kansas City. Santa Fe was an end-of-the-rainbow town that called to a man on the drive and helped to draw him onward when he had neither reason, nor inclination, to continue.

I smiled to myself, thinking how quickly money came to mean little on those drives. A man signed up for work in need of cash. A few weeks into the endless work, poor food, dangerous river crossings, and hostile Indians, he forgot about his poverty and started worrying about his skin. When that happened, he needed a reason to continue, something to look forward to across the vast prairie. If he could not find it, could not believe in anything, he might take off on his own toward any excuse of a town and search up other work. I had known a few who had done just that.

CHAPTER TWENTY-SEVEN

Dandy Jim and I had gone about ten miles with the sun bearing down on us when it seemed about noon. I squinted up at the sun to judge. I had just decided we could go a little further, when looking over the country, I came upon a distant figure flanking us. A few seconds later, whoever it was dipped out of sight.

Wary, I called up to Dandy Jim to veer off to the right. In time, we would pass behind the figure in the distance. Thinking I might be a bit too suspicious, we pulled up and made cold camp.

"What's the matter?" Dandy Jim asked, studying my face and chewing on some smoked beef.

"None of yur damn business."

He shrugged and continued chewing. I had decided that Dandy Jim could talk a preacher out of religion, if he got the chance. The best way to keep him from working his magic on me was not to give him the time of day.

I waited to see if someone would come upon us. I looked all around for signs of movement along the horizon. An hour passed and no one showed, so I felt it was safe to move on. In the meantime, Dandy Jim had leaned back along the ground, propping his head against a rock. His hat was pulled over his face.

"Get up," I said, kicking his feet. He started and rose slowly.

"It's not the accommodations the hoosegow had to offer," he

said, rising. I tied his hands to the saddle horn.

"Can't you find any better place to tie my hands? It hurts my back to lean forward all day."

"That's yur problem," I replied, and we were off again.

This time, the miles stretched out with no surprises. The only obstacle to endless sight was the low range of mountains hovering to our right. I figured by sticking close to the range, we could make it another ten, fifteen miles before dark.

In the afternoon, the wind kicked up ahead of some angry-looking clouds billowing out from the mountains. I could hear the distant rumbling of thunder. Flashes of lightning shot down in thread-like fingers, touching the ground and snapping, then the grumble would roll out along the bottom of the cloud.

I started looking about the landscape for anything that might offer some shelter. Hail could easily come tumbling out of that cloud and I wasn't about to suffer the beating if I didn't have to.

Then, there were the horses to think of. What if they got spooked? Not mine, of course, but I was not so sure of how the others would react to such circumstances.

A good deal off, but closer to the mountains, was a small cluster of buildings. I hoped it would be a ranch with a place for the horses and a sturdy roof to get under.

"See that place to the right?" I asked Dandy Jim. He nodded. "Head over there. By the looks of that storm, we'd better hurry up about it."

We set off at a decent gallop, but we could see the lightning flash brighter and longer and the sound of the thunder came sooner. Then the rain came. I could see it move along the ground ahead of us, sweeping like a white curtain against the dark background of the clouds.

The rain hit us first as scattered, cold drops, then a deluge. We were soaked in a moment and charged our horses harder along the ground to make it to the buildings. My hat flew off and the drawstring caught at my neck, digging into the flesh as the hat caught the wind and spun.

We made it to the house just before small pellets of hail started to tumble from the sky. We stood under elongated eaves, gathering the horses onto the porch with us. The hail bounced all around the dilapidated old place.

"Que pasa?" we heard from within and turned in surprise.

"Quien llama?" I asked back.

He rattled off some words I did not understand, but I picked up that his name was Paco and he was not sure why he had to answer such questions on his own porch.

"Tormenta," I replied, pointing up at the clouds as he came to the window to look out. He was a shriveled old man with pouches at the eyes and a shuffling walk. Several dogs tussled with each other and barked anxiously from within.

The little man asked us several more questions about where we were going, what we were going to do there, etc. I answered none of them with the truth. I evaded and sidestepped as much of it as I could. But the man knew more than I told him. He could see the situation plain enough.

Soon, the storm moved further east and left us with a soggy memory. The air was thick and humid. It grew worse when the sun came out and began to evaporate the rain. The water seemed to trail up into the sky so thoroughly, I figured if I stopped the horse in a puddle, we would be able to ride the stream to heaven.

We thanked the man for his hospitality and walked the horses away from the house. When I figured we were out of eyesight, at least his sight, I retied Dandy Jim to the horse and we rode to see how far we could get before dark.

As we came back to the trail toward Santa Fe, I noticed some tracks, fresh tracks. Some of them had a bit of water in them, others had none, but there was water around the crescent moon impressions. I looked sharply up at the horizon and narrowed my eyes.

There was no one to be seen, but they were there. But who? Outlaws? A group of travelers? Who would ride through that storm, if they didn't have to? The natural thing was to stop at the little ranch, but they had not, they had ridden on through.

I charged up ahead of Dandy Jim and looked the tracks over. Three horses. I was not the tracker others were and I paid for it in worry and wonder at what sort of men had passed. If Little Jimmy Carroll were alive and riding along, he would know more about the riders than their mothers did.

Unable to deduce any more than I could, I settled for another tactic. We rode along the path, as if we had noticed nothing out of the ordinary. The idea was to make camp with a fire and see who came to call.

Camp was made by a small stream eking out of the mountains. Wood was scarce, but I found a few limbs lying beneath an isolated clump of trees. The rest of the fire was made up of dried brush and an occasional cow pie. When darkness came, I made up a false bed, threw the saddlebags on the dun, and swung up into the saddle.

"You sit next to the fire there, Jim," I said. "I'll be able to watch every move you make, so behave yurself." I looked at him a moment. He was figuring something out.

"Give me yur boots," I said.

"My boots?"

"You heard me."

"What the hell for?"

"Do what I say," I commanded, drawing my revolver and motioning for him to hurry. "Right now."

I tied his boots to the saddle horn of my saddle and then jerked the reins around. I left the marshal's horse there to look as if there were just enough men for horses. A little ways away there was a rise and I drew myself and the horse below the rim to watch.

The night drew on slowly toward morning. Dandy Jim sat up with the fire and drank all the coffee. Along toward midnight, he curled himself up on the ground and let the fire burn out. I dozed a time or two for short spells, but when I looked up, the dark forms lay on the ground like sleeping men.

Then, the silence shattered, starting me out of a doze. I shook myself awake and peered over the ground. Three men rode into camp, shot up both bedrolls, and stomped around. Our horses were sent into a panic, stomping around and jerking against the hobbles.

"Where's the money?" I heard one ask.

Another one got down and checked the bedrolls.

"There ain't no one here, Bill."

No one? Where was Dandy Jim? A fear dawned on me like none I had felt before. Dandy Jim was out somewhere loose and knew exactly where I was. He could have slipped up and cut my throat, if he knew I had been dozing. Most likely, he had just made tracks, but killing me would have given him freedom from pursuit. It was an edge I knew he would take if he thought he could.

"Goddamnit!" one of them yelled in anguish. "Where's the money? I thought you said there'd be money!"

"There was. Thousands of it," a familiar voice said. I cocked my head sideways, waiting for him to say something else.

"I oughta kill you right now," said the other fellow. Bill, I guessed it to be.

"By God, I swear it. Hey, look, the dun ain't here." I shook my head at recognizing the voice. George. By whatever deal he had made, he was loose and looking for the bank's money. From the distance of my position, I could barely make out horse from man, but I knew I had to take a shot. They would put two and two together in a minute. I took aim down the length of the barrel, trying to pick out a distinct shape. Then, one of them wandered away from the rest, leading his horse.

"Hell, he must be . . ."

I plugged him. Fire leapt from the muzzle of the Winchester and a piece of lead screamed through the night. The bullet stopped the speculation in his throat. I hoped it was George. Next, shots erupted from the little group toward my general direction. They were blind, wild shots.

C'mon, get on a horse, I thought, staring at the confused shadows moving to and fro about the smoking fire.

"Get the damned horses, anyway."

"Best just get the hell outta here."

That's it, mount up, I thought, as I crawled down the bank nearest the fire, keeping low so as to light their figures against the softer blue of the sky. I could not see if either one was George.

"Goddamnit, I didn't come all the way out here just to turn tail and run. Get something."

I crawled around to another angle from where I had fired, trying to flank them and get another shot. If I killed another one, the one left might just abandon the whole idea.

My heart was thumping a hole in my chest as I crawled. Every move I made seemed louder than a preacher in church.

"Hear that?" one of them asked, stopping dead in the act of searching the camp.

"Let's just git. He's still out there, damnit."

"If he could see us, he would have shot again."

"Damn well saw George," the other responded.

I lay as still as a stone, breathing slowly into the ground and looking up from under my brows.

"The hell with it, let's go," the first one said.

When they swung up into their saddles, I caught sight of a broad back, or was it a chest? I cocked the Winchester, carefully aimed, and let go a shot. He arched back and rolled off the horse.

"Goddamnit!" the last one yelled, putting the spurs to his mount and thundering off into the night.

The other lay moaning on the ground, flopping from side to side. I stayed where I was for a long time, waiting for the other to come charging through camp to shoot me. All the while, I heard the groaning fits of the wounded man. George must've died quick, but this one was taking most of the night.

Not being dead, he might have a revolver handy. If I came up on him in the dark, he might shoot me. I waited and waited, but he didn't stop screaming. Natural sympathy for a wounded man almost brought me out of hiding a time, or two, but I kept my head.

To hell with it, I thought, and crawled back to the horse. Daylight would serve me better than any amount of luck. But I was not about to sit around waiting for Dandy Jim to cut my throat. I gathered up the reins of the horse and freed her legs from the hobble. I rode east to where I felt comfortably distant and slept in the saddle. That way, if anything frightened the horse, I would already be on the move.

Nuevo Méjico was a dangerous place to be rich. It was dangerous enough to be poor. Damn George! Why could he not just sit it out and let the outlaw in him find a better, more legal means of expression? He brought them damn deputies right to us. Maybe he just wanted to kill Dandy Jim. Maybe he wanted the money. Like all things dishonest, it had a harsh end and so did he. But damn him.

CHAPTER TWENTY-EIGHT

When daylight came, I found myself in the saddle, swaying to the movements of the dun as it wandered about the semi-desert munching the short, scarce grass. Dandy Jim's boots dangled from the saddle horn, looking foreign, as if the result of some drunken antic. I reached back into the saddlebag and brought out the bottle of whiskey. A quick swig, then I would get down to business.

The whiskey burned my throat, but cleared my head. I thumped the cork into the bottle and looked around to get my bearings. West was the direction of the mountains. That was easy enough. I tried to figure out which way I had come. I wound up having to cut my own trail before I figured it out.

A mile or so later, I came within eyeshot of the little camp. One body lay near the fire. Off to the left was another one. I went up to the one I figured was George. His hand was torn ragged and tracks were around. A coyote, or something had been chewing on his hand. The back of his throat was a confused mass of jagged flesh. Ants and flies were thick at the wound. It made me shudder to look at it. I kicked the body over to make sure it was George. It was.

I gathered up whatever I thought I'd need: coffee pot, cups, and the little flint used to spark a fire to life. I circled the camp looking for barefoot tracks. The ones I found led to the west. I could not follow the tracks themselves; Dandy Jim would probably have a trap set for me further along. So, I went to catch the horses.

There were four horses, besides the one I rode. I would have given them away, if there were anyone to give them to. I tied them all together and walked over to the other man. He was being systematically eaten by bugs and flies that gathered at the gaping hole in his stomach. I studied the face. He was one of Bowman's deputies; one of those who tried to rob the hotel, no doubt.

I spit and started off in the general direction of the footprints. I had a system of riding across them at certain intervals and checking the horizon for anything unusual. Dandy Jim was a clever man. I figured he could lay a trap better than most.

Two hours of riding brought me to a small valley. The footprints led to a group of rocks. I knew I would lose them there, so I worked my way down to the bottom of the ravine.

The dun made her way through the tangled, rocky terrain with expert agility until she brought me to a small bend. When I came around a jagged edge of rock, there lay Dandy Jim. He snapped his head up to stare at me with the menacing eyes I had seen the first day.

"Well," he said, in a hurt, angry tone. "It's high time you showed up."

"Happy to see me, are ya?"

"Happy to see my boots."

I uncoiled them from the saddle horn and tossed them through the air. They landed with a leathery smack and a puff of dust.

"I like to have froze out here," he mumbled, working on the knotted rawhide. "What was all the firing? I thought you might have been killed and your horse stolen, along with my boots. I could see myself trying to make my way to civilization in this condition."

"I just wanted to keep ya close. No sense lettin' ya get away, not after all I've been through."

"Where would I get away to, do you suppose? Do you see anywhere to hide? Is there a saloon out here? A hotel?"

It occurred to me that Dandy Jim was just that, a dandy. As long as I kept him far from towns and the like, he would be somewhat at my mercy. Whoever rode with him must have been frontier savvy. Without them, he was lost.

"You can lead these horses from here on," I said, unwrapping the reins from the saddle horn. Dandy Jim looked up at me. I thought for a minute he would try some trick, but he took the reins from my hand.

"You're gaining quite a string, Snake."

We rode out of the ravine and back toward the trail to Santa Fe. By evening, I would be done with this duty. Cowpunching never seemed as pure and simple as it did about then.

We rode for an hour before either of us spoke.

"I take it the men who owned these horses are dead."

"Yep."

"This one looks a lot like George's."

"It was."

He turned around in his saddle to see if I were teasing. When he turned back, he knew I wasn't.

"What on earth gets into folks?"

"Money," I replied. "You ought to know something about that."

Dandy Jim did not reply. The silence gave me time to think that I should keep him quiet. I had never let him talk before, but the wild weeks were coming to an end and nothing he could say would change it. So, I allowed the civil discussion because I missed the sound of it.

From working ranches and the like, I had come to appreciate a good talk with another man. So often, a fellow was left to himself and his work. When company could be found, it was brief, usually in the exchange at the end of one man's shift and the beginning of someone else's. It didn't lend itself to socializing. But I liked the saloon talk and to hear stories.

As Dandy Jim saw that I was not going to slap his mouth shut, he grew more talkative. When he talked, he became the man I had read about as a youngster: the daring gambler, the Mississippi gentleman.

Besides, I told myself, Santa Fe was nearly in sight.

"How do you suppose he escaped?"

"George?"

He nodded.

"He had a deputy with him. I reckon he promised to split the money from the robbery. Sounds like something he'd try."

"You killed him?"

"Yeah."

"First man you ever killed?"

"No."

"Who was the first?"

"Mexican back there at Taos. A mob of 'em came after us. I had to."

"Sad thing, killing."

I nodded, but he couldn't see me. He could not see me stare at the ground for a long time, either.

"Only man I ever killed was a deputy in Texas; one of the marshal's deputies. Dumbest thing I've ever done."

That did not sound right. That was it? I heard he was wanted for murder a number of times over the years. Was he trying to tell me the only one he ever killed was the marshal's deputy?

"I heard it was more than one."

"No, sir. Some of the men I used were killers, but not me. Oh, I've threatened a lot of men with death. I can vouch for that readily enough. But, to do it, you see. That's a different thing, isn't it?" He let the question hang there for a minute. "The marshal, he was a different sort. He killed with relish, with flare." Again, silence. "George, he downright enjoyed it, don't you think? And him a deputy. A brutal man, you must agree with me there."

Yeah, I suppose he was right. I had noticed the same sort of things and it didn't seem right that men like the marshal and George were allowed to kill without remorse, without fear of reprisal. They would kill in the name of justice, even. All in search of a man who gambled, cheated, and robbed, but rarely had the gumption to commit murder; maybe only once.

Then again, those around him murdered easily enough and he chose to associate with them. I knew of their ways. I held two dying men because of them and plenty of bullets flew close enough to me that I could have grabbed them.

"What happens when we get to Santa Fe?"

"I'm gonna take ya to jail and turn ya over to the townspeople."

"I mean, do you keep the money, or give it back? How does that work, exactly?"

"I give it back to the bank."

"Even the five hundred?"

Now, that was something I had not thought about since the marshal died. How would I handle that?

"I ain't sure yet. It's sorta mine and sorta not."

"I think you should keep it. Look at all you've been through and you'll be giving most of it back. Right?"

"Yeah," I said, though my voice sounded a bit unsure.

"Well then, just keep it. What difference does it make? No one knows it didn't drift with the wind, do they?"

"No, I guess not."

"It's settled then."

I didn't know about that, but it could wait for a decision.

Santa Fe was still a few miles off and no one had asked about the figures, yet. When the bank started totaling up the amounts, I was sure I would be asked about it. I could make the decision then.

"They'll hang me, you think?"

"Give ya a trial first."

"That's somewhat a formality, I guess. Too many people can identify me as the murderer, but I didn't kill anyone. Do you suppose they'll understand the difference?"

"No."

"Oh well, I look at it as punishment for the one I did kill. God gets his vengeance through men, as they say."

I had never heard that before, but you could put my religious knowledge in a thimble.

"Christian, are ya?" I asked him.

"Not so anyone would notice it, but I was brought up rather strictly. Gambling is a civilized sport of society in the South, not the cutthroat business it's become in the Frontier. A better class of people can be found around the Southern tables."

My mind was working faster than I wanted it to. I couldn't help but feel that there was an injustice to putting Dandy Jim to the scaffold. He was a Christian, a wayward gambler that may have killed a man, but that seemed to pale in comparison with the death and destruction of men like the marshal and George, especially George.

"You know, I've never held a grudge against you, Frank, even though you lied to me in the alley. I don't believe in coincidence often. You slipped one by me there, but only because you're not like the marshal and the others." He let that sit on my mind for a moment.

"What sort of business are you normally engaged in?" he inquired.

"Trail hand mostly, some ranch work. I can blacksmith some, too."

"I thought so. Honest work. Never hurt a man, that," he said and paused. "You like that sort of labor?"

"Hell no one likes it," I replied, knowing that was not the truth as much as it was a cowpuncher's alibi. If anyone figured out how much we loved the work, they would not pay us for it. I could hear men like John Chisum say: "Come on out and play, if ya want. I've got cows and horses and everything." Like a bunch of simpletons, we would probably follow him.

"I suppose this all seems rather strange to you; running all over tarnation, one group of men chasing another. The killing and all."

"Yep."

"Well, I . . ." he started, but I interrupted.

"Since yur so damn ready to talk, why don't you tell me what the constable was doing with the money."

"Well," he said, glancing over his shoulder. "I gave it to him. He was going to give it back."

"Give it back?"

"That's right. I took a chance. I hoped if I gave the money back, they'd listen to me when I told them I hadn't killed anyone. Deke and Buster were with me that day in Santa Fe. They were the ones who fired the shots, not me. I hoped they'd listen, that's all."

I let it settle in my brain for a bit. It made sense. The constable must have realized Dandy Jim had not been completely square with him when I pulled out that bundle of bank notes. I nodded as I thought over all the incidents and could not find a single one that betrayed Dandy Jim's side of it.

"Then, what the hell was he runnin' for?"

"Wouldn't you?"

Maybe I would. We had proven ourselves as desperate men.

"I had the argument going my way, anyway," Dandy Jim continued, "but, when they put together that George killed the bartender, everything I said rang true and he decided to trust me."

"Ya told 'em it was George, did ya?"

"Well, he did it. Right?"

"Yeah, he did it."

We rode for a couple of miles in silence, each of us turning things over in our minds. I sorted through the events of the past weeks and put them together with what Dandy Jim had been saying.

"You know," he said. "If I just hadn't killed that deputy in Texas, there'd be no reason for me to hang. Would there? I didn't kill anyone in Santa Fe. I'm willing to give the money back. Oh, but then there's God to deal with and his vengeance." He clucked his tongue and shook his head sorrowfully. "If I'd only known he was a deputy and not a jealous husband. That's who I thought he was, you know. He scared the devil out of me, him making his way through the crowd with that look. You know the look these lawmen have when they decide on killing a man."

I was starting to feel like I was on the wrong side of the law. Dandy Jim seemed hardly to be in the wrong. He had robbed the bank all right, but he didn't kill anyone. Hell, Jesse James and those boys robbed everything: stages, trains, banks, and who knows what else? No one turned them in to the law.

Dandy Jim killed the deputy, he admitted that much, but it might have been somewhat of an accident. Except for that one try at an escape, he had given us no trouble at all. I just could not see him shooting a deputy for no reason.

Compared to the marshal and his like, Dandy Jim was a saint. He had surely never gutted anyone. At least I didn't think so.

"Justice is a funny thing," he said, breaking the silence. "I've seen where a man killed another, murdered him right in front of witnesses, but they were all too afraid to testify to it. The court had to let him go. Then, some men got together and killed him. Shot him in his sleep. Justice was done.

"That's how it has to be out here," he jutted his chin at the whole West. "Sometimes, men have to do what's right, instead of what's legal. Take you for instance. There's no reason for you to bring me all the way back to Santa Fe. It isn't your job, is it? But you're doing it. I have to admire you for that.

"Not many would take on such a responsibility. Fact is, if you turned around right now and rode off with the horses, no one would blame you. Why, no one even knows you're bringing me back. If anyone even cares, they figure the marshal is bringing me back, but he's dead."

He was right about that. Wouldn't everyone be surprised when I came riding in with Dandy Jim Beudreaux? Me! All I had ever been is a hired hand, a cowpuncher. No one would suspect me of law work, especially not alone. If they knew I had gotten as far as I had with Dandy Jim, they would buy me drinks for a month.

"Of course, you're probably looking forward to that reward money. How much are they paying for my capture? Do you know?"

"No idea," I said and spit.

"Well, has to be up near a thousand dollars, by now, what with them pegging me to the murder at the bank. That's quite a sum," he mused. "Even if I didn't do the killing. You can spend that, can't you, Frank?"

"Shore could."

"Of course, there's nearly five thousand in the saddlebags. But," he said, holding up his hand, "I understand that's dirty money. Ill-gotten gains, as they say. Yeah, bankers, they have names for all kinds of money, don't they? Bet it spends the same, though.

"You know why I robbed that bank? Because I don't like bankers. Threw my dear mother out of her house after the Civil War. Took every dime she had in back taxes to the Union! Imagine that. And, the bank foreclosed on her house for failure to pay on the note. By God, the Confederacy gave her leniency on the taxes as she was helping so with the war effort. Every dime we got went right to the troops.

"That's no excuse, I know. You don't have to tell me that, Frank. I understand there's no excuse for robbing the bank. But now you know why I did it.

"It's just like a bank to take five thousand and dole out one. Anyone, other than you, would hide the money and swear they never found it. They'd probably beat me up some to show they tried to get me to tell where it was hidden. I've already been beaten enough to make that sort of alibi. Not you, though. You know why? It's that honest work of yours. Makes a man understand things that marshals and bankers don't. You understand honesty and integrity. If you didn't, you could kill me right here and no one would be the wiser about the killing, or the money."

I rested my hand on the Colt. It would be easy to kill him and take the money. No one expected me to bring him back to Santa Fe. No one cared about Dandy Jim, just the money he stole. He was right about the bankers, too. Half of them only gave loans so they could foreclose after all the real work was done. One banker might sell the same place three or four times before he got rid of it. I had seen enough of that in Nuevo Méjico.

I was starting to see that Dandy Jim was right about a lot of things I had never thought of before. He had a different way of looking at it that seemed reasonable. But for a little misunderstanding, Dandy Jim would probably not even be wanted by the marshal. He damn sure had not done enough to get hanged; especially not in New Mexico Territory. It was not right that they had to pin the killing on him just because he was the only one left to take the blame.

I wagged my head at the injustice of it all. The circumstances that brought Dandy Jim to the gallows were thin enough and I had certainly seen worse from the lawmen I had been keeping company with. It all weighed heavy on my mind.

About noon, I called for us to stop. We hobbled the horses and sat down to lunch and some whiskey. I figured we were close enough to Santa Fe to go for something a bit stronger than coffee. Besides, I was so depressed at turning Dandy Jim over to the law for hanging, I had to brighten my spirits some.

CHAPTER TWENTY-NINE

My attitude toward Dandy Jim had changed over the morning. I felt he had been dealt a sorry hand. I wanted to do something for him, maybe put in a good word with the sheriff or the judge.

I sat across from him, he on his rock, me on mine. Santa Fe stood in the distance, still not visible to the naked eye, but the traffic along the main trail was lively enough. We had seen a wagon go by and two men on horses headed the opposite way.

"Well, sir," I began, moving the jerked beef to one side of my mouth. "I believe you've been treated unfairly in this business, Mr. Beudreaux. If it's worth anything, I'll put in a word for ya."

"I'd accept any charity you could show."

I nodded my head and ate.

"It's not too late, you know."

"Too late for what?"

"How many head of cattle would that five thousand buy?"

"Oh, no. Now, don't go talkin' that way. This here's the bank's money, like it or not. I got to return it if I've got it."

"Just hear me out," he pleaded.

"No, sir. I'll have none of that talk."

"Tempting though, isn't it?"

"You know damn well it is."

"Do you suppose a chance like this'll ever happen again? To you, I mean? It won't," he said, before I could answer. "This is an opportunity, Frank. Can't you recognize it?"

I looked at him. I knew he was right. There would never be

another chance for a fellow like me to lay hands on five thousand dollars. Life just wasn't like that.

"What do you have to gain by taking me in anyway? Notoriety? You don't want that kind. It'll lead to trouble. You want the thousand dollars free and clear with no risk? I can understand that, but there's little risk to keeping the five thousand.

"Just think how easy it'd be; easier than picking money up off the street."

I shot a sharp stare at him. Did he see me pick up the twenty from under my horse's hoof? No, he couldn't have. What did he mean by that, then?

"You leave me a horse and a few dollars to outfit myself proper and you ride into Santa Fe as if nothing ever happened. Damnit, Frank, can't you see the simplicity of it?"

"I see it."

"Don't let yourself fall for it."

"For what?"

"For their rules. You're smarter than you let on, Frank. Tell me you don't see the ways they keep men like you poor all your lives, while they live in luxury. Tell me you don't see the banker pulling legal jobs of his own. The way they did my mother. You've seen the land offices sell worthless land time and again, drawing people out from the East with lies. Tell me that's right, if you can."

"I can't."

"What do you care if they hang me, or not? You know I don't deserve it. You know the injustice of it. Why do their work? Let the banker come and get me if he wants his money. They're just stringing you along, Frank. They string everyone along with laws they don't obey themselves."

Damn, if he wasn't right. I could not ignore the fact of it. Regular folks could hardly get a square deal in all of Nuevo Méjico about then. There were businessmen who had the lock on cattle contracts to the government. Men like Murphy and Dolan in Lincoln. Even John Chisum, a man I respected, had the fix in for his beef so that small ranchers didn't get a chance and had to do like Jacobsen and drive cattle all the way to Kansas, California. or Montana to get a decent price. The government backed them up on it. Marshals and sheriffs catered to them and turned their backs when trouble would sprout up. Or worse, they arrested competitors.

No, I didn't like the way of things in Nuevo Méjico at the time. Crooks and thieves were abundant and the least damage of all was done by the ones they called crooks and thieves. The men in power were the worst. They did as they pleased and no one gave them a sideways look.

"We're together in that respect," Dandy Jim said. "We're both men struggling at the bottom of society, just trying to feed ourselves. They kick dirt in our faces for our efforts and laugh at our failures. They feed on our failures. You've seen it, Frank. Tell me you haven't."

"I've seen it."

Dandy Jim was getting me a bit riled up.

"The worst I've ever done, is slap them in the face for it by robbing their banks, taking their money on the tables and thwarting their attempts to make an example of me. If you help them now, you'll be hurting the fellows like you and me. Can't you see that?

"Why don't we just slap them in the face again? Let them know we're not to be fooled with. Let's show them the regular guys can fight back. There'd be nothing to it. Their marshal didn't win, we did. Let's you and I win one for all the small ranchers and farmers who get kicked around by these men of power."

Strings of faces flashed before my eyes; faces of men and women struggling in the near desert conditions to try and carve out a piece of the land for themselves and their children. The faces of people I had seen passing through with a fine herd of steers. Envy dripping from every one of them as they tried to count the animals trotting by. They stared at us and our bounty with eyes as big as silver dollars.

As I weighed the decision, I noticed riders coming toward us. There were three of them. I stood up to meet them, my hand ready on the butt of the Colt. But I did not expect anything to take place this close to Santa Fe, not in broad daylight. If it did, I had learned enough pistol slinging from murderin' George to shoot my way out of it.

I was relieved to see a badge on the foremost rider. I glanced at Dandy Jim.

"Well sir, you almost had me. Them's law comin'. Ain't no decision left to make, I'm afraid."

Dandy Jim did not show a sign of his thoughts. His face was set in a stiff line of jaw, his eyes dead to the world around him. I looked up at the riders. I knew the one out front. From where? I tried to think, then it hit me about the same time he recognized me.

"Who've we got here? Frank, is it?" Billy Macon asked, with a note of irony in his voice.

That was all I needed. Wrangling with Dandy Jim wasn't enough trouble? I had to tolerate wild Billy Macon and his shiny, new badge, too? I felt my eyes roll up in exasperation.

"Introduce me, Frank," Billy said, his voice haughty with victory. I suppose he thought being the law was an accomplishment. From what I had seen, it was a bit of a step backward. So, I took pleasure in telling him who I had caught.

"This here's Dandy Jim Beudreaux. He's my prisoner."

"Don't look like your prisoner, Frank. Looks like your partner."

"The hell you gettin' at, Billy?"

"The name's Sheriff William Macon," he snapped. "Dandy Jim Beudreaux, huh? Don't look like much of a gambler."

"You stupid sonofabitch, Dandy Jim here robbed the damn bank. After I split off with the marshal, we tracked him down. I always knew you couldn't find yur ass with both hands, Billy."

Billy started running his tongue over his thin lips. His small eyes darting back and forth between Dandy Jim and me.

"You got the wrong man," he said.

"Like hell, I do."

"I say you got the wrong man. I caught the bank robber a week ago. Hung him for it, Sunday."

I stood speechless. "What the hell have ya done?"

"My job, which is more'n I can say for that cur, Ben Fowler. The lazy old cuss."

"This here's the man, Billy."

"Stop calling me Billy," he said, rising in his saddle, as if to get in a better position from which to pull down on me. "Call me sheriff, if you must, or William. Take your choice."

"Well, ya ain't enough of a sheriff for me to call you that, William."

He started for his revolver, not much, a threat more than the beginning of a draw.

"Do it," I said, narrowing my eyes. "Do it, William, and I'll cut you down, 'fore you get three fingers wrapped around that hogleg."

It was quite a boast, especially since my hand was dangling just above my knee, but it gave him a pause and that's all I needed. Let him think about it. The hot-headed little squirt.

"What makes you so sure this is the man that robbed the bank?"

"He told me."

"That true, mister?" he asked Dandy Jim. "You confessed, did ya?"

"Hell no. Frank and the marshal's men hunted me down for no reason. After they killed all my partners, I gave up. They'd have killed me, Sheriff, and I wouldn't have known why, if you hadn't shown up."

"Look here, William. This man's Dandy Jim Beudreaux. Look at yur posters, will ya? He's wanted for everything from gamblin' to murderin'."

"Not in New Mexico," Billy trumped. "From what I can see, you're both undesirables to Santa Fe. Get anywhere near town and I'll have ya both arrested."

Having said his piece, Billy whirled his horse around and drew his deputies along like friendly pups at his heels.

"Can you believe that sonofabitch?" I asked.

"I believe anyone who says I'm not wanted in New Mexico. You'll be letting me go, now. I suppose."

"Well, you suppose wrong, then."

"Come on, Frank. You heard him. They already hung a man for the robbery. Do you think there's a person in Santa Fe willing to go against that? What for? Why would they want to stir up trouble? Besides, the sheriff said we weren't to go into Santa Fe."

"Look here, Dandy Jim, or Leonard, or whoever the hell you are, I don't aim to let this thing rest. You done it and you know it. I don't expect you to tell him the truth, but I have proof of what I'm saying. I have the money.

"As for Billy Macon, he's a danger to innocent people as sheriff of Santa Fe County. I've got to expose him as a liar. If I don't, they'll hang an innocent man every time something goes wrong and I'm high on his list of suspects.

"Remember all of that right and wrong you were tellin' me about? Well, this is a wrong that needs to be made right. I'll still put in a good word and try to get you justice, but I have to show this Macon up for what he is."

A thought struck me at the same time. If Billy happened upon the two dead men and remembered that we had a couple extra horses, he'd be after me for murder, unless I got things straightened out in a hurry.

Not only that, but feeling that his name was clear in Nuevo Méjico, Dandy Jim would make every attempt to escape. I needed help with all I needed to do and there was only one place to go: Skinny Jacobsen's out along the Rio Chito to the southwest of Santa Fe. In order to speed up the travel, I had to cut the three extra horses loose and take my chances with Dandy Jim riding ahead of me, untethered.

"We're gonna have to ride hard, so keep up. One move to left, or right and I'll kill ya. My skin's at stake here, so don't mess around. Understand?"

"How's your skin at stake?"

"If Billy finds those dead men, who do you think he's gonna find to blame?"

A knowing look came over Dandy Jim's face and he nodded.

"Hell, you might even get out of this without a hangin' if I can swing it. Don't trade a maybe rope for a sure-as-hell bullet."

The Rio Chito was only a few miles south of where we were, and we rode hard along its curving length until the "J/R" brand started to show up on the cattle we met. Then, a cowpuncher spoke with us a bit and waved us through to the ranch buildings.

That old place looked as welcome as home ever did. A wisp of smoke drifted lazily out of the chimney. Skinny's wife would be getting dinner ready by then. We were safe on the ranch and rode slowly up to the buildings so as not to alarm anyone.

In the distance, I saw the lanky frame of Skinny standing out on the porch staring out at us coming over the last few hundred yards.

"Just when a feller thinks the world's workin' the way it ought to," Skinny yelled over the distance, "God goes and pulls a dirty trick like this. How ya doin', Snake?"

Home. At least it was one of the many I had known as a 'puncher.

"Calls you Snake, does he?" Dandy Jim whispered.

"He oughta, he's the one that started it."

CHAPTER THIRTY

Dandy Jim and I were invited to eat at the ranch. Around back of the house, next to the summer kitchen, there was a wooden canopy structure that was connected to the house. Below the canopy, ten men could be fed at the large table of rough-cut wood. The door leading to the main part of the house always stood open, giving the table area a sense of being an informal, open-air room.

The food was good. Mrs. Jacobsen was a fine cook, but she had a couple of helpers, so I wasn't sure how much she still cooked. It was a big job cooking for eight to ten men a meal.

Because the door to the main house remained open to cool the interior, cussing was not allowed at the table and cowpunchers spent most of the time in half-expressed notions.

"Why, that sonofa . . . buck, he don't know as much about cows as he knows about the moon. We had an old dog once was a da . . . durn sight better cowhand than he was," one of the men said, sopping up the rest of the gravy on his plate with a piece of bread.

All during the meal, surreptitious glances shot toward Dandy Jim. Untied, he looked as average as a man could. There was nothing about him that spoke of the years of gambling and carousing he had done. The dirty suit was in tatters from the past few weeks of scrambling over rocks and through miles of dust. It hung on his shoulders like the formal garb of a bankrupt baron.

The boys were duly impressed by my ability to bring him to justice. Only a few had heard of him before, but they quickly told the others who he was. As was usual, their stories were much greater than his deeds, but they acknowledged that Dandy Jim was a considerable man.

"Had a book writ about him," a young 'puncher declared to another in hushed tones before dinner.

When they had gathered into little pockets of discussion, I was unable to resist the chance to get their hearts going. They were busy eyeing the prisoner and mumbling exchanges when I stepped up, casually awaiting my opportunity. Eventually, it happened that they had all taken a break from watching Dandy Jim. Trying to keep the smile off my face, I called out: "Watch him," and leapt into the crowd, causing momentary panic as they searched around for Dandy Jim and found him calmly looking at the sleeve of his jacket.

"Lord almighty, Snake! Ya tryin' to kill us?"

"What'd you think he was gonna do, Fred? Gamble ya to death from behind?"

"Now, Snake, you know he's murdered folks. Don't pretend you don't."

For everything else Dandy Jim was, he had impeccable table manners. He said "please" and "thank you" as often as he asked for some item to be passed, or when passing a plate along. He had a proper way of eating with utensils that boggled the minds of those picking up the last pieces of steak with their fingers and shoving it into their mouths, or reaching clear across the table for a roll, or some such thing.

"I don't care what he's done, you all could take a lesson from him as far as manners go," Mrs. Jacobsen remarked.

"Thank you, ma'am," he replied, causing Mrs. Jacobsen to blush.

Dandy Jim had a way with folks. Even the wary 'punchers

gave him due respect. It was all quite amusing to see him charm the whole crowd of them.

When dinner was over, there was business to discuss. I asked the men to keep the prisoner busy with stories while I talked with Skinny about my predicament. They obliged and I followed the tall rancher into his office.

Even out there on the ragged plains of Nuevo Méjico, some of the ranchers had pretty swank quarters. The Jacobsens's were one of them. Except for the neutral territory of the long dinner table, the ranch house was decorated in a style of wealth. Good wooden floors, rugs, paintings, comfortable furniture, and several bookcases made up the interior of Skinny's office. I had been there before, but mostly just to accept wages before charging off to town.

I stopped this time to look around. There were a lot of nautical things: a globe, pictures of ships, and a shiny, brass barometer neatly placed on the desk. Jacobsen caught me admiring them.

"My family was made of seafaring men before America. I'm the first one to keep his feet on the soil. Sometimes," he said, in a wistful tone, "I can look out over the backs of steers and it reminds me of a turbulent sea. Kind of strange, I imagine."

"Yur that kind, Skinny."

He gave me a look of amused reproach.

"You're not a readin' man, I take it."

"No, sir, cattle and land's what I read."

"Well, if you picked up a book, even by accident, you might find such comparisons artistic, instead of something to poke fun at."

"I've read a book before."

"You mean the one about Dandy Jim Beudreaux, Gentleman Gambler and all of that nonsense?"

"That was one. Mark Twain, too."

"I suppose congratulations are in order," he teased, then his face took on a dark shadow of concern. "What sort of trouble are you in?"

I looked down at my feet and the handsome rug beneath them. "I shouldn't be in none, but I think I am." I looked up at him. "How could you let them get rid o' Ben Fowler?"

"Politics," Jacobsen said. "I've a ranch to run, Frank." There, he was using my real name. It meant he thought I was in a great deal of trouble.

"It ain't as bad as you think, at least I hope not."

I went on to tell him all about the trip, the chase, the guttings, the murder of the bartender, all of it. Then, I told him about having to kill the two men on the way.

"Met up with ol' Billy Macon. If he finds those men, he'll pin it on me."

"Well, you did it."

"Yeah, I did it. But I done it in self-defense. They'd have killed us. Shot right into the bedrolls, Skinny. I can show ya the holes."

"Is that the money?" he asked, pointing to the saddlebags I had been toting around all day.

I nodded.

"Honest to God, Frank, I'd take that money and get out. Take Dandy Jim with you. If you go into town, it'll stir up all sorts of trouble. You might even get hung before it's over."

"Is that what you'd do, Skinny? Take the money, turn old Dandy Jim loose, and go on about your business? Stand by while Billy Macon hangs innocent people to bring glory onto hisself?"

"No, it's not."

"Then, what makes you talk that way to me? You think I'm less able to handle the trouble? I learned a few things on that trip, Skinny. Things I ain't too proud to know, but I know 'em."

241

"I could send some men in with you," he offered.

"Men ain't gonna help and you know it. I need you to come along. I need someone known in this country that's willing to say they believe me."

"Frank, there's thieving going on these days; all sorts of rambunctious activity. Some people say the new sheriff's in on it. Some say he just looks the other way. There's rumors of a private group of gentlemen in town. The folks call them the Santa Fe Ring. No one knows exactly who's involved in it, but if they decide I'm an enemy they could take all I have and run me off."

"So, you won't do it?"

"I didn't say that."

"Then, just what the hel . . . heck're you gettin' at?"

"I just want you to know it ain't easy to discredit the sheriff. He has friends."

"Yeah, but he don't have the money. I've got the money. That means I've got proof of what I say. He's just got his own words."

"Then what?"

"What do you mean?"

"Well, after we show up the sheriff, what then? Do you suppose he'll shrug his shoulders and wander off to the next piece of business? Or, do you think he'll make life as unbearable as he can for those of us who're forced to do business in Santa Fe?"

He saw I had not stopped long enough to think it out that far and that it didn't mean as much to me as it did to him because I could leave. If things got hot, I could just wander off to Texas, or some place like it.

"I live here. Everything I own sits along the Rio Chito. I can't pick the land up and move on, Frank."

"Are you tellin' me no? 'Cause, if this is a yes, get to it."

Skinny broke out with a chuckle, but it didn't last long.

"I'm telling you straight, I'll go, but I won't go all the way."

"Where the h . . . heck ya gonna stop at?"

"Shut up and listen a minute," he snapped, then apologized for it. "I'll go along with you as far as I can, but when I back out I want you to know why. I won't risk the ranch for this. Understand?"

"Wouldn't want it another way," I said.

"Good, then. We'll leave in the morning." Skinny paused for a moment. "Where'd you get that necklace?"

"Traded an Injun for it," I replied, blushing. I rose from my chair then and wandered out to the dining table. The plates had been cleared and several of the men were gathered around it, watching. When I walked up, I saw Dandy Jim dealing cards. I shook my head in disappointment. Didn't these fools know better than to gamble with him?

"Damn," one of them roared, throwing down his cards, then looked sheepishly up toward the main part of the house. He wiped his lips with the back of his hand. "That's all the money I got," he said, rising from his seat and walking toward me.

"He gambles for a livin', ya dang fool."

"Hell," he whispered. "I was winnin', too. Then my luck turned soft."

"Yur head turned soft," I gave him back.

"He can't win every time, can he?"

"If he wants to."

"Think he's cheatin'?"

I laughed and walked away from the man. Anybody that infected with foolishness might be a carrier. I went over to Shorty, a man I had ridden to Kansas City with on the last trail drive.

"Howdy," I said, squatting next to him with our backs to the wall.

He nodded his greeting.

"Ya ain't gamblin', Shorty?"

"I ain't near fool enough to gamble with the likes of him. Lord, he's done everything but make those cards sit up and recite a prayer."

"I'd like ya to come with us in the morning," I said.

"Yeah?"

"Got some business in town. Looks pretty touchy for the sheriff, or myself, depending on how it all works out."

"That sheriff, the young one, he's so damn," he looked around for someone to object to the language, "full o' hisself, he's almost two people."

"Ran into him a couple of times."

"Know what I mean then, do ya?"

I nodded gravely and said: "He don't like me none, anyway. I made him look like a fool in front of old Ben Fowler. You ever know Ben?"

"I knew him."

"Billy Macon said he was a drunk. That true?"

"Time to time."

"Anyway, old Ben, he takes and smacks the young'un upside the head with his rifle butt. Swolled him out pretty good." I thought for a moment. "What happened to Ben?"

"That kid. Next thing you know, Ben decides to quit being sheriff and the kid steps right in. Didn't even let the seat cool down. That's the way it is, I guess."

I nodded.

"You suppose Ben'd take a chance to get even?" I asked.

"If he's sober."

"What're the chances of you ridin' into Santa Fe and keepin' him sober?"

"I don't know anyone well enough to keep 'em sober if they want to drink."

"What if you just tell him a message for me?"

"I could do that."

"Good, just tell him that I'm the one who went with the marshal, he'll know who I am. Tell him I know the young sheriff hung an innocent man. I have the proof and I'm bringin' it to town in the morning. Along with the real robber." I looked at him for a moment while he memorized the message. "See if he can't get a few of his old friends together. I'm gonna need all the help I can get."

"Can't promise it'll make a difference to him."

"I know that. I'll cover yur chores. What've you got left to do?"

He gave me a list of things to check on, typical ranch work, and I promised I would do it. He showed me around the place some and told me how he did certain things. I nodded to it all. Then, he rode off toward Santa Fe.

When I had finished the work, I looked up a bed and a safe place to put the money until morning. Once I had squared away my things, I sat on the porch late at night and checked my weapons over. I felt a hollowness in my gut. I was neck deep in all of it and none of it should have mattered a bit to a drifter like me.

I had heard tell of folks who happened to be in the right place at the right time and it changed their lives forever. I had heard others tell of how they had been in the wrong place at the wrong time and it changed their lives forever. I wondered which it would be for me, good or bad?

When the gambling was done inside, I went in and got Dandy Jim secured to a post. I gave him a pillow, though. Looking at him, I hoped I would be able to keep him from getting hung. I had to keep my neck clear of a noose, first.

"Tomorrow, you sleep in a jail bed. Sounds better than all this tyin' up, don't it?"

"I reckon," he said.

Yeah, caught is caught. I don't know that any sort of caught is better than any other. One might be a bit more comfortable, maybe. I guess that is all a prisoner can hope for: a little comfort in the end.

CHAPTER THIRTY-ONE

Early morning came cool to the cracks in the bunkhouse. I loved the clean, crisp air of a New Mexican dawn. I sniffed at the air and roused myself awake. I looked up at the post. Dandy Jim slept with both hands over his head and looped about the pole. He stared up at the ceiling, his head rested on the thin pillow.

Looking at him, I felt a bit guilty. If it were not for me, he would probably be a free man. Then, I thought again. Naw, hell I had nothing to do with it. It was his problem. He had gambled and robbed and consorted with killers. If that was how he chose to live his life, I had nothing to be sorry about.

"Ready, are ya?" I asked.

He turned his head toward me. Again, those dead eyes as impenetrable as iron. He had a way of locking the world outside himself, as if everything going on around him were of no consequence whatsoever.

"I am," I said and sat up to blink and look around for my boots. They were under the bunk. I brought them up and tipped them over. Nothing fell out. Sometimes, a spider or a scorpion would sleep there, and it was a good practice to shake your boots out before trying them on.

"Don't count on me to back your story," he said.

"I'd be just as grateful if you didn't try to get me locked up. Unfortunately, if I win, you lose. If you win, I lose. Don't be surprised if I cuff ya upside the head when you go to stickin' my head through a noose."

"Fair enough," he said and pulled at the rawhide strips.

I went over and untied him, then walked him outside for a piss. I looked up at the sky. Not a cloud in sight. It was going to get hot, in more ways than one.

"If things work right," I said, more to myself than Dandy Jim, "tonight you'll have a good bed and I'll be on my way to Texas, or someplace."

"It isn't really between you and me, is it Frank?"

"Nope," I said. "Never has been. It's been about doin' a job, doin' the right thing."

"I meant today. Today, it's between you and that sheriff."

I nodded. "Today it is."

I held the Colt on Dandy Jim while he saddled our horses. By then, the others were starting to stir and come outside. In an hour, we were all fed and ready. I looked over the ragged bunch of men and the well-dressed Skinny.

"I hope the day has an auspicious end," Skinny said and Dandy Jim nodded.

"I'd settle for seein' the end of it," I remarked, mostly to myself. "Heeyah," I yelled, and kicked the dun into motion, the others following behind myself and Skinny. Dandy Jim rode just ahead.

There were six of us all told. Myself, Skinny Jacobsen, Dandy Jim Beudreaux, Dick Brown, and the two Benton brothers, Sam and Joe. I was reasonably sure that Shorty Saunders would join us and, hopefully, Ben Fowler. If he could bring a few men we would number ten or better when we got there. That ought to get us a listen. From then on, I would be on my own to explain it proper.

Dick Brown was a quiet man, about my height. No one knew very much about him. He sort of meandered about doing his job, never having too much to say. But he was talented with anything that threw lead and I had seen him wade into a fist-fight on occasion with results. The Benton Brothers were an odd pair, twins. They were up for anything that sounded more exciting than watching cows. They liked their work, but were always up to something that made it more interesting.

On the trail drive to Kansas City, Sam used to throw his loop over two steers at once and climb off his horse and onto their backs. He would stand there, one foot on each animal, until they put up a fuss. We used to count the seconds out for him. The longest he ever stayed up there was sixteen seconds. When it was over, he would let the rope go. Eventually, they would fight their heads free of it, often working it loose and stepping through. Skinny frowned on the practice, but recognized the need to break the boredom.

Joe was a wild one. He would get into arguments a lot, mostly with Sam over one thing or another. Being twins, they knew how each other's mind worked and they would have the most hellacious spats, but they wouldn't finish their sentences.

"I told ya . . ."

"That's another thing . . ."

"Don't start that . . ."

"It was true then . . ."

"If you'd just . . ."

"Like hell . . ."

Then, they would either go to blows over it, or separate from each other only to come rollicking into camp later that night, slapping their knees and talking the cryptic language between bouts of laughter.

The sun rose up at the left corner of my eye. It was bothersome for the first few minutes of daylight and I noticed that everyone looked off to the right just a bit. Every now and then, I would squint one eye and check into the sun for riders.

The way I had it figured, Billy Macon would have just enough time to make it to the bodies and back about the same time we rode into town. I hoped to get there before he did and make his claims of two dead men sound contrived to throw suspicion onto me.

A few miles out of town, with the sun well up, I saw two riders coming from Santa Fe. I held my breath as they approached. Shorty and Ben? It didn't look good if they were unable to get any more help than that. It wasn't. The men rode on by, touching their hats in greeting.

We were only a mile out and my hopes were fading when three men emerged from the buildings along the main road. I waited, hoping. Sure enough, it was Shorty and Ben and another fellow. Well, three was better than none.

They pulled up to us to discuss the situation.

"Howdy, Ben," I said.

"Got him, did ya?" Ben asked, looking Dandy Jim over.

"Yes, sir."

"Good. Well sir, I suppose we'd best get into town."

I nodded. At least he wasn't drunk. Not much, anyway. Shorty looked tired. The other fellow was young, maybe one of the men we had started out with that long-ago day. I nodded toward him in greeting.

"Name's Robert Cunningham," he said.

"You ride with the sheriff that first day?"

"No. Just got into town a week ago. Ben says I can be his deputy if he gets his job back."

Later, Shorty whispered: "Sister's a whore," referring with a nod toward Robert.

"Even coyotes and wolves got to eat," I replied, though I don't think he knew what I meant. I don't know if I did, exactly.

That last mile was the worst. I had done my job. I had been over the longest miles of my life, but that solitary and final mile was the longest, hardest, most intense of them all. Even the thought of shedding my burden was tempered by the thought of getting another in exchange.

At least with Dandy Jim in jail and the money returned, I would feel lighter; nothing to protect, or fear; no one to chase me or kill me for any reason other than one of my own making. If they wanted to try me for murder, let them. I could face it down with facts if I had to. At least there would be no more midnight raids on my camp. Hell, no more cold, fireless nights, either. Even if they put me in jail, I would be out of the rain.

"Okay, fellers," I said, as we neared the main street. "It ain't been much of a ride for you, but me and Dandy Jim here have been through the mill. Let's keep our eyes open and on the lookout for that blamed sheriff. Anything happens, save yurselves. I aim to."

The mood of the men changed. The air about us seemed to press against us, or was it just me? Lord, I felt as if I were riding through the side of a tornado.

Nothing happened. We rode into town as if ghosts. Some of the citizens nodded and tipped their hats toward Skinny, but thought nothing of the man tied to the saddle horn in front. I don't know what I expected. Perhaps, happiness at the return of the dreaded criminal, or angry mobs instigated by the sheriff, but surely one or the other.

We rode up to the sheriff's office, tied up our horses, and untied Dandy Jim. I walked him through the door. A fat little man sat behind the desk, a broom leaning against his chair. When we entered, he looked startled, then settled down to a calm boredom.

"I have a prisoner and I want the reward money."

The fat little man looked up.

"Who is it?"

"Dandy Jim Beudreaux. You must have a poster somewhere."

"I only work here," he said, droll and unimpressed by my announcement.

"Have ya got a key?" I asked, angry at him for his attitude.

He looked up and around. "Don't see one."

"Look in the desk, damn ya!"

"The desk ain't my business." He returned my stare. "You some sort of law, or just a bounty man?"

"A guide for a United States marshal," I replied, hoping to jar something out of him, a spark of some ambition. Then, I grew impatient. I kicked the desk. "Get the hell away from there. If the desk ain't your business, I'll find the damn key."

The man jumped up from his seat and grabbed his broom. I went around the side of the desk and started pulling drawers out, shuffling through the contents.

"I wouldn't do that," the man said, standing a bit away with a tortured expression.

"I know you wouldn't, damnit. That's why I am," I replied.

There was a jingling of keys. I lunged for 'em and pulled it out just as Billy Macon came through the door.

"Whose damned horses are . . ." he stopped in mid-sentence when he saw me standing there, holding the key to the cell. He looked about the crowded room. He snarled at Ben Fowler, but said nothing. He stopped for a moment on the tall figure of Skinny Jacobsen, then turned back to me. "What the hell're you doing in my desk?"

"Your man couldn't find the key and I've got a prisoner to lock up."

"That's my desk!"

"Well, if yur butt would o' been in the chair, I wouldn't have bothered with it."

Macon looked at Dandy Jim.

"I told you once, this ain't the man," he said and then remembered what else he said. "I told you not to show your face in Santa Fe. I'm gonna have to arrest ya, Frank."

"For what?"

"First, for breaking into the jail and going through my things. Aimed to steal something, I figure. Next, we found two bodies out on the road, both shot, both deputies, one a U.S. marshal's deputy. Sounds like one of your bunch. Until I figure out who killed them and what you knew about it, I'm going to have to put you in jail."

"I don't suppose you've bothered to have a look around, have ya?" I asked, meaning he was considerably outnumbered.

"These men are free to go," he said.

I laughed and walked over to the cell. I opened it and pulled Dandy Jim toward the opening. Billy watched me, as if expecting me to step in and pull the door closed behind me. I shut the door, all right, but Dandy Jim was the only one inside. I tossed the key to Billy.

"That's the end of my service to the City of Santa Fe," I said, throwing my chin up and starting for the door. Some of the others had stepped out ahead of me and waited on the porch.

"Don't make a move for that door. You're under arrest," Billy said, stopping me in my tracks. I turned slowly around.

"I ain't done a damn thing wrong, Billy. You got the bank robber in the jail and that's all I was called to do. You owe me a reward, but I aim to take that up with the banker when I hand over the money from the robbery. See, I know I got the right man, because I got the money. Have you got the five thousand dollars? Huh, Billy?"

He stared at me, not knowing what to think. That was the proof I needed and he knew it.

"There's still two dead deputies out on the road," he said, moving his hand a little closer to his revolver. "I call that murder."

"You hung an innocent man and I call that murder," I replied.

"A mistake, at best."

"Self-defense," I countered. "If you figure out who those men are, you might find that one is wanted for murder in Cimarron and Taos. The other's probably not much better." I turned to go.

"Not another step," he shouted.

I came back around in a hurry, with the revolver leveling between his eyes. Just for kicks, I whirled it around the way I had seen George do. It was not as smooth, but effective. I handed the butt toward him, my thumb resting on the hammer. When he reached up to grab it, I flipped my wrist back, cocking the hammer and swinging the muzzle toward him in a snap of movement. The Colt was upside down, but it would fire that way.

"That's enough!" Skinny said, angry. "I can vouch for this man."

"Who the hell're you? Some damn dirt farmer. Why the hell would I take your word? If you told me it was daylight, I'd doubt it."

I had seen Skinny mad before, but Billy Macon brought a whole new shade of red to Skinny's cheeks. Sparks of hatred flew from Skinny's eyes.

"Shoot the sonofabitch," Skinny said, knowing damn well I wouldn't.

I stomped my foot on the wooden floor and Billy nearly went over backward. It took all I had to keep from laughing as he caught himself and firmed his knees. It didn't take him long to bring the brass back to his voice, though.

"I'll have you all hung!"

"Better check the due process clause, Sheriff," Skinny said, turning to go. Some of the men had drifted back in and Skinny shoved them toward the door on his way out. I backed toward the door of the little room with the Colt held high. I covered the others while they got the horses ready.

"I'll bring you down," Billy swore.

"Yur makin' enemies, Billy. I brought you a prisoner, you'd best leave it at that. You ain't no match for my Colt, nor Skinny's weight in this town. Just 'cause he don't lord it over everyone, he has powerful friends. More powerful than a no-account sheriff."

I expected to ride out of town in a cloud of dust and thundering hooves, but we didn't. Instead, we rode calmly to a house lying on the outer rim of the town. It was a grand old house with a sign out front.

GAYLORD R. WILSON, ESQUIRE
Attorney at Law

Old Skinny, he knew his stuff all right.

CHAPTER THIRTY-TWO

I didn't like the looks of the attorney's office from the start. The smell of doom seemed to hang about it. Doctors were the same way. They would stand before a fellow calm and reasonable and talk about having to cut an arm off, or take his guts out. Well, there was nothing calm or reasonable about amputation. Nor was there anything calm or reasonable about getting hung.

I studied Mr. Wilson as I was introduced to him. He was a bright, vivacious man, lunging here and there for his chair, a book, a pen. He encouraged Skinny and me to take seats in the chairs provided before his desk. I could hear the other men out on the porch, keeping guard. I wanted to be out with them, not stuffed into a fancy chair. They mumbled discussions and occasionally erupted into nervous laughter. At the same moment, I felt the weight of the books lining the shelves. In there was the law, I thought to myself. God, there were a lot of laws. I wondered how many of them I had broken without knowing it.

Skinny Jacobsen told the story better than I could have to the nodding Mr. Wilson. When they were done, it seemed as if I were included in the conversation.

"So, all you wanted to do was return the money and the robber to Santa Fe?"

"Yes, sir."

"You should not have drawn your weapon. That looks bad."

"Not as bad as the inside of a cell."

Wilson raised his eyebrows.

"You have the money with you?"

"Yes, sir," I said, unloading the saddlebags from my shoulder and dropping them heavily to the floor. "This is all the money he had when we caught him," I said, skirting the issue of the five hundred dollars in my saddlebags. "Also, I am still employed by the U.S. marshal folks. At all times, I was acting in my official capacity as a guide and posse member." I threw in that last bit to let him know I wasn't just some bounty man.

He nodded, then looked up at Skinny.

"You two wait here. I'll take the money to the bank and see which way the wind's blowing in town."

When he left, Skinny looked at me.

"When you jerked that Colt down on the sheriff, I wanted to kill you, Snake. But two seconds of listening to his mouth and I wished you'd shot him. This lawyer, he's a good one and he'll get things straightened out, if they can be."

If they can be? Was there really a chance I would wind up in jail over this? Well, now, that just wasn't right. I had not done a thing to deserve such treatment. Every time a fellow brushed up against the law, he seemed to come away dirty.

Skinny and I went out to the porch to stand with the others. I was grateful for the fresh air. All of those books sucked the life right out of me. When we came out, the others were smirking some. Then, Shorty looked me square in the eyes.

"Damn, Snake, where'd you learn to twirl a Colt like that?"

Behind him, the others broke into laughter. There was some joke afoot, but I couldn't figure it out. I told them about the best pistol slinging man I had ever seen, George Brimson.

"They say Mace Bowman over to Cimarron's the fastest in these parts," Joe Benton said, trying to start an argument with me.

"He is now," I replied, thinking of George's corpse being picked at by coyotes and wolves.

Dust in the street swirled up into an inverted cone, twisted mightily, then died down, like breath from the nostril of an underground beast.

"Riders!" one of the men yelled from the corner of the yard. All of us snapped alert and ready. "It's the sheriff," the man said, rushing back to the rest of us.

"How many?" I asked.

"Four."

At least we weren't outnumbered. Of course, they had the weight of law on their side. But law mattered only so long as it could be enforced.

Skinny was getting the worst of it in my mind. He had the most to lose and the least to say about it. Whatever decisions were made, they would be made between Billy and me. Maybe the lawyer, if he hurried.

"This is just exactly what I didn't want," Skinny whispered to me. "I didn't want it looking like my men against the sheriff."

"I'm sorry," I said, feeling guilty for having brought him into it. "But look where I would be if you hadn't come along." He had to agree that he had done the right thing. "Ya don't have to tell me how bad doin' the right thing is," I said to him and winked.

A huge smile broke out on his face and then melted away as Macon pulled up to the yard and dismounted. They came armed. The four of them fanned out to take in the eight of us. Some of the deputies carried shotguns. Billy stopped his crew ten feet from our line and threw his chest out.

"I'm takin' you in," he said.

"Speak to my lawyer," I replied.

"Sheriff, Mr. Wilson's handling this man's defense. I imagine he's having a talk with the judge by now. Maybe you ought to wait . . ."

"I ain't waiting a damn minute. You coming along peaceful, Frank?"

"Soon as the lawyer gets back," I said.

"You'll come along now."

"No, I ain't."

Billy reached for his revolver and I had never heard such a rattling of iron and leather in my life. Up came the shotguns, out came the revolvers. Everybody stood peering down blue steel at someone else. The tension was so heavy in the air a man could weigh it in his hand. It seemed as if we were all waiting for the one thing that would start the lead flying back and forth. I couldn't imagine what might bring it to a peaceful end.

That was all right, I had consigned myself to my own death. I didn't want to die, but it looked like I was about to. Better to do it fighting than sitting at the mercy of Billy Macon. The only regret I had was that others were going to die along with me. In an attempt to avert that, I spoke up.

"Look here, Billy," I said, watching the temper flare in his eyes. "Let's you and me settle this. Ain't no reason yur deputies and my friends have to die. How about it? Just you and me."

"If you want to save their lives, I suggest you set that revolver down and let me take you in."

"I'd be happy to do just that," I replied. "Except, you ain't known for worryin' none about the truth of the matter. As long as you got someone to hang, yur happy as a dog sniffin' shit."

"Hold it!" someone yelled from the side of us. He nearly got killed for his efforts at peace. All of the weapons moved toward the voice, then shifted quickly back to their original targets and eyes did the moving.

"I've got the judge with me," Wilson said.

"Sheriff, lower those weapons," shouted the judge.

"No."

"Mr. Whittaker?"

"As soon as he does," I replied, but as soon as I got the words out, Skinny released the hammer on his revolver and put it in the holster. His men did the same. What could I do, but go along with the move?

"All right, that's the spirit," Wilson said. "Now, Sheriff."

Billy lowered his weapon and so did his men.

The judge moved to the center of the group, addressing Billy.

"I've been shown indisputable evidence that this man, Frank Whittaker, has rightfully fulfilled his duties as a sworn member of U.S. Marshal Dayton Howard's posse in search of Leonard Braswell, also known as Dandy Jim Beudreaux, also suspected in the bank robbery and killings of a few weeks ago."

"What about the dead men on the trail?"

"I don't know anything about that," the judge said. "But unless you have evidence that it was either Mr. Braswell, or Mr. Whittaker . . ." he let it hang at that.

"I know they had something to do with it," Billy blurted.

"Like you knew those other fellows committed the bank robbery?" Skinny asked, sending a wave of red up Billy's face.

The talking went on for a moment more and the judge asked us to disperse. Billy and his bunch reluctantly went back to their horses and rode off. The judge followed them on foot, leaving the rest of us to look awkwardly at each other.

"How much do I owe you?" I asked the lawyer.

"Your life," Wilson said, without batting an eye. "But I'll settle for five dollars."

"Five dollars? You know how long I have to work to make five dollars?"

"Just be thankful you're alive to make it up," Skinny interjected.

"Four," I said.

"I'm not here to bargain with you, Mr. Whittaker. It's a set price for criminal defense."

"I ain't no criminal."

"See how successful I am?" he threw back.

"Why, it's robbery. You should be in jail," I said, but dug into my pocket and shamefully had to pull out the wad of bills totaling somewhere near one hundred and sixty dollars. Fortunately, the five hundred was still safe in my saddlebags.

"Why, Frank!" Skinny said, surprised at the cache. "Boys, don't you think Frank owes some rounds?"

"No, now. This has to last," I objected. "I can't go throwin' my money around. Someone might rob me if they thought I had more'n a nickel."

"I always knew you squirreled it away, Frank."

"One thing," Wilson said, accepting the five dollars. "This is not the end of anything, it's merely the start. We've won the first battle, but don't fool yourselves into thinking the war's over."

"It's over for me," I said. "I brought the robber back and the money. Whatever I had to do with it, I'm done."

"Well, be careful," he said and went into the house.

I looked over at Skinny.

"One drink," he said. "Then, we have to get back to the ranch."

We walked through the streets trailing our horses behind. The citizens went on about their business, unaware that the real bandit had been apprehended.

As I thought about it, I started to see what the lawyer had been getting at. When the people became aware that the sheriff hung the wrong man and began to put pressure on him to justify himself, he would look for someone to strike out at. That someone, I felt assured, was me. There would be people to take my side, but more powerful men to take his.

I could see the whole swell of it growing before my eyes like a dust storm on the horizon. I looked around at the group of men walking with me. Were they there to drink whiskey, or as my protection until the news spread and opinions could be formed?

Old Skinny, he knew more than he seemed to. He used the pretense of celebration to disguise his armed escort, giving news time to spread. Once people had a chance to digest the facts, I would have my own supporters and he could withdraw without leaving me helpless.

"Thanks," I said, looking up at him.

He remained stiff jawed but glanced down at me. He briefly smiled, glad that I had been smart enough to understand his motives.

We came to the saloon where it all started. I looked up at the adobe structure. There was a bit of foreboding in my heart. What else would transpire there? Would public opinion be with me, or against me? How would the people see it? How would the sheriff try to interfere with their reasoning?

I led the way in. It was deserted in the morning hours. At noon, the place would start to fill with those looking for a way to finish the day. By evening, it might be crowded two deep at the bar.

"Service here!" I yelled out to the back room.

In a moment, the fat bartender waddled out. He narrowed his eyes at me. Memory of some past trouble registered on his face.

"You, behave yourself," he said, pointing a stubby finger in my direction.

"Look at the business I brought," I said, hoping it would quell any hard feelings.

"Hold onto your hat," Skinny joined in. "Before today's over, he'll bring you a boon you haven't seen in a while."

The bartender cocked his head at Skinny for a moment and looked at the rest of the men gathered around.

"What'll ya have?"

CHAPTER THIRTY-THREE

As the day passed, more people came to the saloon looking for the cowboy that brought in Dandy Jim Beudreaux. I suppose I liked the notoriety a little more than I expected to. I leant myself to telling the whole story of the trip to get folks on my side of the argument. Skinny was right to think that if I were available to the people, they would flock to me and congratulate me. I felt a bit like a politician at first and didn't like the feel of it, but Skinny pushed the importance of it.

"I can't be here to hold your hand, Snake. You've got to make your own allies for the upcoming fight."

I couldn't argue with that, so I plunged into it with energy. I shook hands with the men as they straggled into the place. I listened to their speeches about what's right and getting the bad guy, even when everyone else thinks he's been hung. They admired my determination and perseverance. I admired their morals and ethics and insisted that they would have done the same thing, were they me.

When afternoon came, Skinny packed up.

"I can leave you one man," he said, preparing to go.

"Are there any that care to stay?"

"Are there any that care to leave?" he asked, nodding at the men who were busily laughing and talking with friends and sporting girls.

"I know Shorty the best," I said, though I didn't know him very well. I trusted him the most.

Skinny left me with Shorty, Ben Fowler, and Ben's friend, Robert Cunningham. As he said goodbye, he shook my hand. I felt as if I were slipping into a grave. By the way he took my hand and got a little misty-eyed, I realized that he might have been able to talk a good line, but deep down he thought I had seen my last sunrise. Knowing that, I started to get a bit more serious about defending my life.

The others left us to the din of the saloon and the continual drinks being purchased by the men coming in to show their gratitude. When my knees went a bit soft with drink, I figured I had better slow down. I started pouring the drinks out into the spittoon as the others drank. Soon, it was full and the black sludge ran over the top. I kicked it aside and brought another over.

Shorty, Ben, and Robert were staying sober to the best of their ability, which was remarkable considering the circumstances.

"I aim to get my job back, what do ya think, Snake?" Ben asked.

"I'll put in a word, if I can."

He clapped me on the back, and I started to worry about his sobriety.

"Keep sober, Ben. There's liable to be trouble when Billy thinks we're drunk enough."

Shorty came back from the door, after being relieved by Robert. He made his way through the festive crowd. It occurred to me that it was only festive because it was a crowd. The occasion provided an excuse to get together and put a few drinks through themselves. I had no delusions about that.

"There's a protest outside," Shorty said, and watched my eyes grow wide. "The relatives of the Mexicans they hung are carrying banners and all."

"For a minute, I thought they were protesting me."

264

"Naw," he said, looking for somewhere to spit, but all the spittoons were overflowing. He looked at me. He was a little white at the cheeks, then he swallowed. "They had a lot of friends. I saw the mayor go over to the jail."

"Yeah?"

He nodded. "Oughta start any time."

The bartender, red faced and sweating profusely, slopped another shot glass in front of me. I looked at it for a minute and tipped it up. I slapped the glass down on the bar and looked at Shorty.

"I drink one out of every four," I explained, and pulled the Colt out of my waistband. I flipped through it to make sure I had enough cartridges.

Shots rang out from the street and I jumped. Shorty put his hand on my shoulder, and we watched a drunk skitter across the boardwalk in front of the batwing doors.

"My nerves're a bit raw," I said.

He nodded.

I looked about at the crowd. Each man had stopped by to speak to me for a moment and went on to find others to talk to. I wondered if any of them were willing to stand up when it counted. I knew they would be no help with the sheriff, but if they would make their feelings known in public circles, I would be happy.

The Ring could buy themselves a sheriff, or intimidate the one they had, but they couldn't vote one in. Somewhere along the line the people had to ratify what they wanted. Public opinion stood for a great deal at times such as that. I had seen it before. A group of men could shove a lot down the throats of the people, but on occasion the people would refuse to swallow and the whole shebang would come tumbling down.

It happened in Texas, before it was a state. It happened in the Civil War and up in Montana when the Vigilance Committee got rid of Jack Slade. It could happen to the Ring, too, and they were stupid if they didn't realize it. I hoped the protest would prove that the winds were changing for their sheriff. I hoped they would abandon him before he pulled them all down. Mostly, I hoped I would not be hung for what was about to happen.

Robert pulled back from the doorway and looked over his shoulder on his way toward us. I knew what it meant. I gave a whistle and caught Ben's attention. He looked up from the man he was talking to and broke off the conversation.

"Ready, Shorty?" I whispered.

"Hell, no."

I grinned at him. Neither was I. A moment later, there was a crash at the door and the crowd began to part up the middle. Startled onlookers dodged out of the way of the oncoming shotgun barrels. I saw their faces coming out of the crowd. Billy's was first in line, with the others pushing at the crowd to make them stand back.

"Howdy, Billy," I said, grinning tightly.

"You're instigating a riot," he snapped.

I broke out laughing.

"You think you can shoot me for that?" I looked around at the men who had purchased my drinks. "What do ya think, fellas? You suppose that's good enough reason for this sodbuster to shoot me?"

"No!" they roared back.

"Billy, if I wanted to instigate a riot, we'd run you out of town."

"Is that so?"

"I reckon it is."

He looked at Ben Fowler.

"How's it feel to be standing upright, Ben?"

That was the wrong thing to say. Ben walked right up to him

and smashed him in the jaw. Billy went to the floor with a thump and the men with me jerked their revolvers. Fortunately, the deputies trailing along with Billy were overawed by the whole set of circumstances and kept their shotguns silent, waiting for orders.

Billy looked up from the floor with a bulging eye. Ben gathered together a glob of spit and sprayed it into his face. The crowd erupted into laughter and a mocking chant of "Ben, Ben, Ben!" He must've been popular as hell in his day. The deputies took a step back, looking wildly around at the jeering crowd. Public opinion is a powerful thing when it gets something to latch onto.

"Git!" I yelled at them and they hightailed it out of the saloon. It's a good thing they were green as hell and I said as much to Ben.

"He's fired all the best men in the territory," Ben replied.

We disarmed young Billy and sent him out of the saloon by the seat of the pants. When it was over, I looked around with great satisfaction and slapped Ben on the back.

"Good work."

"It ain't over," he snapped. "They won't come to talk, next time."

Next time! Why did it have to go on and on like that? I studied Ben.

"Does someone have to get killed over it?" I asked, sarcastically.

"Yes," Ben replied as quick as he could. Then he took a deep breath and let it slowly leak out. "That's the way of things. I've seen it enough."

The crowd sensed that it wasn't over. They also seemed to sense that the next time would be worse. I watched as several said their goodbyes and touched their hats to their friends. A few of them came up to Ben and whispered something.

"Watch the door," I said to Robert.

He scampered over to the door and peered over the little flaps of wood. I watched him for several minutes and looked about at the other men standing next to me.

"Will it be today?" I asked, hoping that it would not happen at all.

"Who knows," Ben replied, then amended it to: "Probably. I think it's Billy's last day and he figures he'd best get all the use out of the badge he can."

I shook my head, unable to understand that sort of thinking. Why not just clear out of town while he still had his skin? Would that not be a great deal smarter? Then, I looked back at my situation. It would have been smarter for me to take the money and turn Dandy Jim loose, but I did not. I suppose he felt some of what I had, in a different sort of way.

Our only warning that they were coming back was the sound of a shotgun blast and Robert flying away from the door, his body ripped open like a grain sack. He hit the floor hard. I had the Colt in my hand and cocked before I had time to think of pulling it.

Then, silence. No other sound or movement that didn't belong to the dispersing crowd of men. We waited for a second before we all realized the situation at the same time and dove for the floor. The bar was peppered with shots. The fat bartender was thrown backward into the wall. I could only hear the great mass of him hitting the floor.

I crawled along the beer-soaked, spit-puddled floor toward the window.

"Come on out, Ben," Billy shouted in through the door.

"Come on in, Billy," I called back.

"Ya bunch a damn cowards!" Billy said.

I was near to the doorway by then and took a peek around the corner from the floor. It took a moment to locate the men standing on the other side of the street. They hid behind some horses, waiting for us to exit.

Robert's sister came out of the back room and stopped short. She cocked her head in surprised recognition and rushed to his side, smearing her fancy clothes in the blood. She started to wail from the floor, looking around for help, or those responsible.

"Is there a back way outta here?" I asked Ben.

"Could make one."

We crawled back toward the bar and around it. As I passed the space between the bar and the wall, I saw the fat man lying in his own blood, staring up at the ceiling. Two bartenders inside a week, I thought. Before long, a man won't be able to buy a drink.

From the back room we could hear Billy's voice going hoarse from screaming into the saloon. There wasn't a door to be found, but there was a small window. We pried it open and I looked all around to see if anyone was smart enough to cover the back. They were not.

I crawled out, scraping my backbone on the windowsill as I lurched through. The other two crawled out and we worked our way between the buildings. When we got to the front corner, I hazarded a glance around.

"They're gone!" I urgently whispered. The last thing I wanted to do was sneak around town hoping to see, before being seen.

"Boom, Boom, Boom," came the sound of revolvers inside the saloon.

That gave us our best chance and we seized it. We rushed around the corner and arrived at the door. I stood in the middle, Shorty to my left and kneeling, Ben to my right and doing the same.

"Give it up, Billy," Ben said.

Instead of doing as he was told, Billy whipped around. I can still see that desperate look of anger and fear on his face. He and his deputies moved as one.

My first shot went into a deputy's shoulder, spinning him around. Ben fired next and I saw Billy snap forward and stumble backward. Another deputy dropped one of his six-shooters and sprang to the left. Shorty shot him in the leg as he began to raise the other weapon.

The deputy I shot recovered long enough to send a bullet ripping through Ben's side. Ben whipped around with the bullet and sat down facing the street. Billy tried to raise his Colt. I kept a bead on him. He looked frustrated for a second and knew it was no use. I wanted him to just stop it and get to a doctor, but he seemed compelled by force of pride and raised the revolver.

The Colt jumped in my hand. The bullet struck his thigh and I watched him drop to one knee.

"Stop it, Billy," I shouted, knowing my next shot would be the last.

The deputy to the left had enough sense to put his weapon down and lie still, waiting for the event to conclude. Shorty, no longer interested in that target, took a turn at the other deputy.

"Boom!" went his .44 and the deputy's head came apart.

I saw it from the corner of my eye, as I was busy keeping the revolver trained on Billy, waiting for him to see if he could raise his weapon one more time. He struggled with it, bleeding from his stomach and shattered leg.

As this drama took place, Shorty had presence of mind to go over to the deputy to the left and disarm him, then pull him out of the saloon by the legs. A crowd was forming behind me. I could feel and hear them grow in number. Someone called out that the doctor was on his way.

"Don't," I said again, as Billy worked on raising the pistol. He had to push as hard as he could to move it an inch. I thought about going over and taking it away from him, but I figured that would give him just enough energy to bring it to bear. A lot could happen in ten feet. Billy's face was red with exertion and his cheeks were puffed out, trying to squeeze the energy into his hand. Amazingly, and shamefully, he happened to get it up and cocked just enough. I shook my head.

"Damn, Billy," I puffed and squeezed the Colt's trigger. "Boom!"

The bullet ripped through Billy's chest and flung him backward into the shattered bar. His revolver clunked when it hit the floor, harmless.

I stood in the center of the bar, blood all around, and looked down at the bodies of men. The events seemed to have a life of their own, a predictable life that men like the marshal and Ben Fowler could recognize, anticipate.

I left when the crowd started to sneak back into the saloon for a final drink on the house.

CHAPTER THIRTY-FOUR

The aftermath of the shooting was almost as confusing and hectic as the event itself. People milled about the street, staring unashamed at the mangled people lying about the boardwalk. Shorty and I hurried to help the doctor with whatever chores needed to be done.

The undertaker stopped by to measure the dead men, then scurried back to his office to start construction. The mayor appeared long enough to hem and haw and wring his hands. To be useful, he tried to shoo the townsfolk to their homes, but they moved as a pack of chickens, clucking and strutting only far enough to get out of his reach, then filling in behind him as he made his way down the street.

"Goddamn," Ben said, rolling back and forth as the doctor tried to clean the wound with alcohol. Sweat rolled down his face to the tip of his jaw and dropped silently onto his bare chest.

We got Ben into his bed. It was dark by the time the doctor went to look after the deputy who had been shot in the leg. I gave some comforting words to Ben and handed him the bottle of whiskey from my saddlebags.

I caught up to the doctor and Shorty at the hotel, where they hired a room for the deputy. I went to the sound of the shrieks and opened the door. Shorty was pushing on the deputy's chest, while the doctor bent over the exposed leg with a saw.

"Give us a hand," Shorty said.

Taking hold of the man's foot, I pulled the leg straight and fought the deputy's attempts to get free. Holding onto the ankle, I could feel the vibration of the leg as the saw began to cut. The deputy remained conscious for the first few strokes, then passed out. But we followed the doctor's instructions and kept hold of him.

"When I hit a nerve, his leg will jerk. I don't want that," he said.

I could hardly look at what was happening to the man. It was too easy to put myself in his place and every stroke brought bile to the back of my mouth. I held onto the leg through nerves and bone, but I wasn't ready for the sensation of holding onto the severed limb. When it came loose, I nearly threw it out the window to get it out of my hands.

Then, a thought came to me. What do they do with all of the severed limbs? I thought about all of the amputees I had known from the Civil War. "Christ," I said aloud, thinking of piles and piles of arms and legs. Is there a cemetery for the pieces of us we lose on the way to death? Are they kept in alcohol to be buried with us when we die? A shiver ran up my back when I thought of dogs romping through the streets with arms or legs dangling from their clenched jaws.

"What do I do with it?"

The doctor glanced up from his work at cauterizing the wound and dressing the stump with a tired, exasperated expression. "Whatever you want," he said.

"Here, Shorty," I said, thrusting it toward him. He jumped back from it.

"Keep that damn thing away from me."

"You shot him," I argued.

"That'll teach me to shoot for the head," he replied.

The doctor, not amused by our antics, grabbed the leg from my hand and tossed it to the floor. "Knock it off, you two. You can go now," he said, releasing us from the duty.

Shorty and I made time getting out of that little room. Once outside, we breathed in fresh air unclouded by smoke and blood.

"Thanks, Shorty. If there's ever anything I can do for ya . . ."

He waved me off with his hand.

"Glad to do it," he said. "That Billy Macon was a sure-fire pain in the ass. You never got to see him for his regular self. Used to strut around like the cock's own crow. Had no use for him. Made comin' to town a downright chore."

I thought we were alone at that time of night, with all the bodies picked up and the saloon stripped of every bottle. I realized we weren't when a man stepped out from between two buildings. He was dressed in fine clothes and puffed on a cigar.

"Which of you would be Mr. Whittaker?"

I narrowed my eyes and pushed on the butt of the revolver.

"I would."

"Seems we're without a sheriff," he said.

"Were yesterday, too," Shorty shot back.

The man nodded his appreciation for the quip and turned his attention solely to me.

"You caught the real bank robber and brought back the money he stole. Did it ever occur to you to keep the money and kill the man?"

"It occurred to me a lot," I said.

"But you didn't."

"No, sir."

He nodded and took a deep pull on the cigar.

"I'll send for you tomorrow."

"For what?"

"I'll put a motion to the commission to hire you as an interim sheriff until we can hold a special election. Can't have the bad men thinking we no longer have a lawman in Santa Fe County. We wouldn't want to turn out like Cimarron, heaven forbid."

"Well," I said, hating to ask. "Who are you?"

"A friend," he said and walked back into the shadows.

"Who the hell was that?" I asked, whispering.

"Governor Axtell."

"What do you know about that?" I asked, without expecting an answer.

"Word is, he's in the Ring."

That night, I got a room at the hotel and slept long and heavy. There were moments when the feeling of holding a man's severed leg in my hand crept up my spine and woke me temporarily, but I found sleep easy to come by.

The next day, I spoke with the banker. He offered me one thousand dollars for bringing Dandy Jim to justice, but I only accepted five hundred. The rest of the thousand was in my saddlebags.

Next, I accepted the position as interim sheriff, but declined a campaign that would make the job permanent. I had time to think about it and I didn't want to be a lackey of dirty deeds for the Ring. I professed to be a Texan and told him I wanted to give it another try. He accepted my reservations with dignity and thanked me for my tireless work in bringing Dandy Jim to justice.

"If you'll just do one last service to this community," he said, drawing me in. "I'd take it as a personal favor if you'd stay on until Dandy Jim is tried and hanged."

I nodded and walked from the little office in the Palace of Governors with a badge on my chest. My first official act as sheriff was to fire the little man that cleaned the place. If he had just given me the damn key when I asked for it, I thought things might have been different.

That left me alone with Dandy Jim. I pulled a chair over to his cell.

"Read a book about you when I was a kid," I said, trying to

break the ice a bit. "I was real impressed with it. Even thought I wanted to be like you. I gambled and beat all my pals, but lost when it counted. That's a good thing, I reckon, to get past the dreams and on to honest work."

"Gonna hang me?"

"I reckon so."

He swung his legs over the side of the bed and put his hands up to his face. I thought he was crying, but he just rubbed his face and leaned back against the wall.

"I shoulda killed you in Trinidad when I had the chance," he said. "I just didn't think you were that much to worry about. Ironic, isn't it?"

I shrugged my shoulders, mostly because I didn't know what "ironic" meant. It was a strange word that I had heard used a time or two by educated men, but there didn't seem to be an obvious definition. It wasn't a word like dog, or cat, or something like that, so I shrugged.

"Well, Snake," he said, standing up and pacing the floor. "I've lived an interesting life, I suppose. I've been to places you couldn't get into with a load of buckshot. I'm better than this." He waved his arm at the interior of the jail. "But I suppose it serves all the petty purposes of the little, greedy politicians to hang a man like me. It galls me, though, that a puny weasel like you got to me."

I listened to what he had to say. I let him get it off his chest. He was facing the gallows and needed to make himself feel better about it. I didn't begrudge him his last fits of pride. The thought occurred to me that he was trying to make me mad, to force my temper.

"I kept thinking you'd cave in to the greed. I'm usually pretty sharp at reading a man." He ran his fingers through his hair. "I'm glad you killed that sheriff, though. He's the one who blew it. I had you going when he rode up and spoiled it all. I could see it in your eyes. A minute more and I'd have gotten you to turn me loose."

"That's right, Jim, I would've," I said and rose from the chair. "I'm not the thinker you are. I'm just a 'puncher in the end. I ain't been to any fancy places, nor rubbed elbows with the rich and powerful. My fare is a campfire and a few good men to swap stories with.

"And yur hangin', you got me beat there, too. When I die, it'll be by the horns of some nasty steer, or a fall from an old cayuse. I might even freeze to death in the jaws of winter. But your death will attract people from all over. It'll make the papers and all. Yes, sir.

"Trouble is," I said, "we'll both be dead."

During the trial Ben Fowler recovered and announced his candidacy for sheriff. He was popular, but I didn't think he would win. The Ring put up their own candidate. By the time the hanging was scheduled, the campaign was in full tilt.

"It'd help me a bit if you'd let me stand up there on the platform when ya jerk the gambler's pin," he said.

"Least I could do, Ben."

The morning of the hanging, I walked Dandy Jim to the scaffold. The townsfolk waved at me and hollered. I didn't pay much attention but had the decency to nod in their direction. I was somewhat of a celebrated citizen that day and felt the pull that politicians must feel. It was nice enough, but not worth the headaches that came with it.

I walked Dandy Jim up the steps. Ben Fowler stood smiling and waving at those below. When I looked at the gambler, it was the first time I'd seen anything besides conceit in his eyes. He was scared, even if he wouldn't admit it.

The crowd thronged the square. A man with a camera stood forefront of the scaffold and readied the box for taking pictures. I stood up there with Dandy Jim. The executioner had just put the noose around his neck and I leaned over to him.

"Last night," I said, "I kinda felt bad about the way you've been treated in all of this and, well, I left the door to the cell open. I guess you didn't check it."

Then, I nodded to the man and the trapdoor opened up beneath Dandy Jim. He didn't have time to remember if he checked the door or not. He died in a frantic search for the truth, the way he had left so many others in his wake.

ABOUT THE AUTHOR

T. L. Davis began writing short stories as an outlet to life experiences in the early 1990s. While taking some college courses he made contact with a production company and began working on stage plays, having *Chosen Realities* performed locally. Davis was interested in all forms of writing and continued to pursue his interests through writing articles for several Western-themed magazines including *Western Horseman, Cowboy Magazine,* and *American Cowboy.* The juxtaposition of the Western culture with Western artists led him to write several articles for *Art Revue.*

Davis has gone on to write novels, screenplays, plays, and short stories.

The employees of Five Star Publishing hope you have enjoyed this book.

Our Five Star novels explore little-known chapters from America's history, stories told from unique perspectives that will entertain a broad range of readers.

Other Five Star books are available at your local library, bookstore, all major book distributors, and directly from Five Star/Gale.

Connect with Five Star Publishing

Visit us on Facebook:
    https://www.facebook.com/FiveStarCengage

Email:
    FiveStar@cengage.com

For information about titles and placing orders:
    (800) 223-1244
    gale.orders@cengage.com

To share your comments, write to us:
    Five Star Publishing
    Attn: Publisher
    10 Water St., Suite 310
    Waterville, ME 04901